Nkosi's Little Warriors

LAUREN CAMP

FOR JONATHAN

Who walked 1836 miles for his salvation, and for his
late mother, Maxiline, who he lost the day the LRA
stole him.

.

CONTENTS

ACKNOWLEDGMENTS

Huge thanks to Julie Sutherland for her editing wizardry, to Amanda Lee smith for her attention to detail, and to Tyler Quarles, without who, this story would have no face.

INTRODUCTION

Hiding in the foreboding interior of this world's most melancholic continent is the bleeding heart of Africa: the Republic of Nkosi.[1]

For decades, one thuggish kleptocracy has ousted another, resulting in anarchy, leaving only two militias still standing. Still killing.

Nkosi's civilians trudge on, desperate for a break from the cataclysmic history that has robbed its young. The war children of Nkosi's conflicts are at once the most harmed by – and the most harmful in – the Republic's dreadfulness.

Some of the children to be stolen from their families, to be brainwashed by drugs, manipulated and exploited, were recuperating at The Princess Marina Hospital in Nkosi's capital city, Baobab, when It happened.

The medical records, interviews and personal journals of these once child soldiers have finally been reviewed. The children's psychic dams did not hold. Awful histories flooded forth.

One may presume to understand, but it is only presumption. How could one possibly empathize with such lives lost?

This is a dramatization of their story. This is the story of the Little Warriors.

---

[1] Nkosi is the predominant word for God in Africa. It used by a variety of tribes in several African nations.

Name: Dorian (Dodo) Mwesheni
Age: 12 years old (estimate)
Date of Birth: Unknown
Month of Admission: September 2009
Session: #7: Held by Dr. Mandeep Jain
Minutes by: Sophie Le Roux, Nurse
Dr. Jain: Dodo, today I want you think about a memory that makes you very, very happy. Do you have a memory that makes you happy?
Dorian: Yes.
Dr. Jain: Can you share it with us out loud?
Dorian: I don't know if I can say it out loud.
Dr. Jain: It's OK. Take your time. We will wait for you...
Dorian: When I need to feel better, I picture myself flying towards her.
Dr. Jain: Towards whom, Dodo?
Dorian: My sister, Helena. She is standing in the watering hole with her arms stretched out, waiting for me to jump for her. I feel myself being tickled by a thousand bubbles – the way I did whenever I hit the water. I loved how that felt. And how she would wrap her slippery hand around my arm to pull me up for air. That was a nice feeling too. She taught me how to love the water because she knew I would follow her into it. I wanted to be wherever she was. When I want to feel happy, I think about the way Helena taught me how to swim.
Dr. Jain: What else do you remember about your sister? Is there another memory that comes directly to mind?
Dorian: The day they came and stole us.
Dr. Jain: Can you tell me who stole you?
Dorian: The Militia for Minerals. Anthony Zaza pressed a gun into my forehead.
Dr. Jain: Who is Anthony Zaza?
Dorian: The man who runs the MM. He told me he would shoot me if I didn't kill my mother. He held her down in front of me-on her knees. But I got lost in my head.
Dr. Jain: Then what Dodo?
Dorian: I think Zaza was going to kill me because my sister screamed really loudly. She took the knife and did it for me ... She cut my mother's throat. She cut our mother's throat.

THE MEETING

The Republic of Nkosi
13 July 2008

Nkosi is a sweeping country-land that occupies the middle part of Africa. Its borders stretch along its Atlantic's breaking shores. Its rolling mountains of the north pour southward into the farmlands in the valleys. The land expands hundreds of miles easterly, digressing into the Karoo, a brittle plateau in the horn of the Republic's shape. Magically, in Nkosi's southernmost regions, a great jungle rises upwards. It protects the country on its other side from the Republic's sacred silliness: social upheaval.

From the jungle, growing north, stretching between the wetted valleys and the mountains, a dull, dry place takes up its centre space. Nkosians call it the Nothingness. This desert, home to the vultures and the bones of refugees is an ominous pan over which the desperate trek. They leave all that they know. Forced from their giving earth and traditional ways, they seek out the country's capital, Baobab, for salvation. Many do not make it to the city, an old trading post on the most northwestern cape of the Republic. It is there where the Government's supporters reside. Or dare anyone say, hide.

From the mouth of Baobab's sea stews a stinking lagoon. It is where the children of the Republic's largest and most decrepit displacement camp clean and feed themselves. Out of this smell oozes the Crocodile River. It slides along the coast, meanders between the hills and into the jungle, where it slips its way to the southernmost clearing of the country – the long-forgotten plateau. It is rumoured that a gathering of rebel warriors are learning things there that no man should learn.

The mines that were, in the days of colonialism, the jewels of this once promising place, hold steady and lonely long past the brink of the farmlands in the east. No one goes there. Only those enslaved by this country's 'Freedom Fighters' see and feel the depths of such dirt.

The Republic is colourful. Through her four generous seasons, Mother Nature stupefies. She starts damp, grows hot, cools, and finally, though tarnished, manages to sweeten into spring. There is no natural reason for her people not to stay fed. If only they could 'stay put,' then innovation would be their grace. Yet, war cripples such progression and disease toys with the nation's children, and so the wandering Nkosians go hungry. Very hungry.

Before this most recent and brutal conflict, life was their kind of normal. People pretended to be happy. People pretended to strive for a better way. Now such pretending is impossible. Hope is a hungry word, one Nkosians have no means to feed.

Amongst these people from not so long ago was a fine group of men. Men whose idealism drove them into the bush hunting for thieves.

Every Friday, the men rose early to escape their city lives. They piled into an old Land Rover and wound their way through Baobab's old quarter, watching flickering gas lamps in derelict windows ignite the drowsy morning. They moved through the alleys of the sleepy town, sipping at their flasks and listening to the murmurs of mothers that drifted through the Rover's windows.

Then, passing the Displacement Camp and its vile lagoon they escaped Baobab by heading south along the Crocodile River. Embers burned the horizon as the Rover ambled up the hillside. They toured through shack-clad villages and climbed higher, continuing up to the faraway trees. At these heights, the men looked down on the plains to find a graceful valley and its scattering buck.

On one of these habitual Fridays, a little time after their steady assent, the Rover stalled, forcing the men to begin their hunt at a fateful location. The driver, accepting the irony of Africa: Western tools often break under its pressures, softened the gears down to first. "Of course." He pulled up to a clearing that would cast a shade over the vehicle.

The men, four African, one Dutch, climbed out of the car and pulled off their button-ups, relieving themselves of their undershirts. Changing into their khakis, they surveyed the view. The lowlands swept eerily green before them. If heaven had a view.

These expeditions weren't for the faint of heart. Fear lingered unspoken in the men's hearts. Tensely, they asked one another, "Ready?" Five fists met in a circle and began to pump. "One. Two. Three." Four scissors and one paper flew out on the count.

"Damn." Stefanus, the only blonde stepped out of the circle. Fate had dealt him the hand of isolation. He would stay with the truck as it cooled and guard it. In a few hours, after an old fashioned rest, it would start again. The trackers patted Stefanus on his broad shoulders. One of them gripped his skin as he did so and muttered empty words of consolation. "Safer out here than in there, though!" Stefanus chuckled back, "Get in there!" He pushed his comrade gently towards the jungle. The Nkosians Against Poachers (NAP) checked torches and slapped at mosquitoes as they went. Then they were gone and he was alone.

A loss was a loss. Stefanus leaned against the Rover. He ran his hand along its metal and tapped on the bonnet to sound out some noise. This scenery was too quiet for him. It was not a good feeling to be left lonely in the middle of that beautiful nowhere. He began to hum, covering the eeriness of his discomfort with noise. He opened the door of the driver's seat and pulled a blanket onto the grass. He lay down and stared up at the sky. It stretched above him, caressed by dusty clouds. If one were to look down upon him from way up there, his body would be so infinitesimal that his fear could not strain one, that his rampant thoughts could not stir one. Not from way up there.

He tried to stay awake. He was not supposed to sleep on these expeditions, for his own safety and the safety of his team. Soon though, regardless of his resistance, the silence stole his waking and he faded away. Hours passed as the others tracked for poachers.

A vibrating voice woke him. Delirious, he made his way to his feet and stumbled towards the car. A screeching voice crackled through the radio. A tracker from NAP had found something in the bush. The transistor blared with static. "Stefanus – we' found----- we ca-------blo!---------------."

Alarmed, Stefanus' breath cut short. He fiddled with the dials. Static irritated his ears. He hit it with his fists and breaking it. The radio went dead. He steadied himself against the Rover and watched the jungle. He would have to wait for a clear sign to make a move. Uncertainty derailed his body. At this point he had to reason with himself and try to conclude why he chose to be on this expedition:

Every Friday, he tracked missing lions with the men from the NAP. There was a theory, a rumour, that the lions had not left the Republic of their own accord, but had been taken by poachers from the country next door. On a social level he understood. Everybody has got to eat, and a lion rug goes for a pretty penny. Yet, after many expeditions, no evidence of lion poaching had come to fruition. Sometimes, when the men were lucky, they found a lonely baby silverback. The gorilla would moan out its longing for its Mammi all the way back to Baobab, where the team would spend weeks nursing the baby before finding it proper care.

The NAP was run purely out of the goodness of the trackers' hearts, as there was no government funding for such endeavours. Hell, there was no government in Nkosi. Sure, its buildings were here. They rose wide and white, architecturally influenced by races come and gone: the Arabs, the Dutch, the French, the English, and the Belgians. The country had been everyone's whore. Baobab itself, and its sweaty alleys, bore much likeness to those cities of the north, resembling those found in Tunisia, Egypt, Morocco – even Sicily. Though the Republic had been inhabited by every kind of human, only those born from its soil could endure its strife. Cursed? Perhaps. Stefanus thought this possible.

A shift in the breeze brought Stefanus back to his current reality. He glanced around, looking for anything out of the ordinary, but drifted back into thought to busy his mind whole he waited for the trackers to return.

He thought of President Mfundisi, the man in hiding who was supposed to be running the show. Then, he thought of his own show, his own mess ... He thanked God he was out of the Princess Marina Hospital and all its bustling sorrow, if even for a day. Stefanus kept a small office at Princess Marina where he drummed over the hospital's finances, keeping it running on whatever he could, however he could.

Stefanus slapped a mosquito from his leg. Blood smeared over his shin.

Looking at the deadly insect reminded him that he had the tedious task of divvying up the donated blood between Princess Marina and the displacement camp on the outskirts of town. That would cost him. Everything was about greasing the hands that lifted; Nkosian hands do not work or cut deals unless they are paid to do so. NAP was the only exception to this rule, and he reveled in their generosity. Africa's general greed had exhausted him. Forty-three years old, tall, strong and blond, he was conspicuous, but well respected by the people. They knew he had paid his dues. His CV was written on his leathery face. His trials resonated in the faded colour of his eyes. Once brightly blue, they had become foggy, disenchanted by Princess Marina's daily hell.

He had lived in Africa a long time, having been drawn to its mysteries years before. Bored with life in the Netherlands, he sought adventure and found it as an aid worker in Rwanda after the genocide. He was young then, in ideology and physicality. Now he was tired. He had grown skeptical and conservative, but he could not return to the developed world now. He was bound to this land. Knowledge was his greatest captor. Too empathetic to leave, he cycled to work every morning earlier than the cuckoo burrow's call, because quite frankly, he hated the sound of a calling cuckoo burrow. He rode through the mist of Baobab's winter mornings when the alleys were quiet and smelled of sweet, milky tea. He enjoyed the breeze on his quiet commute. A luxury. By noon, the sun had melted the city's winter, an African idiosyncrasy that had always annoyed him.

His morning ride first took him through a decrepit and unsanitary cluster of buildings. Once he made it to the main road, the cityscape shifted into the spacious remnants of colonialism. There, he would raise his brow to the crystalizing rustles of jacaranda leaves. His heart slid in sync with the chain. Cycling reminded him of being at home in Amsterdam, as did the Dutch-gabled roofs of the buildings that stood close to ruin. As he moved past them, he felt somewhat at home. Then he would turn into the Princess Marina Hospital and roll through its courtyard. There the early risers sat, taking in the warmth of the rising sun. Patients' heads hung low, mourning lost limbs. At the building's grand doors, Stefanus would drop his bicycle, and with it, his optimism. He didn't need to lock it. He could leave it there for days. Nkosi is a country where hypocrisy thrives. It is a confused place where they will steal parts of your body, they will steal your children, but not a soul should take a belonging. It is against their religion. What that religion is, Stefanus was uncertain. Everyone operated by self-made rules. Stefanus, having grown up Methodist, couldn't understand the fragmented ideals that constituted the nation's belief system. He often cursed these as the root of Nkosi's self-made suffering.

For instance, the cities' religion was a cross-contamination of the world's worst beliefs. Out in the boonies, they do as all tribal Africa does – they worship their ancestors. This tradition is not all that bad, despite its witch doctors and the immeasurable amount of trouble they cause with their corruption and greed. They wait on special children, the colourless ones – the albinos. The medicine men bide their time with patient, stagnant eyes, like cruel crocodiles. Then one day, one hut's colourless child is gone. Its mother is heard throughout her village, crying the song of mourning. "Wayayayayayaya!" She wails over her torn-apart child. It has been brought back to her in pieces – pulled apart by the jaws of the 'healer.' Guiltily, the villagers withdraw into their huts, because it was they who asked the doctor for a potion for this or for that. They know that his recipes are greedy. It is widely known that one cannot cure a migraine without a pinky finger of an albino boy. The mother's calls sliver towards the retreaters. Her mourning enters their mouths and slips down their throats where it coils itself up in the pits of their stomachs.

Her sadness hibernates there, poisoning their morality.

With fragmented fundamental principles like this, how can Nkosi possibly thrive compassionately and justly?

These thoughts drew Stefanus away from the current anxiety he felt over his friends and his broken radio. Regardless of what the NAP had found, Stefanus was relieved to be in the jungle and removed from his stuffy office with its ticking, useless fan. He pulled himself away from the car and approached the jungle. Peering into its depth, he wondered ... As he scanned its greenery, his thoughts returned to Princess Marina. He wished fervently that it was a place where supplies and competency matched those of hospitals in the developed world. Most of the time, his efforts to sophisticate the place were wasted. At times like these, he found himself wishing he had never become an aid worker. There was far too much blood to mop up and far too few educated people who could possibly begin to know how.

These excursions with the NAP helped him escape. The Nkosians Against Poachers was his raison d'être in Nkosi. For one, it kept him out of the bar and away from the temptation of the round-bummed women who saunter through its crowded tables. There is something about the Nkosian women. They are wild-eyed, as if they have not yet learned humility. In their Eden, they frolic. Cheekily, they refuse to emerge from the garden of naivety. "Oh no Sah, you don't need a rubber. I am clean-clean." False vows made to expatriates all too often. Fools are those who, lost in lust, believe them.

The women walk around the crowded bar, hiding their red and swollen lips with brown lipstick, the signs of illness exposed in their sickened skin. How could one not instinctively know by the way it slides over their sharp scapulars that the women of the night in Baobab are sick? Oh, so sick.

Yes, he was happy to be in the wilderness, and away from the seething city and its oppressive temptations.

And then she emerged from the jungle. The trackers came running out of the leafy depths strewn with her blood. She was tiny in the men's arms. Her head dangled from her neck and her legs were cut clean off below her knees. The NAP men moved roughly past Stefanus as they struggled to open the Land Rover's back door and settle her in the seat. He gazed on this little girl who lingered on death's hearth. Grotesquely, she cradled her dismembered limbs against her chest.

Stefanus' stomach heaved. He had never witnessed such a fresh case of the brutal tactic used by the Militia for Minerals and the Liberating Land and Life Stealers. He had never been so close. "What the hell is this?" he cried.

"We found her in the jungle, Sah!" The girl, awoken by the conversation, fluttered her eyelids and spread her arms wide. Her disfigured feet pushed into the air as she lurched awake and cried out, "Severin!" Stefanus wiped the sweat from her brow with an unsteady palm. She fell back into her own puddle of blood and fainted. She could not have been older than five. The trackers ran for the other doors of the Rover. As one of them slammed shut, the little girl unfolded. Her limbs rolled off her chest and onto the floor of the cab. Instinctively, Stefanus picked them up and returned them to her chest. He started when his hand met her small breast. Horribly surreal, the mere action sent him into a wild panic. He let go of her shins and slammed the door. Stumbling backwards, he noticed his hand was sticky with her charred blood.

The Land Rover started after Stefanus' third aggressive turn of the key. They made a hurried retreat from the jungle towards Princess Marina Hospital in Baobab. Stefanus barely watched the dirt road, being too drawn to the feverish little girl in the back. He whispered to the man beside him, "Will she even make it?"

"I don't think so."

"Shouldn't we stop so she can go peacefully?"

"No. We must try..."

Stefanus' heart fractured. Great shrieks of emotion galloped up his throat and down his arms. His mouth fermented. Choking on air, he cried out and frustration poured from him. He shook in his seat, bereft of hope. One of the trackers, noticing this unusual outpour spoke directly. "Just drive, Stefanus. Just drive."

And so Stefanus drove, shamelessly crying. He tried to keep his eyes on the road and not on the little girl who was losing her battle in the backseat. Her breath strained as they pulled up to the hospital. Still crying, Stefanus pulled her into his arms. Her lithe spirit cooled his Nordic savage raging.

11

He pressed his mouth to her forehead. The residue of her fever stuck to his lips. Entering the ward, his wild eyes caught the startled gaze of his friend. Dr. Jain who strode towards him and relieved Stefanus of his burden. Holding her shins, he tried to explain, "The NAP guys found her in the jungle. These are her feet."

"We aren't equipped to do anything with those," Dr. Jain remarked as he rushed off with the little girl. From the end of the hall, he called back, "Well done Stefanus!" But the praise didn't resonate. Stefanus felt empty. He already felt the ache of loss as he watched the little girl being rushed down the hall to a place where she would probably die. He wondered what they called her, this girl whose family would never see her again.

In spite of his shock, Stefanus remembered he had to go to the displacement camp to pick up the load of blood that had been donated by CIDA. A nurse came to him and relieved him of the little one's severed limbs. Stefanus asked, "Where will you put them?" Her reply was soft and low, as she recognized that this was not the Stefanus she knew. He had folded inside of himself. She spoke as if to a child. "I suppose we can bury them?"

"Yes, I think that's best. Where will you bury them, Sophie?"

"How about under the thorn tree in the back, where the orphans playground is? I assume that is where she will play from now on, Sah? If she survives..."

Stefanus dropped his gaze, not wanting her to notice his swollen eyes. "You know best Sophie. You always know best."

He left the hospital as quickly as he entered it. His eyes stayed on his feet as he passed the men from NAP who stood waiting for news. He picked up his bike that lay on the colonial building's stoop. "She's in Dr. Jain's care. I doubt she'll make it. I need to go to the camp to see Deborah. I'll see you next Friday. Good night gentlemen." The men shook his hand and bid him farewell.

Silhouetted by the slipping sun, Stefanus rolled his bike through the courtyard, and for the first time, while passing the rehabilitating men and women sunning themselves, he allowed himself to soak in their destroyed features. He wondered what their stories were. Who took their ears, noses, fingers, arms or toes? Who rescued them? How did they make it to the ward at Princess Marina? One question above all taunted the prisms of his logic: How in God's name did they survive? Not only the stealing, but the healing.

TIMES LIKE THESE

In a burning village in the Valley of Nkosi
6 JULY 2008

A group of women were corralled into a hut that had been doused in gasoline. Flames rose, hungrily licking at its walls. Trapped, they panicked; fearing their children in the lineup outside would be picked off, one by one, just for fun. Women were shot if they tried to escape the torching. The boy-soldiers took their jobs very seriously. They stiffened their faces as they massacred the Mammies.

The sound of mourning rushed from the mouths of the dying women. They sang, "Wayayayayayaya!" The stench of burning flesh seared at their children's noses as the harping of their mothers loving voices died out with the scorching of their hearts. Nyla, a little cripple hiding herself at the end of the lineup, thanked the ancestors very much that she did not have a Mammi to watch burn.

Thirty children down the line from Nyla, an older girl named Helena, whispered urgently to the boy next to her. "I want you to be brave, Dodo." The child nodded.

The heat of his village in ruins burned at his back.

"I want you to remember everything about this village. Remember your home." Dorian turned to find great fires heaving into the sky.

Taking hold of his shoulders and drawing his attention back to her, she added, "I want you to remember me, and how I was here. Please do not forget." Dorian stared blankly back at her. "I want you to remember how you were here. Promise me you will remember everything. Remember the legacy of our warrior father. Remember the face of our mother." Helena trembled as she shook him, "Say that you promise!"

From Dorian's taut throat came the lie, "Promise." He turned from his sister to look for Nyla. He could not find her through the smoke and stench. Instead, he caught the eye of his best friend, Severin, and placed his hand on the other boy's shoulder. Severin, certain that Nyla was dead, fell away to his knees and whimpered in the dirt.

A shadow loomed over them. Little Dorian squinted upwards. Backlit by the sun, he found a man wearing a charming smile. A moment of false relief calmed the child.

The man laughed. Throwing his head back, he revealed the girth of his neck. His cackles made Dorian think of the hyenas that hunt at night.

Dorian's chest heaved, realizing that things were – unfortunately – what they seemed. The man lowered his face and turned to gaze on Dorian.

A premonition cooled Dorian's blood. Blood that he desperately wished would leave his body and take him away from this place – his village's market square – and this time, a heavy afternoon in his ninth dry season. He didn't like it when the women screamed their song of mourning. Wayayaayayaaa! Their yelping overcame him, alarming his tender heart of danger.

Ignoring the women's pleading from inside the hut, the man cast out his palm. A young boy from the group of intruders ran over. Wearing an eager smile, he handed the chuckling man a rusted knife. "Here you go, Anthony Zaza!" shouted the boy.

"This is a very fun game," the man called Zaza said to Dorian. "You are going to show us that you are a man. You are going to take this knife and cut the throat of the bitch at our feet. She says I cannot kill you. In fact, she demands that I not kill you. So, we will kill her."

Dorian looked down to find his mother's pleading face. She looked more frightened than when his Pappi had not come back from fighting the Country Men, the 'Freedom Fighters.' He felt her sweaty hand tighten around his. Her pulse ravaged on in his palms, as, beside him, his sister's spirit grew numb. The other children in the lineup, the ones who had also survived the bloody morning, watched the family in horror. The market square stilled. Its remaining inhabitants stood breathless, waiting.

The man had to be joking. This all had to be a very bad joke.

Anthony Zaza wove a knife before Dorian's nose and sneered, "Come on boy."

Sound drowned and time stretched out over the silver of the knife. Dorian felt as if he was dying in the jaws of a crocodile. He could feel the stranger grow impatient. He managed to force out a defiant reply. "No."

"No? You have ten-seconds you little shit." Zaza's barrel bore into Dorian's forehead, singeing his skin with its hot tip.

Looking upon his loving mother, Dorian accepted his fate. His heart's decision was made: They would die together.

The man began his countdown, seemingly enjoying himself. His voice reverberated above Dodo's fragmented recollections.

"TEN."

Mornings: Sweaty on Severin's mat, they giggled into one another. He thought of Nyla's eyes, two large circles of light. He pictured the five-year-old, cooling herself against the clay wall, watching Dorian and Severin tickle one another. He heard their laughter. It chirped inside his mind.

He remembered the feeling of Severin's heavy palm as it pushed him out the door. He was bound to get in trouble again, as he did every morning, for not sleeping in his own hut with his elder sister. As punishment for this, his mother always smacked him with her bare hand. He secretly loved the way her skin stung his behind.

"NINE."

Sunrises: He recalled his morning runs through the village, how its small buildings glowed an amber hue. He dreamed of his breath on the crisp morning air as he skidded around corners and hurdled fences. He thought on his entrances at his family's gates to find Helena already home from her chores. He would watch her lift a large ceramic pot of water off her head and place it at her feet. Especially memorable was how her strong back manipulated the weighted clay. How lucky it was that his village had a well. A few months ago, he was sick and his mother brought him to the clinic in the neighbouring village. He noticed through his fever how the young girls there walked, crooked-backed, like old men, bent by years of traipsing heavy miles to quench their families' thirst.

"EIGHT."

Helena: He could see in his mind's eye the sun's apricot shimmering against her chocolate skin. He thought of the high cheekbones she had received from her mother and her golden eyes – the same ones Dorian had inherited- a gift from their warrior father. Behind those eyes beat a courageous heart, and 'in times like these,' they would surely be in need of one. So said his mother when they watched the sun slip down the sky and disappear behind the hills at the end of the valley. They did this every night while singing for the lions, calling them home to the Republic.

He concentrated on the image of her generous smile – that graceful smile that held his heart. His sister was special, with her tiger-stone eyes. He didn't want her to be stolen in the night, like everyone said could happen on account of her exquisite beauty. When they were smaller, it was a running joke. People would squeeze her cheeks and say they'd take her when his mother was not looking. Now, though people said it coyly, and only meant it as a compliment, he noticed that their cheek worried his mother. 'In times like these,' she would say, 'they could very well be right...'

"SEVEN."

<u>Being a warrior</u>: He pictured himself playing with Severin in the jungle. He thought about how they climbed trees and mimicked the monkeys. How they hunted for snakes and were mischievous, as little boys are roguish the world over. Their favourite game was to pretend that they were warriors.

Dorian's late father was famous for his skills. At night after dinner, when the chief told the villagers tall tales, Dorian's father would often be the leader's muse. A legend, he was called upon to tremble over Nkosi's hills, to fight all the 'baddies'.

Dorian's father had helped conquer the White Men, the Arabic Men and the Country Men – the 'Freedom Fighters.' He had driven the intruders from the hinterlands and returned victorious to their village in the valley.

Stories of his heroism are told around the fire. Drums celebrate his successes. The entire populace pounds the earth with their feet. They dance, shaking the night.

"SIX."

<u>History lessons</u>: When his father did not return home, their chief came to Dorian. He said, "No matter your father's successes, Nkosi will never be safe. It is the only place in the world where we use the same word for death, for love, for celebration and for woe." When the French had taken Nkosi for their keeping from the Dutch centuries ago, they brought with them yet another language. Its subtle nuances had confused the Nkosians. This is how l'amour and la mort, given the illiteracy of the people, became 'lamore,' and so death overcomes an Nkosian in any moment of elation. "So young Dorian..." said his chief, "we must celebrate his passing just so."

With lamore and admiration, the boys had replayed how his father had helped ruin the White Man when the Country

Men rose up to fight for independence. Then they had replayed how he fought in hand-to-hand combat with the Arabic Men who tried to turn them all into something – though what, the boys were not sure. Perhaps baboons? Finally, they reenacted when he fought the 'Freedom Fighters,' who did not know how to use a knop kiri,[2] a spear or an axe, but who knew how to fire a gun – whatever that was. The boys were never certain. They had heard it makes a scary noise, and only cowards fight with them.

"FIVE."

Fathers: Dorian didn't mind sharing the role of his father with his best friend. They each took turns pretending to be him, the victorious warrior. He would share anything with his best friend, and the same was true of Severin. The boys felt similarly sad about the absence of their fathers. Severin's father only came home from working at the mines across the border every few months, and of course, though Dorian did not yet understand death fully, he knew his father had not yet returned, and people kept telling him that he never would.

When Severin's father did return, he brought home fancy presents like Seiko watches, or plastic toys for both his son and Dorian. Severin had to pretend some of the gifts were for his little sister, Nyla, for whom her father brought nothing. She was ignored. There was never a dolly for her like the ones other little girls' fathers brought for them from the country next door.

Severin was always embarrassed by his father's disregard for Nyla. Out of all the girls in the village, he believed that she deserved a dolly the most. It would be the perfect present to accompany the little cripple during her days spent with the village women. Both Dorian and Severin knew how she studied them, with her twisted shins and her mangled

---

[2] Knop kiri: A club used by Zulu warriors. The term directly translates as a 'head smasher/cracker.'

feet, taking in the warm voices of the women in her village. They both knew that it hurt her to not play with the other girls, who did not invite her to skip rope – how could she? – Or dance to the drums at night. Dorian noticed how she bravely smiled when she watched the other girls pound the earth with their able feet.

"FOUR."

<u>The intruders who found them in the jungle</u>: They lay smoking cigarettes on the patch of greenery that extends from the jungle to the edge of the hill. The boy's bounty of firewood lay scattered in the grass. Having emerged from the thickets, Severin and him had stood, machetes by their sides, surveying the strangers' machines that were slung over shoulders, along backs or carelessly strewn about in the grass. The men were larger than those they had seen in their village. They looked well fed and teased one another with stories that irritated the air. Dorian noticed that they all shared a tattoo on their upper right arm. It looked like two upside-down birds.

A man wearing all black rolled onto his stomach and caught sight of the two boys holding one another's hand. He had teased them, "Oh, hello." An oblong object dangled from the man's neck, glinting in the sun. It looked expensive. Something about it made Dorian feel uncomfortable.

He remembered he had felt too shy to speak, but Seve had managed, "Good morning Rra."[3]

The stranger smiled wryly. "Do you see these boys? They are well-mannered ones. They have addressed us in the old-fashioned way, using the title that young boys used to address gentlemen before independence. Very nice. Yes, you'll do. Come," he said, gesturing at Dorian and Severin. "We must all see how it is going."

"THREE."

---

[3] 'Sir.'

<u>The dead man</u>: Guns at their backs, Dodo and Seve were walked down the hill towards their burning village. They passed the big hut where all the stock for the dry season was kept. They watched as a man on his knees cried for mercy from a group of intruders. One of the intruders pulled out a knife and, with a vacant expression, slid it across the beggar's throat. Menacingly, the corners of the killer's lips curled upwards. The group of intruders then began to load a truck with the village's locked-up harvest. The dead man's wife came, hollering the mourning cry. Her voice shrill in everyone's ears, "Wayayayayayayaya!" She stumbled towards her lost love. The group of boys stopped their looting and watched her fall over her man. She convulsed over him, heaving her heavy heart. Another child took his machine and pointed its end at her head. CRACK. Her mourning ended. A sudden understanding came to Dorian. He whispered to Severin, "That machine is a gun."

"TWO."

<u>Nyla</u>: He thought of her most favoured ritual – how she would sit and listen to the conversations of the women while they weaved baskets and pounded millet. She hadn't a mother, she had only a despondent father, so she preferred to spend her days with the women while the other village children played catch or skipped rope. Nyla would pretend one of the women was her Mammi. She had shyly confessed this secret to Dorian, asking him if it was OK to 'make pretend.' Dorian thought there was no harm in her having an imaginary Mammi now and then. Nyla would sit by the chosen's side and listen to her banter with the other women of the village. The day would bleed hotly into dusk, and all the while Nyla would cool herself with the thought that today's pretend Mammi loved her very much.

"ONE!"

Anthony's sweaty finger tightened against the trigger.

Helena's voice rang out, "Please no!"

Dorian felt the man give in to his sister's call.

Helena knew it was too late. She knew that her family could not escape their fate. She snatched the knife from the man's hand. Their eyes met. At this, Dorian's senses were stirred, coming to as Helena raised the edge of the knife to her mother's throat and drew in her last innocent breath. She could not bear to lose her mother and her brother, and the men would inevitably kill her mother anyway – something she and her Mammi both knew. Although Dorian began to cry and Helena could not bear the sound of his misunderstanding, she pushed the blunt blade into her mother's flesh. All the while, Dorian kept shrieking the screaming song of a kite, "Helena! Helena! Stop it!"

She could not stop now. Her mother was already choking on her own blood. With numb hand and numb heart Helena pressed on and in until it was done and her mother's spirit was gone.

Dorian flung himself over his dead Mammi. Growing sticky with her blood, he whimpered in the dirt. He wished that one of the intruding boys with the weird markings on their arms would come and shoot him in the back of the head already. Trembling, Helena handed the knife to her new master, Anthony Zaza. He wrapped his hand around Helena's arm and pulled her up to her to feet. She stood, silent, in front of him. Anthony moved in on the girl.

Her eyes shot to her feet.

He brought his nose down to her cheek. Zaza inhaled her scent, picking up musky traces of dust and apples.

Her lips shivered from fear.

He whispered into her ear, "I like the way you smell, girl."

And as quickly as Anthony Zaza had come into their lives, he was gone, stepping away from them and into a truck. Its engine roared and it sped away, leaving the line of children coughing in its dust.

Helena softly unpeeled Dorian's arms from their mother and tried to hold him. He pried himself free and glared at her, white heat emanating from his raging eyes. Her broken heart cracked even further – he had already forgotten how they loved one another.

. . . .

The survivors, led by the branded boys and their machines, were herded through the ash of their village. Nyla found Severin amongst the raided and took his hand. Greatly relieved to find her alive, he helped her hobble beyond the limits of the village for the very first time in her life.

The children were marched up the hill towards the jungle. At the top, Severin looked back on his tarnished home. Night was coming, and he knew the farmers would soon be back from the fields. He imagined them finding their wives burned and their children vanished. One of the branded boys poked the end of his machine into Severin's ribcage, urging him forward. The two children met eyes. The boy with the machine recognized Severin's vulnerability, so he softened and advised, "You have to walk now. Say goodbye and then put one foot in front of the other, over and over and over again. Don't think. Just walk." Though he didn't want to, Severin understood and appreciated the other boy's lenience. He gave Nyla's hand a good squeeze and turned away from his home. Then the hungry mouth of the Nobody-Knows-How-Vast Jungle of Nkosi swallowed brother and sister.

SMOKE & WATER

Victoria Falls Hotel, Victoria, Zimbabwe
8 July 2008

Mfundisi stood at the bottom of the gardens at Victoria Falls Hotel.[4] Behind him lay luscious grounds. They rolled, brightly manicured, to the stoop of the white colonial hotel. Its gables swept the roofline sweetly, like the curls of European children. And just like those curls that turn golden in the African sun, these gables had tarnished over time, looking burned and tired at their edges.

However, the hotel's windows gleamed, offering gateways to vistas for the people indoors, who relied on the air conditioning to take in the view: the Chobe River Delta's mighty end.

Dramatically situated, the hotel's garden blooms as the smoke from the plummeting water thunders. A violent beast breaths between the cliff off the garden and the place where the second gorge of the Falls pours and then cuts its way into the rock. Carving tirelessly at Victoria Fall's great, tall walls.

---

[4] A colonial hotel built for those commuting from the Cape to Cairo on the Red Line.

The Victoria Falls Hotel, revered as one of Rhodes'[5] finest accomplishments, is built along the Red Line's steel tracks, which he hoped to lay from the Cape to Cairo.[6] Leaning on his cane, Mfundisi watched the Chobe River slip over the cliff's edge. The noise of its falling moved the nervous old man. Held in a trance, the tumbling water gushed like the rivers of his disheartened heart.

Disturbed by its rushing, he wished for a million wishes, each one borne within his greatest muscle. Those collective desires heaved at its chambers, and together they fought with its seams. He would give of his blood, he thought. He would give of his life to make it all go away. Then, releasing himself from the water's hypnosis, he resurfaced and thought on how the Freedom Fighters wanted his heart on a stick.

Talking to himself, he murmured, 'Why are you hiding here, Mfundisi?'[7] He shook his head. Giving up his heart wouldn't have helped. "It would not have resolved in one resounding peace. It still won't." He had often repeated these words as a sort of mantra, whenever he grew tired of the guilt. If he were to die, who would have Nkosi then, The Militia for Minerals or the Liberating Land and Life Stealers? Taking one power out of the struggle between the three, the MM the LLLS and the Government would not bring back the dead.

Guns had certainly changed things. Before, when the people of the Valley, the Nothingness and the Jungle united with the Government, they were still able to control the uncontrollable – the 'Freedom Fighters.' Sadly, these new

---

[5] Cecil John Rhodes was the founder of the state of Rhodesia, another name that Zimbabwe has had through its colonial history.

[6] It was Rhodes' dream to connect the Cape to Cairo via the Red Line, part of a rail system that would run through the colonies and foster trade. It is mostly completed and operational despite some missing links in Sudan and Uganda.

[7] A Swahili name meaning 'wise one.'

militias soon equipped themselves with enough machines to vaporize the traditional warriors of Nkosi, whom the Government needed in the fight. Needed not only as a reckoning force, but also as a means to rally the energy of the people. Only with the warriors could traditional patriotism prevail.

Uncertainty rang out to Mfundisi's fingertips as he recalled their united losses. He tapped his cane in the grass and turned his eyes back on the falls. Again the smoke and water rattled him. He peered down to the end of the chute. Water exploded. A crescendo of droplets erupted. Through them, the demonic River God of the Zambezi mocked him. The old man dragged his cane to the end of the grass and peered deeper into his fate. Sadness harped on him in this moment of accountability – he had failed his country.

From where he stood, he took in the flowers in the garden. They were an indescribable joy, and the magnificent scent of the flora lingered on the humid air. Still they could not help Mfundisi find peace. Laughter from the American children further tested his uneasiness. Sinisterly, the ruler of Nkosi cast judgment over his shoulder. Unaware of his scorn, the children splashed about in the hotel's pool that looked over Victoria Falls. Africa's longest drop. The best place in the entire world for a scenic suicide.

Mfundisi shivered slightly and to stave the melancholy, shifted his train of thought to his history. Mugabe was an old friend. They had simultaneously fought the good fight. Each of them struggled for independence from colonization. Each of them had buggered up thereafter. Before embarking on an ambitious war in Angola, the Russians had taught them guerrilla warfare in a little country called Mozambique. Who wasn't taught how to terrorize in those times? Cubans, Nigerians, Vietnamese, South African conscripts … everyone learned things they shouldn't have. The Reds, in exchange for allegiance, had funded all of their ambitions, and from such giving, Communism was implemented in Zim', Tanzania and post-independence

Nkosi. What other ideology could Mfundisi and Mugabe
integrate? Having followed them to freedom, they trusted
the Russians. The old ruler sighed, thinking about the Cold
War. A war quiet everywhere else but Africa. Mozambique
was where Africans learned how to enforce their freedom.
Even members of the ANC[8] were there. Mfundisi wished
that he had been forced to be patient like old Rhiololoh[9].
Mandela was forced to wizen before being instated as
president of South Africa.

The USSR taught many of them terrorist tactics to drive
out the White Man. In an effort to win popularity in Africa,
the Russians had promoted Socialism through promises of
liberation for all black men. They had not, however,
explained how to run a country properly upon the winning
of it. How disingenuous. What lack of foresight. What greed.
Mfundisi's intentions had always been good. Naïve, but
good. He followed Stalin's five-year plan. He introduced
pockets of Socialism in the public sector. The Government
took back the mines. He de-privatized schools. He de-
privatized hospitals. Everyone worked for the people, and it
went terribly because, well, his people were not very
enthusiastic about working.

A traditional folk, they preferred to continue living
tribally. As the population of whites, with their disliking for
Socialism, thinned post-independence, Nkosi's worth on the
international market inevitably faltered. With an ailing
economy and the onset of three deadly diseases – malaria,
tuberculosis and the socially crippling HIV / AIDS –
Mfundisi wavered. So did his people, disillusioned by
Communism. They could feel that their leader was lost and
tired. However, Mfundisi was a good man. Unlike so many
other African leaders he did not suffer from the sin of pride.
Instead he had humbly asked for help. He met with his

---

[8] African National Congress Party.

[9] Nelson Mandela's Xhosa name.

generals, and his Government officials, all well-educated
men. None of them had been Freedom fighters, of course.
They were too young during the initial plight. Those men
who survived the War of Independence from Mfundisi's
generation had chosen to return to their land in the heart of
Nkosi, uninterested in politics.

He now realized they had been wise. They had lived out
their lives without the weight of accountability.
Unfortunately, his younger politicians had taken advantage
of his meekness. They had stolen from the country. They
stole medicine and sold it to refugee camps over the border.
They jimmied the numbers from the mines and sold Nkosi's
coal, gold and tantalum on the black market for personal
profit. Nicking little bits of funding from the health system
and the education system, they grabbed money from
wherever they could.

Greed reigned amongst his men, and Mfundisi, having
trusted that integrity surrounded him, found himself run out
of the Republic during an attempted coup d'état. The
generals were subsequently punished, executed in Soviet
fashion. Having been driven out of Nkosi, Mfundisi had
given the death order whilst sitting on Mugabe's farm in the
Lowveld of Zimbabwe. The tyrant had advised, "You must
be ruthless old friend! Make a spectacle!" The news of the
executions rattled the nation and triggered wild ideas about
the country's taxes going to Mfundisi's off-shore bank
accounts. Headlines ran, "The executions are a sham! Where
are the missing funds?"

Two rebel forces opposing the president were borne from
these conspiracy theories. One of them took the mines by
force. The other patrolled the jungle and shared their
theories with the villagers in the boonies.[10] With the mines
being the greatest source of wealth for Nkosians, the
country's economy spiraled further out of control as this

---

[10] The 'boonies' is a synonym for 'outback.'.

rebel army became very, very rich. For security, what taxes were left untouched from corruption went to the Nkosian Army to protect the governing body and keep the Militias away from the cities. Education and health care took a backseat to chaos – all at a time when order was of utmost importance. A country needs to protect and educate its young. Mfundisi knew this, yet it was impossible to achieve.

The Republic of Nkosi unravelled. Mfundisi had called out to the Western powers, begging for guidance. They gave him none because of his alliance with the Eastern Bloc during the Cold War. What a hard lesson to learn. A lesson thousands of young Nkosians would pay the price for. What could he do but run to a place where the rebels could not find him? So he had run ... all the way to Zimbabwe. Here, from Victoria Falls Hotel in the southernmost part of Zimbabwe, where the Chobe River flushed into the Delta, Mfundisi and his most trustworthy officials ran Nkosi. Or pretended to. He knew that the most important infrastructures had been taken over by NGOs. They ran schools, brought in doctors and aid to hospitals, developed social programs and fed his people. How long would they stay, though? They could not go on like this forever.

The old man headed up to the terrace to take his tea. A sickly, white-gloved Shona[11] boy pulled out the president's chair. Mfundisi sat down and tucked himself closer to the crystal and silver-clad table. The boy settled a white linen serviette over the old man's lap.

"Simon, you do not look well."

"I am fine Sah. It is a flu ... it is just a flu."

Mfundisi watched the boy knowingly. "Simon, I need my stationery and a ball point pen please, and I will have scones this morning with good old-fashioned Golden Syrup."

"Yes Sah. It is Saturday after all, Sah."

---

[11] A prominent tribe in Zimbabwe. Their opposition are the Matabele. These two have been in conflict for centuries.

"It is indeed, young man."

Mfundisi tapped the table lightly with his palms, subconsciously drumming out a beat he had learned in his childhood – one his older brother had taught him on the goat-skinned drums.

Simon returned and placed the paper and pen next to him, poured his tea and unsteadily buttered Mfundisi's scones as another boy, also wearing white gloves, rushed over with a silver pot of Golden Syrup. As Simon turned to leave, Mfundisi took hold of his forearm. "My boy, you must go home to your mother. I do not want to see you here tomorrow. I can butter my own scones. Go fall asleep beneath the stars you were born under. Go say goodbye to your brothers and sisters."

The boy's eyes glistened. His words were breathy and fearful. "It is just a flu, Sah."

Mfundisi squeezed the boy's arm and, upon releasing it, said again, "Tomorrow I'd better be buttering my own scones."

"Yes Sah." Simon backed away from Mfundisi and bowed slightly before adding, "Thank you Sah, thank you."

Mfundisi studied the dying boy, who was walking off the terrace and over the grass to deliver a Malawian Shandy[12] to the noisy American kids in the pool. Mfundisi, irritated by their shrieking, looked contemptuously in their direction as he picked up the pen. After taking a bite of his scone and upon tasting the sweetness of the syrup, he began a poem:

> But I feel it – no, I hear it:
> a long whistle or a moan.
> Like a falling pebble,
> a plummeting rock,
> a dropping bomb.
> I look up to catch a glimpse …

[12] A popular mocktail.

He dropped his pen to the table. He sat back in his chair and again looked upon the falls. Losing himself, he thought of his young days in the guerrillas.

He wondered if the little boys who are stolen now to fight for the MM and LLLS are trained in the same way he was. Cocking his head, he imagined a young boy handling a Kalashnikov. The thought made him chuckle at first. Then, swallowing his laughter he turned his attention back to the American children playing in the pool. Watching them, he wondered how young boys were capable of killing. He himself, even with his undeniable resentment for the White Man, was scared as hell when he first took a man's life. And the guilt? The guilt never tapered. His stomach weakened at the memory.

No longer hungry, Mfundisi pushed his scones aside. Though he was once idealistic and determined as a soldier, he was now an old disillusioned ruler. All that he had fought for had turned his country to ash. What a folly. What a sad state of affairs. And the blame that should be on the Freedom Fighters lay perversely on his shoulders. An infuriating burden to bear.

THE GREAT TREK

In the Nobody-Knows-How-Vast-Jungle of Nkosi
8-13 July 2008

Captives and conscripts, the children marched, as slaves
have done for centuries. Like those stolen before them, they
trudged farther and farther from liberty, away from their
before-lives. Memories of old freedom, of family, of
humanity, flickered frame by frame in front of their noses.
On their journey with the MM through the Nobody-Knows-
How-Vast Jungle, the stolen children were witness to the
pillaging of countless villages. Over the days, the number of
those enslaved accumulated.

Lucidly, the nightmare burned on, and their memories of
happiness incinerated in their wake. Severin carried the
youngest captor, his crippled-at-birth sister, Nyla. He felt her
little heart beat into his chest. He breathed her in. Her soft
scent with its traces of dust kept him struggling forward. As
little Nyla cooked in the heat, she perspired and slipped
against Severin's skin. He gave way to his knees, at which
point Dorian took hold of their favourite little girl and began
to carry her.

It was her first time in the jungle and it was just as Dorian
had described it: gloriously dark – the cruel irony smirked in
the shadows.

In the afternoons, before this nightmare, whenever the boys came back from their wood collecting, Dorian would lay with Nyla and tell her of all the things her brother and he had seen in the jungle. He described the way the monkeys played and toyed with one another. He talked about what flowers were in bloom. He spoke of their smells and colours. Nyla's eyes would grow wide with intrigue. Her heart felt as though it would burst from yearning. She wished she could walk there herself. She noticed now how quiet he had grown. He was not his usual self, Dorian, the 'chatter box.'

Looking up at him now she murmured, "Dodo, are we going home soon?"

Kissing her forehead, he replied, "No Nyla. I don't think so."

"Tell me a story to make me feel happy." Dorian dropped his head back. Squeezing his eyes closed, he hunted for all the legendary tales his mother had shared with him: how the zebra got her stripes, why the warthog eats on his knees and how the monkey learned to swing. Yet all he could see was his mother's face and all he could feel was her steady embrace. And so in searching, he suffered the whispering taunting of her name, Maxiline, and could only say, "I can't Nyla. Not yet."

Before they were stolen, Dorian had promised that one day when it was not so hot he would piggyback her up the hill to the jungle, so she could finally get to see where the monkeys play. He had said that he would carry her, the way he was carrying her now, to the waterfall. Then they would take their lunch – the dried meat Dorian's mother would wrap in banana leaves.

They won't have that lunch ever again because Helena killed Dodo's Mammi. Dorian thought of the look in his mother's eyes as the knife moved into her skin. Saliva collected in his mouth. He wanted to throw up, but what was there to throw up?

Back then, in afternoons in the village, he would talk and talk and talk about the jungle, all the while massaging Nyla's crippled limbs. It calmed her very much. Not all his talking, but his touching.

"I miss our afternoons in the doorway Dodo."

"Me too Nyla. Me too."

In this moment, with Dorian heaving and salivating and cursing under his breath, Nyla couldn't understand why he had changed so much. She couldn't understand how he had grown so far from himself. She turned her attention from his misery and wondered at the natural world. The jungle was quiet for the most part, but roused itself from silence as they passed the pouring waterfalls and coiling snakes or when the leaves rustled from the group's moving amongst the trees. The men's voices and their periodic laughter punctured the air from time to time, but she dreamed above and beyond them, draped over Dorian or Severin's back. The strained breaths of either boy carrying her lulled her to sleep. They would shake her awake and remind her to push against them.

For the most part, the trekking children didn't look at each other. Their eyes hung low beneath furrowed brows. A great thirst overcame them all. Their throats were naggingly dry, as they had been walking for a very long time without any refreshment. Some wondered if they would ever be given any. Their minds conjured up tableaus of their homes and images of their mothers and fathers. Smells and touches scratched at their senses. Interrupting these recollections were the harsh utterances of the man's speech before they were marched from their village.

On that day (that now seemed so far away), he had smiled upon the children. He had told them that they were now part of the Militia for Minerals. He said that their job was now to protect the country's natural resources so that they could no longer be stolen, so that the resources could not be used by anybody else, or for any other purpose, but for addressing the plight of the MM against President Mfundisi. "The President whose government is starving the people of Nkosi with its Socialist policies and greedy pockets!"

The children didn't understand. And in any case, they weren't really listening, deafened by fear.

Yet, after a few days of being herded through the Nobody-Knows-How-Vast-Jungle of Nkosi, and especially when they were given time to rest, they finally mustered the strength to work together to make sense of their circumstance. When they did turn their attention back to Anthony Zaza's rhetoric, they would try to piece together what parts each had comprehended. As a group, they came to the conclusion that they were never going back home. They understood that the Militia for Minerals now owned them, and they were being taken to the MM's camp in order to start working against the President Mfundisi.

Days of walking stretched into nights. Friends fell from exhaustion and were left behind.

While their captors laughed over their lunch, the stolen children sat withered from lack of food and water. One of them asked the rest, "What is a president?" No one knew the answer, but all of them understood that knowing wouldn't help. They were going to be warriors, just as Anthony Zaza had hollered.

Another boy asked, "Aren't we too little to be warriors?"

The rest of the children nodded solemnly in affirmation.

Finally, a sack of dried meat was dropped in the middle of the children. It was the meat that had been hunted by their fathers and cured by their mothers. Helena and the eldest girls divided it equally amongst the children. The girls reminded them to eat very little, for if they gorged they would become very thirsty. The children obeyed, and this is how they thwarted the great thirst that had taken the many stolen children who, unknown to the group, had trekked before them.

Naively, they thought they were the first. They thought they were the only.

On the eighth afternoon, while passing a small waterfall and its pond, they were instructed to first drink as much water as possible and then get into the pond to wash the shit and urine out of their shorts or skirts. The children were relieved. The residual fecal matter had embarrassed them. They were very grateful to their captors for letting them drink and wash. No one thought to blame their abductors as the cause of their need to defecate in public. Critical thinking is, after all, not a child's forte. The process of manipulation is a delicate one, but the MM prides themselves on an art they have mastered: tricking children into trusting.

After the children drank, washed and ate some more dried meat, their spirits rose. Like their captors, they started joking with one another. Jokes that existed in their villages had followed them. They teased the same kids and laughed at the same idiosyncrasies that they used to in the village.

It was just as they were wavering on the blurry edge of acceptance that they saw him again. He pulled into the clearing, having cut through the jungle in a buckie.[13] Three older boys and Anthony Zaza climbed out of the truck. He shared some quiet words with those who had been guarding the children who all recognized the three older boys from the thrashing of their village. They moved through the children, bearing their machines proudly. Fingers on triggers, they stalked and then encircled Helena.

"You're coming with us." One of them spat on the ground and smiled a knowing smile. The children from her village flickered with fear, like those candles lit for loved ones in cathedrals about the globe – golden teardrops of light wavering in the darkness of God's houses.

Helena rose and let the boys lead her back to the truck. As she went, Anthony Zaza watched her with a hungry eye as the boys commanded her to get into the back of the

---

[13] Buckie: a small farm truck most commonly produced by Izuzu or Toyota.

buckie. Wearing a stony face, she obeyed. Her brilliant eyes shone back at her friends from her village. She climbed in and sat down, demure.

She stared back at the mass of silenced children. She looked for Dorian's face, but could not find it. His newfound apathy for her had caused him to settle listlessly into the grass, apparently unaffected by her re-stealing.

Anthony Zaza made his way to her and leaned on the cab. He looked upon her for a long time before saying it. "Hello."

She nodded cautiously in reply. She could feel something dangerous about the man who had smelled her for too long in her village. She knew now that her journey would be a different one than the rest of the children's. He reached into the cab. His hand caressed her thigh before grasping a machete.

She stiffened.

He smiled.

"Don't worry, it's not for you."

Anthony handed the machete to one of the MM guards before getting into the cab of the buckie and driving Helena off into the thicket.

Dorian felt relieved by her thieving. He couldn't stomach the smell of her. He couldn't handle the sight of her. She was no longer beautiful to him, but rather a disfigured reminder of his mother. He didn't think of anything much besides his growing hate for his sister who stole their mother from him. He lay grinding his teeth as she disappeared. The other children watched his reaction.

Their faces were blank. Their minds were busy.

Dorian looked at Severin. Severin looked at him. They shared their feelings with the tightening of their mouths, the sharpening of Dorian's breath, the wringing of Severin's hands ... and then they turned their heads from each other, unable to 'speak' with one another anymore.

The children's captors began to build a fire. One of the men ignited the stack of wood with a bag of burning rubbish and then lit his cigarette. He picked up the machete and walked towards the enslaved as the fire erupted behind him. The movement roused Dorian – his nerves tightened and sang.

With hammering hearts, the children sat waiting– all of them except for little Nyla, who slept idly in the grass. She was awoken by the grabbing of her crippled shin and pulled from the group of children. Too soon after waking, her throat dry from sleep, she was unable to voice a cry. Only soft noises escaped her mouth. Severin jumped to his feet and ran after his sister. He dove for her forearms and grasped them, pulling her back in the direction of his friends. Feeling the sudden tug, and hearing Nyla's shriek – sharp like a desperate kite – the stranger turned and glared over stretched-out Nyla and into Severin. Severin in turn carefully looked into the man and watched how his smoke escaped his lips and became a slipping serpent, slithering its way upward. The smoker raised his machete and slashed at Severin. From fright, the young boy let go of his sister and staggered backwards, but stayed on his feet. Nyla fell to the ground with a heavy thud. Severin grimaced at the sound.

The man pointed his weapon at Severin and threatened, "I can do you both if you want." Seve stood, unmoving. He was a stagnant body, rotting with fear. Like a little bird, Nyla's head twitched, her glance darting from Severin, to the children, to the machete, to the man with the cigarette, and then down to her twisted shins. She tried to get up but the man pushed her shoulders to the ground.

He held her down as he spoke through his cigarette, "Watch carefully boys and girls. I'm only going to show you how to do this once." Dorian jumped to his feet and ran for Severin, covering his eyes as the first chop separated shin from knee. A unified gasp from the group of children confirmed Severin's fears. However, she did not scream. She could not. Severin pulled Dorian's hands from his eyes and across his own chest. He squeezed them tightly into himself. An excruciating current ran between their two bodies. The man whistled nonchalantly to the other strangers and nodded at the fire. Nyla tried to get up again, but this time fell back because of her own weakness. The man lifted the machete and threw it into her again. This next chop was not as clean. The blade got stuck in her knobby kneecap. Blood pooled beneath her as the man struggled to reclaim the dismembering tool from her limb. On the second blow, the stubborn shin was off and her shill voice rattled the surrounding leaves.

The children watched on as she shivered. Before they could begin to process what they were witnessing, they were rounded up by the other MM guards and told to start walking.

Severin and Dorian fell to their knees and cried into one another as a guard chose a burning branch from the fire, patted out its flames, took her thighs and singed the bludgeoned ends. "No reason for her ta die right away. Might as well keep her meat fresh for the hyenas, hey boys? You two betta get movin' with the rest of dem group else I'ma gunna cut you a new face!"

Dorian looked over his shoulder at the group of children who were being marched through the jungle. He dragged his hysterical friend away from the scene and back into line. The children put their arms around Severin in an attempt to calm his crying. They took turns holding him as they walked. He pushed himself into their bodies, thinking they could absorb his anguish. As he walked, bloodlust rose up in his gorge. He thought about how he wished he could murder that man. He thought about how he wished he had a machine to shoot him with. He'd shoot him right through the heart because that's where Severin hurt the most – right inside his small and fractured heart.

. . . .

Back at the scene, the smoking man scoffed over Nyla's suffering and dropped her shins onto her chest. Looking at her bloodied body, he muttered, "You're disgusting," before he spat his cigarette into the grass beside her and turned to rejoin the group. The smell of stale tobacco sickened her further. Eyes shut tight; she could feel the man leave her. She could feel all of them leave her behind.

IN DREAMS

In the Nobody-Knows-How-Vast-Jungle of Nkosi
13 July 2008

Calmed by the delicate sounds of leaves, she faded away. She was not in pain. The shock was too magnificent. It swallowed her whole, so she swam in the acid of its stomach.

Nyla found herself sitting in the doorway, looking down at bent shins. Her eyes followed down their contours to her twisted feet. Enticed by the sound of laughter, baby Nyla looked up to see her Pappi and brother kicking a soccer ball back and forth. A ritual: something that was done at the end of her father's visits home, before he left them and returned to work in the mines in the country to the south of Nkosi.

She sat in the doorway tormenting herself with fantasies of what it would feel like: the sensation of her father's hand on her shoulder, the sticky sweetness of his lips on her forehead, or his dry fingertip upon her nose.

Dreamlike, her family played behind soft curtains of dust that rose with the volley of the ball. She sat wondering what would happen to her if her Pappi smiled back at her before he picked up his scuffed suitcase to leave. Would her legs unravel? Would her toes uncurl? Stranger things have happened in her sleep.

Her father drew the ball to a stop under his steady shoe and rubbed his large palms over his son's head. He pulled Severin in

41

and held him tightly before picking up his bag and walking out the gate. He did not look back at his deformed daughter. She sat lonely in the doorway of their thatched hut watching him go – in the same way that she watched everything, every day, in the village. The witness to soccer games, the big girls cooing over the big boys, the goats whom she named after their various personalities: Happy, Precious, Gentle ... Crier.

Studying her father's shrinking silhouette she wondered if he ever caressed or held her when she was littler, or had he always pretended she was not there? She knew she was different, this little girl with braids in her hair. She knew that she could not run, jump and play like the others. She also knew that it was not because she was the littlest child in the village, but rather because she was broken.

She would never skip rope the way the big girls did, no matter how tall and strong she got. Neither would she shake to the rhythm of the drums at nightfall. Suddenly the scene changed and she saw herself, a bright-eyed child, sitting and watching on as the fire breathed light into the gigantic blackness of the middle of nowhere. She nestled herself between one of the elder women's legs while the others danced. The smoke plumed upwards, draping itself between the celebrating villagers and the shimmering sky. The stars vibrated above her as the drums rattled the earth. Her heart listened to their guiding beat. Cradled as she was, she imagined what it felt like to open one's arms and undulate one's back. She imagined what it felt like to bend at the hips and let one's bum loose.

The forever-spectator, she watched the other children wiggle their hips and jostle their chests and hands, beating like the wings of king fishers, praising those ever-shifting stars that hang like twinkling dreams above. Encouraged by them, she lifted her hands and tried to fly like the rest, but no one took much notice of her. Feeling stupidly small, even in this dream, she stopped dancing and reverted to observing. She understood that this was her fate, to sit and be a witness, forever and for always.

Then she was sailing, freely above, at the height of day. Typical of any small village in the Republic of Nkosi, a cluster of huts surrounded a square where the community gathered for lunch, for dinner, for bartering and trading, for meetings and for, of course, celebrating. She watched the children bartering all the things their fathers had brought back from the mines. They squabbled cheekily. The village itself, like all Nkosian villages, was encircled by idling goats, which the older boys shepherded. She saw them standing strong with their staves, ensuring that the kids did not wander aimlessly into the bush and get taken by hungry hyenas. Then, suddenly sucked into a black void she pictured one, its teeth snapping at her little face. Her heart was racing now. Pumping inside its chest. Hyenas were a problem in those parts as there were no lions anymore to keep them in line. No one knows where the lions went. Even on the great hunts that take the men away from the village for weeks on end they'd come back bringing sad news, "The lions have all gone." Some say they wandered south to the Serengeti. Others believe they went north in search of the wetlands. Nonetheless, the great cats no longer prowled in those parts. Nkosians were sad for this. At night, they danced to bring them back, calling to the ancestors to send their prowling pets a message of their longing.

She crawled away from the frothing hyena, which, chained up to a fence, snapped at her lifeless legs. The older girls skipped rope as Nyla tenaciously crawled for the foot of the village well – another one of her favourite spots to get stuck. When she finally made it, she turned around to notice that the hyena was gone and the chimes of its chains had stopped. Relieved she started to speak to one of the Mammies. She was quite talkative, little Nyla. Her words were precise, and no one could deny that she was remarkably cute with those tightly woven braids in her hair.

"Who plaited your hair, little Nyla?" the mother of one of the big girls asked.

"Ah! It was Dorian! You would not think it, but he is a good platter of hair. I am very proud of his work this week!"

She shined at the women, and with such a compliment Nyla suddenly forget all about her contorted little feet until it was time to relieve herself of the midday heat and hobble back to her hut. From there, she sat in its little doorway and look out onto that little

43

village which lay in the valley beneath the Nobody-Knows-How-Vast-Jungle of Nkosi. That jungle with its waterfalls and humming birds ... with its banana trees and tricky tree monkeys ... with its dark, scary nights when its snakes slip and its crocodiles snap ...with its vivacious days when orangutans whoop and holler from their vines ... with its hippos who yawn and roll in the mud beside their puddles of muck. That jungle where Dorian and Severin fell in love. The jungle where they learned how to run and jump, to be feral and strong. That jungle where they became blood brothers when Dorian fell and bloodied his knee. Where Severin swooped in on his crying friend, slit his own knee with his machete so they could bleed together and so that Dorian would no longer be afraid. She knew all these things because Dorian had whispered them in her ear whenever he plaited her hair.

The villagers heard that on the other side of the jungle was Nothing, and Nothing went on for as far as the eye could see. It is in the Nothingness where the ominous creature, the vulture, lurks. No one, of course, has seen one, besides the warriors who had many times over been forced into the Nothingness. The warriors who were skilled enough to return home brought with them despicable descriptions of the humpbacked cretin.

"The vulture is a hideous beast. It feeds on the fallen with its horny bill and tough tongue. Its feathers are ghastly, and it has claws like swords. It marches thirstily over the sand, stalking from one dead tree in the ground to another. It eats and eats and eats ... children!"

The veterans would then hold their bellies, chuckling at the naivety of the young ones who shrieked in horror from these tall tales. They became terrified of this creature that lives on the other side of their Nobody-Knows-How-Vast-Jungle. It was these warrior stories about the Nothingness that taught the children of the village how to taunt each other thusly: "If you do that one more time, the vulture is going to come and get you!"

The vultures of Nkosi are well fed. They needn't prey on Nkosian young. Littering the Nothingness are the picked-apart skeletons of Nkosi's refugee runaways.

Lovelessly, her Pappi walked away with his old suitcase in hand. Sitting and watching her father head for the mines, little Nyla wished a vulture would come and get her already. Nyla then dreamed that her Pappi opened his suitcase and pulled out her brother's machete, walked back towards her and instead of leaving a kiss on her forehead, cut off her useless little feet.

Slipping deeper into unconsciousness, tears moistened her moonlike face.

. . . .

Hours later, and far from where little Nyla had been left all alone in the Nobody-Knows-How-Vast-Jungle of Nkosi, Dorian and Severin lay huddled together not knowing what had become of their favourite little girl.

"Seve. Seve. Are you sleeping?"

"No."

"I'm starving, Seve."

"Really? I'm not hungry at all."

"Do you think anyone is sleeping?" whispered Dorian.

"None of us are."

"Seve?"

"What Dorian?"

"I ... I ... I think I hate her."

"I think I hate myself, Dodo. I just left her. How could I leave her all alone?"

"What could you do, Seve?"

"What could Helena do, Dodo? Here, give me your hand."

"Thanks Seve ... Seve?"

"Yeah Dods?"

"I really love you. I love you lots."

"Don't make me cry anymore Dods. I'm so tired of crying."

"Sorry Seve."

Sighing out, "I love you lots too Dodo. Let's try sleep, okay? Come closer." Dorian snuggled in. Severin felt his

45

friend's drenched cheeks wipe against his shoulder as he whispered, "Okay. G'night."

Severin's heart wrenched. Saying those words would confirm that this horrible day had truly happened and that a horrible night was waiting for him, but he forced himself to reply. "Good night Dodo."

And so they held on tightly as they suffered together, loving the hell out of one another. And then they pretended to sleep.

VIEW FROM A STOOP

The displacement camp on the Crocodile River,
outside of Baobab
20 July 2008

Deborah sat in the sun on the cement stoop. Her colleagues trouble shot in the square cell of an office behind her. She leaned against the pillar of the stairs and cast her nose upwards into the heat.

Her arms hung exhausted between her thighs. Too tired to think, her mind bronzed vacantly in the afternoon sun, like white skin. When she closed her eyes, the colour orange painted her inner lids. It was a silk drape, masking her memories of this place. It hid her disillusionment with the human race.

Washed away in her moments in the sun was her desire to stay in Nkosi. She often imagined what autumn days would be like in Canada, where the head office of the NGO she worked for was located. She had visited once many years ago and sometimes thought of Canada's brittle foothills, its golden leaves and pumping rivers. On rough days here in the camp, she would sit on the stoop and recall when she had been taken into the Rockies, and her Canadian colleagues had put her on horseback. She recalled roaming along a simple cedar fence. Beyond it stood the mountains. Hanging idly over them, a violet sky. She had never seen the sky so brilliant as it passed from day to night. Finely lit, the day met twilight. Her trip to Canada brought a new understanding. An understanding that there are places in this world where no one has to lock their doors at night. Places where murders make newspaper headlines. Places that felt guilty for understanding peace.

While she had been in Canada she longed for home, despite the startling beauty of the northern wilderness. Yet, she dreaded returning at the same time. An uncomfortable quandary. She understood that the work she did at the displacement camp was because she wanted Nkosi to one day have the opportunity to know the peace she had felt on those auburn days in Alberta, Canada.

Deborah had grown up in Baobab. Daughter to a lawyer, she was raised in a middle class home in the old French quarter. She went to an Nkosian primary school where she learned both Nkosian and English. Many families like hers sent their children abroad for high school. It was the thing to do. Her parents didn't quite have enough money. However, they had sent her to a French immersion private school close to home, where she excelled.

Her mother's family was from the Valley, where they often went on school holidays. Perhaps it was those visits that compelled her to stay. So many of her classmates counted the moments until they could escape Nkosi and attend a university far away. Not Deborah. Those visits to the Valley tied her to this home. They got her hands dirty. They entrenched in her adoration for her land, an unbreakable respect. There is an old proverb in the Valley: "Once Nkosian dirt is under your fingernails, you will serve the land forever. Not because you are a slave, but because you understand that it is your way to freedom."

Deborah was a child of this proverb, however imprisoning. She lived her life in accordance with it. She loved her country, even for its disheartening downfalls, and she wanted it to get better. So that's why she stayed in Baobab for university, and that's why she took an internship after graduation in the displacement camp on the Crocodile River with a Canadian NGO rather than taking one in England or France. Her parents, perceiving that Nkosi's civil wars were not about to calm, begged her to leave, but stubbornly she stayed.

Her life became the camp. She worked her way up the ranks until she was promoted to the top. After a decade, she was named the Country Director. In all sense and purposes, she was the camp's chief. The people of the camp were lucky to have her. Every afternoon, when people passed her as she indulged in her daily sun tanning ritual on the stoop of her office, faces blossomed, opening up in wide grins of thanks.

These afternoon breaks were not driven strictly by a need for sun or the deep desire for a pause. Here, on the stoop, she took in the daily operations of the camp rather than being consumed in her office about what needed to be done, worrying about what a mess everything was, being devoured by fatalistic thoughts. She took this time to watch the little ones as they skipped rope. She smiled at the thought that they were happily doing so because of the work she did. This is what kept her sane.

Today, three teenage girls wearing blue tunics and white-collared, capped sleeved shirts came around the corner of a shack. They leaned into one another, giggling. Deborah cocked her head to read the books they held against their chests. Jock of the Bushveld by James Percy Fitzpatrick. Matilda by Roald Dahl. The third was a Rudyard Kipling compilation.

"Haaaaiii Miss Deborah!" the girls in uniform sang.

"Afternoon girls." Deborah's heart fluttered as they passed. She was amused by their likeness to all teenage girls everywhere. The girls, who were verging on puberty, had flirtatious skips in their steps and giddiness ubiquitous in that age group. They laughed their way down the lane. Deborah leaned her head back against the stairs and closed her eyes again.

One of her new employees came running down the alley, disturbing her reverie. A Cockney accent soiled the air. "Deb! Deb! Snake!"

Opening only one eye, she examined the flailing young man as he ran. Shouting towards him, "Say that again?"

He skidded to stop and pointed down towards Section C. "A woman has been bitten by a bloody snake!"

Unstirred, Deborah replied, "Well, that's fine. Can she describe the snake?"

"Umm … I didn't ask … I just came running. She's swelling up like a balloon and sweating like a baboon!"

Deborah chuckled at the young Brit's half rhyme. Agitated by her apathy, he protested, "It's not funny Deb! She looks like death!"

Deborah dug in her pocket and, pulling out the keys for her ragged old Rover, said, "Here, take her to Princess Marina and ask for Doctor Jain. Be sure to know the kind of snake it was so he can give her the correct anti-venom. In the meantime, I'll spread the word for a reward. I'll hand out some shovels and we'll have a snake-killing spree. Can't deal with this sort of shit every day can we?"

The newbie looked stricken. Nervously, he took the keys and looked at them, stalled at the spot.

"Well, off you go! You came here to save lives, didn't you? Hurry up and save one."

Trembling still, he murmured, "Umm ... okay, Deb."

As he ran for the old Rover, Deborah picked herself off the cement. Her head rushed slightly upon standing. Thirsty, she decided to wind her way through the camp to the little shack-shop in Section E for a bottle of Coke. It was mid-afternoon, and as she progressed, she pushed through the tides of homecoming school children. They swarmed her, chanting sweet everythings. Smiling upon them she felt a richness unknown to kings. Little hands pinched her lovingly. Chins pressed themselves into shoulders as bright bold eyes shone up at her. Some fingers went into mouths to convey shyness, while others tickled her in the ribs. She found some little bodies amongst the crowd and tickled back. A child shrieked, enchanted by the affectionate exchange. She was released on the other end of the current as if she had been sucked into the eye of a churning wave and washed clean.

Emerging on the other side, she looked back at the gaggle of kids as they giggled themselves further away from her. They carried their homework under their arms as if a piece of paper and a crayon were the luckiest things to own.

A boy's paper slipped to the dust. "Non, non, non, non, non!" The little one saved it from trampling, blew hard upon it and waved it clean in the air. He noticed Deborah was still watching him and he grinned guiltily. He grinned magnificently. Deborah tripped over a rock and stumbled gently into a filthy puddle. "Shit." She laughed a little, realizing her curse had been literal, and shook her ankle free of the sewage.

Continuing on her walk, Deborah passed by the makeshift community. Grandpas sat on haunches smoking pipes. With an air of importance, they talked to the young ladies whom they had obliged into listening to their wise lectures. Mothers pounded millet that had been provided by the World Food Program. Babies crawled with flies about their yellow eyes. Distended bellies hung from exposed ribs.

Unaffected by the sights, Deborah continued down the hill. She watched her step as she went. Her hiking boots, heavily worn, skidded. The pebbles on the hill tumbled down the slope. Falling here would not be fun. She laughed at her own ineptness and wondered how all the mothers with babies strapped on their backs managed to achieve such balance as they descended the same hill. It always amazed her how the women who grew up in the fields moved with balletic poise. The women from the city had little elegance. Their shoulders drooped from the stress of their bookkeeping jobs. They hobbled about on feet blistered from high heels.

At the bottom of the hill, Deborah braced herself for the sickening lineup at the little clinic in Section B – a part of the camp where babies howled and mothers helplessly tutted. It was a heartbreaking part of Deborah's daily journey to her bottle of Coke. She tried to ignore the horde as she passed. She still struggled to look at women of her age in the eyes. Those eyes which bore the weight of finding food to keep their children alive. Children conceived in rape. A burden of love forced upon these young mothers.

Deborah's eyes found the dirt and her hands sulked themselves into her pockets as she passed them. Her shoulders drooped, defeated. Her throat cracked from thirst. Or from a sore heart. She couldn't tell which.

Sniffing back on her snot and wiping her eyes, she passed the tribunal. A place where old chiefs hold the people's hearings. They were usually interesting, and Deborah would catch herself hanging around to form an opinion on the people's matters. Will Man A get back his radio from Man B? Whose water canister is it? Today, a chicken had been stolen, and they were trying to find the culprit. Deborah could tell because the usual musical scene was playing out before her. Intrigued – how could one not be, given such a show – she found a spot beneath a thorn tree that provided some dabbled shade. A witch doctor was performing centre stage before the seated audience – a semi-circle of suspects, for someone had eaten a chicken that was not theirs. The witch doctor dripped with feathers and bones. The dry shells around his ankles shook sacrificially as he pounded his heels to the rhythm of the audience of suspects who were clapping their hands in a steady rhythm.

The semi-circle vibrated. Every one of them knew who the culprit was. A community knows one another's strengths and weaknesses. They know who is malicious and who is innately good, and so this daringly beautiful procedure is all done for show. Rituals are all they have left from their old ways of living. Almost everything else is gone. The land, the huts, the people.

The witch doctor waved his arms wildly in the air and spread his wriggling fingers towards the crowd. He sent his arms to the right of the semi-circle and cried, "The wrongdoer! He is in this part of the crowd!"

The applause stayed steady. The man continued to pound his feet. He brought his writhing fingers to his temples and his eyes rolled back in his head. Calling upon the ancestors, he spoke in tongues. His arms suddenly waved to the left, and he cried out, "The evil thief is here!"

The beat from the clapping hands drummed on. In a rage that the ancestors could not lead the witch doctor directly to the supposed chicken eater, he broke out into a bulging-eyed fury. Uncomfortable, Deborah adjusted herself against the tree and looked about to see if anyone else was concerned for the man's sanity. Instead, members of the community stood entranced.

The man danced, flailing, embodying the messages the spirits from above released into him. Striking both arms towards the centre of the semi-circle, his hands trembled. His eyes opened gigantically and focused on the group of people sitting before him. Hissing, he released his news, "He is here!"

There was a shift in the rhythm of the applause. One clapping suspect's heart skipped a beat. Shaky nerves had broken the suspect's rhythm. With a wide gait, the witch doctor moved closer to the group. Deborah saw it on their faces, the excitement for the moment when the thief would finally succumb to the torment and break free from the charade.

It was time for the Witch Doctor's melodramatic finale. The audience was lapping this up. He slowly approached the gaping crowd, sauntering the edge of the half moon. He came right up to the seated clappers and waved his hands over their heads as he jiggled his legs. He clucked his tongue in correspondence with the ancestors as he lowered his hands. His ten digits were a mere whisper from the audience of suspects' heads. He moved his hands from one head to another, and eventually broke into the seated throng, walking and clapping amongst them.

He concentrated on a person for a long while, feeling their aura. As he did so, he asked the ancestors, "Is this man good or bad?" He stuck his ear into the air so that he might hear the spirits' secret answer. Then he would move on to the next culprit to cast yet another fantastical judgment.

Deborah noticed a young man amongst them whose skin was wet with stress. His eyes followed the witch doctor's every shimmy, followed his every shake. From the thorn tree, it was evident that this boy, whose clapping was playing its own guilty tune, was the thief. Deborah's stomach fell. She ached for him. He was young and he had been hungry. It was just a chicken! Then again, a chicken was worth a hell of lot in these parts. She knew what would happen. The boy would finally, engrossed with fear, break for the winds. He'd dart from his seat and run from the inevitable beating.

The Nkosians are harsh and unforgiving when it comes to thievery. It is against their religion. What that religion is, Deborah was uncertain.

The clapping grew louder and the people's voices started sounding out assertions – "Yes, Doctor! Hai,[14] Doctor! Find him, Doctor!"

Deborah, knowing how the proceedings would end, turned from the spectacle. She stepped out from the shade and into a tall man. He was highlighted by the sun, his body, and an enigma. She squinted her eyes and refocused them. "Stefanus? Hi!"

The man extended a bottle of Coke. "It's that time of day."

"Dunkuwel,[15] Stefanus"

"More than welcome."

---

[14] A Southern African term meaning 'yes.'

[15] 'Thank you' in Dutch.

The crowd erupted behind them. Turning back, Deborah found that her predicted scene was playing out. The psychological wringing of such a ritual propelled the boy from the group and he made a run to salvage his pride. The crowd picked up and chased him. He made it quite a ways into Section E, but the throng closed in on him about a hundred yards later and began to give him a great lashing.

Perplexed, Stefanus remarked, "Such a weird place, your country. They will steal a body part. They will steal a child. But no one gets away with stealing a God damned thing."

Not taking offense, because she knew it to be true, she replied, "Funny, Stefanus. I was just thinking the very same thing ... I'm sorry I was not around to receive the blood the other day. I was dealing with something."

"No, no, don't worry ... I was dealing with something myself."

THE TRAINING

A school day on the Crocodile River
July 2008

"Drink it," the boys sneered, thrusting a cup of blood at Dorian.

The bullying exhausted Dorian. Those stolen by the MM before him had teased him ever since the group from his village had arrived at the abandoned school.

The stolen walked from the jungle through the low veldt[16] along the banks of the river and ended the trek standing before wrought iron gates. The architecture of their new 'village' reeked of colonialism. DOORNBOS was written upon the gates above them as they entered their makeshift training camp.

"Drink it Dodo." Severin urged him on, knowing that the bullying was a way to weed out the weak.

The child brought the cup to his lips and opened his throat. He threw his head back, trying to manipulate the blood so that it would miss his taste buds. It didn't. The tang of death ruined his senses. Its metallic flavour made him dizzy. Its consistency offended his stomach.

"Yuck, yuck, yuck, yuck, yuck!"

---

[16] Veldt: a term used to refer to certain wide-open spaces in Southern Africa.

The older boys started clapping and laughing. They danced around like crazed monkeys and then ran off, wielding their AKs. Seve wiped some residue from Dorian's lips. "Yuck ...Whose was it?"

"I'm not telling. It doesn't matter anyway."

"Of course it matters! It was my breakfast! Now tell me whose it was?"

"One of the big girls' – Patricia. They performed a ceremony last night for the commanders. Supposedly if you do that thing to a girl, her innocence protects you during battle. She died because too many of them wanted her help."

"I don't understand. How could she die?"

Pointing at Dorian's drained cup, "She bled to death, Dorian."

"Seve! Where are we? Who are these people?"

"You are one of these people Dorian! You are a MM soldier. Get used to it. Remember the rule in this camp – kill or be killed, okay?"

"I got it. I drank her stupid blood didn't I?"

"Don't hesitate next time. Just drink the stuff. The bigger boys will beat you if you don't. They like to play with the weak ones. It's fun for them, and I'm not gonna let you be wussy."

"I know, Seve!"

"Do you Dorian? Do you?" Severin pushed his best friend to the ground.

The fallen boy looked up at him angrily. "I know Severin," came his unwavering reply.

"Good."

Dorian stood up and dusted himself off. He watched his friend walk towards the rest of the children who milled hungrily about the ammunition classroom. "Stupid Seve."

Leaning against the wall was his sister, Helena. She held herself with her arms. Breathing like a little dragon, Dorian grew fierce. He locked eyes with his sibling and marched towards her. She watched him warily as he approached. His hands turned to fists and Helena, knowing better than to try, picked herself off the wall and made her way back to her and Anthony's room. Zaza was speaking to all the children about what guns they were about to see and how they were going to practice with them.

Dorian marched to the front of the crowd and interrupted his commander, demanding, "Give me one!"

Anthony Zaza found the angry puppy entertaining. He hushed the child with a tender laugh. The rest of the children began laughing too.

"No, seriously! What's so funny? I want a big gun, Mr. Zaza!"

"Dorian, my child, you are going to get a gun, and then you will have some fun."

"Give me one now! I have a lot of shooting to do damn it!"

Severin leapt towards his friend and covered his mouth, fearing that Dorian's attitude would set the commander off. He'd seen the cruelty Anthony was capable of. He'd counted the number of children who had been beaten into breathlessness in the two weeks the boys had been there. The number was twenty-seven. Anthony Zaza had killed twenty-seven children in fourteen days. That was nearly two a day. The odds scared the hell out of him. He stayed clear of the commander if his day allowed it. Dorian threw Severin off him and into the group of attentive kids. More laughter filled the air. Anthony smiled down upon his children, and then presented the children with the gun that was slung over his back.

"Okay, Dorian. Here. This, my child, is a Kalashnikov designed by the great Russian, Mikhail Kalashnikov. It was the gun that helped us win our country back from the White Man, and it is the gun that is good for killing people who don't have any respect for their country. It is lightweight and reliable."

Dorian was handed the gun. He beamed down upon the weapon. "It is mine, Mr. Zaza?"

"Yes Dorian. Everyone is going to get one, and you'd better take care of them. The big boys will show you how to take them apart and clean them, but first we are all going to fire them."

Anthony waved over one of the big boys who leaned against the chained fence of the tennis court smoking a rolly.[17] "Give me your daga[18] for the kids."

"Yes Sah."

"Everyone take a big inhale on this, hold the smoke in and then let it out. It is a magic herb that is going to make you very good at firing the Kalashnikov."

Dorian snatched the droll.[19] He dragged in its smoke with surprised eyes. He coughed it out. The droll was passed around, and then the kids were led to the old soccer field where the bigger boys had set up targets. They had been rather artistic, stenciling their bodies with the big kokis[20] that they found in the art class. Some of the stenciled faces had smiles or mouths in the shape of big Os, to depict surprise. Yes, the big boys had had fun.

The art was placed on top of desks, which were lined up side by side on one edge of the field. On the other side were the kids and their gritty hand-me-down AKs.

"Okay everyone. Come get ten bullets from me, and I will show you how to load them." The kids swarmed their Zaza. They collected ten bullets by stretching their T-shirts from their bodies, making little sacks with the pulled-at cotton.

Zaza's instruction began. "So, you're going to take the butt of the gun between your legs because it's a bit big for you to hold under your arms."

---

[17] A joint.

[18] Marijuana.

[19] An African word for a joint. It is also a synonym of 'shit.'

[20] Felt-tipped pens.

He swatted a fly from his cheek as he spoke. "Remove this big circle thing by unclipping it here." The kids studied Anthony's directions with interest.

"See how it opens up to reveal this wheel?" Little heads nodded. "Now, what we're going to do is wind this wheel to the right because when you fire, it is going to magically turn to the left, pushing out a bullet every time you pull down on this thing here, called the trigger."

The children pretended to understand.

"Once you've managed to turn this wheel all the way to the right, until it can't go any farther, then you have to lay this circle thing on the ground and push the button in the middle of it all the way down with your whole body weight."

Anthony demonstrated, speaking at the same time. "I can do it standing, but you are all still small, so you need to work a bit harder. Once you push this button, it's really easy to load bullets into."

He then grabbed a fistful of bullets from his pocket. "You just pop them in one by one wherever there is space in the cartridge. Once you've put all your bullets in, you close it back up, making sure to clip it closed, snap it back in to the AK, and then you can start firing. Place the butt against your shoulder. Point the nose in the direction you wish to shoot. Stare down the barrel. Take aim …" CRACK.

The kids jumped at the sound of the firing, and then, because they were high, laughed at their fear. They all lined up side by side and were helped by the older kids to practice loading the circular cartridge.

"Whoever hits his target all ten times gets a chocolate bar. And remember – we are not shooting each other. Do not point the guns at your friends!" boomed Zaza.

He sat back and watched Dorian giggle with excitement over popping his bullets into their spaces.

"Peter?" A young soldier came running. "Go roll another for the kids. They've been good."

The tween nodded and took off as the first futile rounds were fired.

Dorian rolled onto his back and exploded into hysterics, crying out, "No chocolate for me!"

Severin smiled over at him, and all of a sudden they were laughing together – just like old times. As though they were looking at life through a kaleidoscope, the world twinkled and shifted. Firing guns sounded like tinkering symbols, and everyone glowed under the sun.

"Melted chocolate looks like poo," said Severin, amidst their fit of giggles. They laughed harder and harder and harder until their tummies hurt, until tears of joy spilled from Dorian's eyes.

He pumped his fist into the air and screamed, "Lamore!"

Severin pumped his and screamed it back. "Lamore!"

Zaza reclined in a wooden chair Peter had brought for him from one of the classrooms. He watched his kids fire and miss. He was not angry; he knew they would get it right. It didn't matter much yet that they had no aim. What mattered was that their attitudes were slowly turning. That they were falling into their roles as his children. That they were starting to see him as their Pappi. That they were aligning with the cause.

"Mfundisi is a bad president! He has stolen all of our country's resources! He is the reason there are no schools. He is the reason there is no food. All those people who don't fight against him and his army are against the good of the Republic! The LLLS cannot be trusted either, my Little Warriors! If they are able to take hold of the Government before us, then nothing will change, for they are just as greedy as fat old Mfundisi!"

Brainwashing is where Anthony Zaza had his most fun. He performed it artfully. With every group of stolen kids, he learned more about the human condition. Regardless of love, hate, adamancy or loyalty, there is a part of a child that is incredibly easy to confuse then warp.

Reward and punish, reward and punish, and eventually you have yourself a child soldier.
One who will do anything for you. One who will die for you. One who will even kill for you.

CAGED

In Anthony Zaza's bedroom
August 2008

All her nights were the same. She sat up in bed as he breathed deeply and apparently guiltlessly by her side. Sleepy, yet not willing to succumb, she stared into the blackness of the damned room.

Everything hurt. Her back ached from being thrown against the wall. Her vagina screamed out from the harming. Her hands were tight from their efforts to squeeze the pain away from her crotch. Little cuts marked her palms where her own nails had pierced her flesh.

She pretended it helped expel him from her body while he raped her.

It didn't.

Her lips were scabby from his biting and sucking. Her tongue tasted of metal and her face hurt from his orgasm. He hit her when he came. Anthony said it made him relax. "I work very hard you know..."

With each blink, she tried to cast the images of her nights away. Every so often, she had to softly shake her head to keep herself awake. Her nightmares bore an unfair likeness to her reality. They were bloody, excruciating, and sexually vicious. There was no point in sleeping.

Yet, she had it better than the rest of the stolen girls. She didn't have to train as a soldier, nor did she have to serve many soldiers. Her battle in being Anthony's little wife was the struggle of holding onto an iota of her authentic self. Of course, she often lost this war and would spend days in a daze, waiting to be swallowed by his insatiable desire for her.

At night, with her back against the wall, she recalled it all: the squeezing of her eyes so she might hide away from the devilish sight of him; the holding of her breath to suffocate the trauma; the wincing to keep herself from calling out in horror; the stiffening of her spine mid-arch and then the pressing of her head into the only bed in the camp so that she might stop the messages her nerves sent to her brain.

"Yes," she says to her body as she drives her head into the mattress. "I know it hurts like hell, but there is no helping it, so please go numb. Please stop feeling, because feeling does you no good."

After he undulates on top of her ... after he hammers it home ... the torture ends, thank God. Her body and face have twenty-four hours to find any resolute moment of calm before being incarcerated by his injustice all over again.

Every night, after he hurt her, Helena sat in the darkness. If she was lucky, the moon illuminated the little cement room, and she felt the glow of the faraway planet as it sought out the little spirit that she had buried within.

It was on one of those nights when she was keeping herself from the terrors that awaited her in sleep that she noticed him. Paris. He was gazing at her through the window. His face was silhouetted by the radiance of the moon, but she knew it was him. She could feel him adoring her, and for the first time in months, she felt as though someone was protecting her. For a fleeting moment she felt safe, and the aching that aggravated all the parts of her body faded into that gaping hole inside of her where her happiness used to be.

Paris had struggled to sleep since Helena had arrived at
Doornbos many weeks ago. The thought of her kept him
awake at night. The first time he saw her, she was sitting – a
proud lioness – in the back of Anthony's truck. A strange
feeling overcame him. He couldn't quite pinpoint the last
time something had warmed him so. Paris could tell that
behind her stern and seemingly unbreakable facade swam a
silky soul, and he wanted to reach out his hand so he could
stroke her.

He had been the MM's keeper of the sex slaves since he
was twelve. Sixteen now, in the four years of watching over
them, the girls' duties as part of the movement had never
perturbed him. He had been told that older men had needs,
and he too would develop them. The older soldiers had told
him about desire and how it pulled at a man, but he didn't
want to make a woman cry or hurt her the way the other
men did when they loosened their sexual enthusiasm.
Rather, he wanted to hold her. He wanted to wipe her tears.
He wanted to calm her pounding little heart.

At night, he would find himself on one of the school
chairs in the centre of the playground. He would look up at
the stars and try to remember his long-ago life. He recalled
how he was not like most of the boys here. He was never
captured. Paris came to the MM of his own accord.

That, however, did not mean that he could leave of his
own accord.

Paris had voluntarily joined the fight because he had
been hungry. His parents had died young, leaving him
behind. And because they died of a disease that everyone
said was despicable, he was ignored by the community from
which he came. In much of Nkosi, the orphans of a family
are traditionally taken in by the extended family circle.
However, given the community's distaste for AIDS, young
Paris paid the price. Nobody cared for the little boy, and so
at the age of twelve, given his tenacity, he walked into the
jungle, hoping to find either the MM or the LLLS. Both were
rumoured to take in orphans who then worked for food and

shelter. He arrived five years ago, before any of the armies had thought to use the children for fighting. This was when the war was not as gruesome as it had become. When men were men and children were children. Paris became the shoe shiner, the kitchen helper, and the gun cleaner.

To get to the MM, he froze at night and burned during the day. Just when he was beginning to think it was useless, he found a group of soldiers smoking cigarettes in the thickest part of the jungle. He watched them talking from his hiding spot in a tree. He listened in on them and, feeling as though they seemed gentle enough, he climbed down from his tree and stood quietly before them.

Their chattering stopped. They took him in. This emaciated lost boy. They brought him back to Doornbos, where they branded him and gave him a meal. Anthony Zaza had been kind to him and had given him simple jobs. He was never asked to fight – not even when Zaza started stealing children for the sole purpose of turning them into soldiers. He was Anthony's go-to, his errand runner and his woman watcher. Yet this time round, he had fallen for the watched-woman, and he found himself hating his master.

If he did fall asleep he would dream of killing Zaza. Images of himself sliding a knife across the commander's throat rattled his nights. Like Rambo, he'd rescue his damsel and save the day, and he would have his first kiss, and she may have hers. He was sure Anthony didn't touch his mouth to hers. He was too busy forcing himself inside of her. Though he may have been wrong, Paris couldn't imagine a man such as Anthony to have a romantic mouth. That night when Helena looked back at him through the window, Paris was determined to make her his. He did not know how, nor did he truly believe it would ever be possible, but having that moment where her sad eyes met his, a memory was restored: that of his family he lost so long ago. He imagined Helena as his wife. He imagined them living a normal life with their children. He imagined them anywhere but here at Doornbos Preparatory.

THE CONVERSATION

A bar off Jacaranda Drive, Baobab
August 2008

Stefanus and Mandeep sat at a table on the outskirts of the bar. It rained behind their backs. Periodically, thick droplets would make the fall from the thatch roof and splatter upon their skin. The two of them had been sitting for a while with cans of crisp Castle lager, staring tiredly at the swarm of city people. All of them were laughing over beers and screwdrivers.

The two of them made internal judgments about the partiers. They studied the people's bright smiles, seductive gestures and charming conversations. Every one of them agitated the two hospital workers. How could these people do this every Friday night? How could they play this game, knowing what happens in their bush? How could they celebrate, knowing that they have no real government and no secure future?

Dr. Jane took a swig of his beer as he remarked to Stefanus, "Perhaps they're trying to have as much fun as possible before the rug is completely pulled out from underneath them?"

"Perhaps they're just selfish, Mandeep?"

"No, no I don't think so. The way we come and sit in silence and drink Castle after Castle is our escape. Perhaps this is theirs? Everyone here needs a little break from their reality."

Stefanus watched a man laughing as he grabbed a woman's bottom. "Whatever," he said as he made a disgusted face. "At least we put in the hours during the day. What do they do?" He knew what Mandeep's answer would be. He knew he was being flippant.

"Well, they are like people anywhere else. They are teachers, lawyers, doctors ... You know, we don't have to keep coming to this bar if you don't like it. We can go to one of the holes in the wall in the old quarter where the poor people drink the shit that tastes like petrol."

"Nah, we can't get a good cold beer there."

"Exactly, Stefanus so drink up and shut up."

"You've been thinking the same thing Mandeep. You're just too nice to show your distaste on your face."

"Maybe so, but I also sympathize with the people in this bar. It must be terrifying to have no control."

"I too have sympathy for everyone. That's why I'm here. I'm just exhausted, Mandeep. I know – I'm acting like a baby."

Stefanus continued to watch the man who flirted and grabbed at the woman's body across the room. "I especially have sympathy for these women. None of them are these men's wives – and even if they were, the way they're treated is despicable. They are all maids by day who spend their whole week scrounging to find stockings, high heels and a new dress for Friday night so that they may trick some man, any man, into paying for sex."

"Isn't it up to people like you and me to fix these social problems, Stefanus?"

"Mandeep ... we need a million of us to fix what has happened here."

The two of them sighed back into their chairs. The young Nkosi women in their little dresses had begun to sway with one another on the dance floor. New age music originating from a safe place far, far away crooned above the working women. From beneath the hoods of their eyes, they lured clients. One by one, the weak joined them on the floor. Crimes commenced. Viruses were given yet another opportunity to spread.

Mandeep gestured to the waiter for another round of Castles and said, "You know, this specific problem – prostitution – it is everywhere, Stefanus. Not just in Nkosi. You are tired, aren't you?"

Stefanus looked at his friend and heaved a dejected sigh. "I am. I'm so tired. I'm not tired of the place. I'm not even necessarily tired of my job. I don't know what's wrong..."

Mandeep sucked in his breath and found the courage to speak. "Stefanus, the little girl you brought in..." He paused before he found courage to continue, and Stefanus interjected, "The one I've been trying to not think of?"

"Yes, Nyla."

"She has a name?"

Stefanus covered his face with his hands, and Mandeep found it hard to utter his suggestion. "Yes, well, I think you should come see her tonight. She made it."

Stefanus leaned closer to his friend and whispered in relief, "She's alive? It's been weeks, Mandeep. You could have told me sooner."

"I wanted her to be strong enough, to have weathered the worst of the recovery. She is alive. Shinless and kneeless now, but alive. I think you should come see her. I think she is ready to tell you her story."

Stefanus sat back in his chair and stared at the table. "What if I can't handle her story? What happens if it devours me? The memory of her pain is hungry. It's been feasting on me ever since that day."

Mandeep studied his scarred friend. He knew he had to choose what he said wisely to persuade him. He spoke slowly, thinking before every word. "Her story may eat you, but if you ignore it then you are just like the people in this bar. You're choosing to ignore something real. Something terrible. She remembers you. She said you held her very tightly and made her feel safe. You owe it to the little thing to see her."

Stefanus drummed his fingers against the table. "Tonight?"

"Why not? She does not sleep much, and you've had a couple of beers, so it will be a little easier to take." Mandeep hoped he had used words of encouragement.

Stefanus closed his eyes and breathed deeply. He tried to overcome his nervousness. He concentrated on the sound of the rain that tinkered upon the tin tables on the patio behind them, trying to ignore the noise of flirtation seeping out of the bar. He thought about how promising the day had been when he ventured out with the boys from the NAP. All he had wanted to do that day was to help save gorillas and find any trace of a lion. "You know, I haven't been out with the NAP since that day. I don't think I'll ever go again. Before we found her I had this wild fantasy that I could find meaning here beyond that of manipulating numbers and bullying people into doing good for their country. I thought the NAP would be something that could relax me. I thought it could help me feel as good as you must feel at the end of each day. Now I'm so terrified of ever leaving Baobab that I don't see myself heading into that bloody jungle ever again."

Mandeep put his hand on Stefanus' shoulder. "At the end of each day I am terribly tired Stefanus, and like you, I have no holiday to look forward to. Who is going to take over? I'm waiting for some young buck to be sent here so that I can take my precious wife" – and here he paused for a moment to dwell upon his courageous Shalini – "and leave this place. So that we can go back to India and I can drink a good Kingfisher instead of this South African shit, watch a little cricket and send my kids to private school."

He seemed to be picturing the scene in his mind's eye. "That will never happen though," he added. "Shalini feels bound to this place now and to the children at the orphanage. I keep telling her it is not safe here. I keep saying that her day will come, and with it the breaking of my heart, because when she is raped or killed, I will never be the same. I won't be able to take her home. I'll be too ashamed for having brought her here in the first place. God, I can picture the distress on her mother's face and the raging of her father. The disappointment from my own parents, Indians hold grudges, you know." Mandeep looked at Stefanus from beneath a furrowed and distressed brow. "I'll never be forgiven." He sat back in his chair and folded his palms in his lap. Looking down at them, he softly said, "So I will have to walk into the jungle and wait for one of your gorillas to rip me apart, limb from limb."

Stefanus wryly added, "Or guerillas."

With eyes still lowered Mandeep agreed, "That's right – or guerillas."

Trying to lift his friend's spirits, Stefanus added, "Mandeep, maybe we're being a touch skeptical. Maybe no one will ever hurt Shalini? Maybe they will respect what she does for the babies who lose their parents to AIDS, malaria and everything else that steals parents here. She is well respected in Baobab, and so are you. The people appreciate the two of you. No one even knows about me. I sit in the back office and talk people from far away into sending the hospital the things it needs. Half the time I don't even get it right."

Mandeep looked back up at Stefanus to assure him. "I know your job is draining, but you are vital to my work. Not that it feels like what I do is nearly enough. Most of the emergencies that come through those doors die on the floor under flickering florescent lights. It's just gotten so difficult though, Stefanus. I remember when the most we got in Emergency were leopard attacks, gas-stove explosions or dismemberments from drunken driving. Now things are different, and neither of us has been asking why. We have just been going with the flow. You, because you're numbed from Rwanda and me because I always tell myself, 'Hey Mandeep, at least you're not in the Congo.' But I think it's time we realize it. We're as bad as the Congo, if not worse, and if we aren't careful we're going to end up just like Rwanda."

Stefanus now lowered and shook his head, frustrated. "You think I don't know that? I'm petrified of what could happen here, but it has nothing to do with us. We can't do anything but what we are paid very little to do ... I just wish I could save someone, Mandeep. I wish I were clever enough to save a life, like you can. That is why I wanted to start working with the NAP, but I can't bring myself to go back out there after finding her. I don't want to know what else is hiding in those jungles, Mandeep."

"Yes you do. You want to know, just like we all do. We need to know what's happening out there, Stefanus, and this little girl says that she will tell you. What I'm getting at is that I think Nyla has some answers. The child may be young. She can't be older than five, but these Nkosians from the bush are forced to perform adult tasks from a young age. They are wise and able-bodied beyond their years."

Mandeep leaned forward. Stefanus could see that his friend's passion was rising. The doctor continued in a more heated voice. "She is perceptive. She knows something. Others have told us what happens to the villages. I think she knows something more. She says that there were other children, that she was not alone, and that they were being taken somewhere by the people who pillaged her village. We have to find those kids, Stefanus, because if what my gut is saying is right, then these kids are being used to fight for the MM or the LLLS. Just like children are being used everywhere else over this continent and I'll be damned if we don't at least try to catch them doing it. This is your chance to save a life, Stefanus."

Stefanus scoffed a little. "How? How am I going to save a life?"

"By figuring out how to get some of them back. We can steal them back! Really, we could steal every single one of them back."

"Jesus, Mandeep. You're insane. These are rebels we're talking about. If I can't manage to bring myself to help the NAP, how am I going to go into the scary jungle and scout around for a bunch of kids who may or may not have guns of their own in their bloody hands? Child soldiers are scary, Mandeep. They are warped beyond repair. It took years for some of those little Hutus to forgive themselves, and now come to think of it, I think they were lying to us when they said they had. I don't think they'll ever truly forget what they are capable of. The kids in that jungle will willingly take my life, and probably enjoy doing so. They're probably hopped up on this or that, if these bastards who took them are anything like the LRA or the rest of them. Also, how would we find the MM or the LLLS? Don't you think if we all knew where they were, the war would be over by now?"

"I heard the only reason Mfundisi has not launched a full attack is because the West believes the rebels have cause. It's up to us here to help, Stefanus!"

Stefanus continued to laugh in disbelief. "You talk as if this is your country, Mandeep. You know, you could just leave, and it would all be gone from your life. You would never have to think of it again, and what if their cause is the right one? What then? What if the Government deserves a coup?"

Mandeep placed his palms firmly down on the table and stood his ground, "Regardless, my conscience would remind me every day that I didn't try to stop something the very thought of made my stomach churn. They're children, Stefanus. Children. Ethically, no matter which army is in the right, you can't force a child to fight your war for you."

The two fell silent for a moment as the waiter replenished their table with cold beer. Stefanus looked around the bar. He was a big, thick man who got in everybody's way. He glanced at the dance floor and felt, to his surprise, a twinge of jealousy towards the Nkosian men who were being propositioned. He had not been with a woman for a long time. His disgust was taking a backseat to his loneliness. He felt as if he could take any one of those girls home tonight, sick with AIDS or not. Surprised at the thought, he realized he had to leave before his lust brewed to a point where he could justify the act. He drank his beer while it was cold. Long, hard swigs cooled his frayed nerves. He started getting fuzzy around the edges. He placed the empty beer down and finally decided his friend was right.

"OK. I will go and talk to her. When is Shalini coming to get us?"

Mandeep tried to hide his relief. "In about ten minutes, I think."

"OK. Well, can we wait outside? I'd rather get chowed by mozzies[21] than witness the exchanges in this place."

"Yes, me too. Let's go."

The two of them pushed through the crowd of tarted-up Nkosians. At the bar were a few others like them. Deborah from the displacement camp was there with a couple of younger recruits. She looked tired, but beautiful in the traditional Nkosian way. Her dark skin, her high cheekbones, her wide set eyes. He wished that he had known she was here. She didn't come into town often, mainly because there was never a shortage of troubleshooting for her in and around the camp.

Whenever Stefanus felt like he was drowning in the amount of work he had at Princess Marina, he took a drive out and offered Deborah a hand. After spending an afternoon with her, the world was always put into perspective. No matter the duress she was under, Deborah always smiled brightly when he came to the camp offering a hand. She shrugged at him saying, "Oh, don't be silly, I've got it." Stefanus took up room in her shack of an office and watched her go. She buzzed from one problem to another: the latrines needed replacing; there was another rape in Section D last night; some of the kids weren't going to

---

[21] Mosquitoes.

school, but were running an ingenious money-making scheme stealing and reselling mosquito nets in Section Y; the supply truck wasn't coming for at least another six days; a young girl died giving birth in Section J yesterday – where do we take her child that has no name and no relatives?

At which point Stefanus raised his hand. "I can take her to Shalini."

"Oh would you, Stefanus? You are so kind. Thank you."

Tonight, she was smiling brightly as always, despite the incredible stresses that compromised her quality of life. Stefanus suddenly realized that he too had given up a life of his own. When did he sign it away? Was it the flight to Rwanda? Was it from the moment he thought he needed adventure? Was it when he took the second job here as a hospital coordinator? Or was it now, after saying that he would talk to this little girl, knowing that doing so was going to lead to something very scary? The two hospital workers nodded at the aid workers and wished them a good night as they slipped out of the bar. Deborah touched Stefanus as the men moved to leave. Her hand felt giving and warm. Protective even.

Outside, the crickets had begun to chirp. Behind the softened rain, the stars looked like a swarm of shining bees moving about the sky.

Shalini was already waiting in her buckie. She had her head back against the seat. Her beauty had all but left her. Stefanus remembered when Mandeep and Shalini had first arrived six years ago. He had been profoundly jealous of Mandeep's luck in finding such a gorgeous wife, not only in physicality, but in heart as well. She was exquisite then. When she moved, bold dark curls tossed about her sharp face. She had fierce grey eyes contrasted with caramel skin, and a coy little nose ring above a wide grin.

She never smiled anymore. At least not when Stefanus was around, and he recognized that she was now a burden to Mandeep rather than an angel. She had encouraged the move, convinced that she had what it took to get off her lollipop train in upper class Delhi to be a doctor's wife in the Developing World.

They didn't foresee the problem that a woman can be stronger than a man in places like these. A woman can tolerate the heat for longer, can cry and then keep calm and carry the hell on. Men burn during the day and suffer because they're not trained to indulge in a release.

Shalini had started small. After she and Mandeep had tried to have their own babies to no avail, she volunteered at the orphanage. She changed diapers and gave her love until she was soon running the show. She had done wonders. She built a centre for women. It was a sexual education clinic that grew into a new orphanage over time.

Of the three of them, Shalini was the most successful at really doing something. She was helping, keeping babies from being conceived or, if they were, ensuring they didn't scare the shit out of their new, poverty-stricken Mammies. The problem was that she loved too deeply and was too proud of her work. Mandeep was no longer the only one who reaped the benefits of her goodness, and Stefanus could tell he had grown resentful of the little orphanage and clinic at Princess Marina.

Pushing these thoughts aside, Stefanus smiled through the window and called out, "Hi beautiful!"

"Sorry, boys. I know I'm late," she said in response. "One of the new babies is colicky and just won't go down."

"No, you're bang on time. Listen, is it alright if you drop me at the hospital?"

"Yes, Mandeep already told me." Mandeep smiled guiltily over at Stefanus.

"Oh so you already knew I was to meet Nyla again?"

"I am his wife. I know all this man's tricks."

Shaking his head, Stefanus swung himself into the buckie and lay down drunkenly. Shalini reversed over the dirt road. From where Stefanus was lying, the stars seemed to slide, silver, across the sky and continued to jostle above him as the car fell into numerous potholes along the way to the hospital.

The jolts decreased as they pulled onto Jacaranda Drive. Staring up at the leaves, Stefanus realized that even though his life was infuriating at times here, there was no other place he could imagine himself living.

They pulled into the hospital. Stefanus hopped out, ran past his bicycle, up the steps and through the heavy doors.

Shalini called after him, "We'll wait here okay?"

"Yup!" His voice rang out, deceptively relaxed.

Inside, the lights were stark, but the energy was soft. The hospital was calm at night. Yes, he could feel the sadness of the sick people from their measly cots, but night-time was not as harsh as the hospital's days.

He walked down the hall. His flip-flops echoed through the wing. Sophie heard him coming and poked her head out of one of the rooms.

"She is in room 12, Sah."

"Jesus, does everyone know?"

Sophie smiled in reply.

Stefanus continued down the hall until he came to the room. He sucked in his breath before slowly pushing the door open. Inside were several cots. Every one of the inhabitants was sleeping except for a little girl in the corner. She sat on her cot with bandaged nubs. Her hair had been done differently, probably by one of the nurses. Two plaited pigtails stood upright on her crown. Even with these devil-horns she was undeniably sweet. He approached, quietly, to not awaken the others in the room, and noticed she was colouring by torchlight. Closer still, he saw that it was a Little Mermaid colouring book, and that Nyla had a lot to learn about staying inside the lines. He was reminded of the Little Mermaid statue in Copenhagen. He first saw it on a family holiday when he was about her age. He loved that statue. There was something about her eyes. In them was a lost and vapid expression. He wanted to save that little mermaid way back then.

Stefanus sat down on the floor next to Nyla's cot. She put her crayon down, Grape-juice Purple, and lifted her tiny chin. She stole his senses with her eyes, and then gave them back when she revealed her gap-toothed grin. He fell in love for the first time. He wanted to save this little mermaid too.

"You be Steffi!" The child did not seem to care that others were sleeping.

He whispered back, "Stefanus, yes. We should try to keep it down so that we don't wake the others."

"Oh they old people. Old people sleep through anytin'. Look!" She waved her torch around the room and giggled.

Stefanus shocked himself by smiling. He had not smiled for a long time.

"How are you, Nyla?"

"I'm okay."

"You are not too sore after your surgery?"

"Nope, the nurses call me Sweetie. I did not have a Mammi before I get here. Now I have lots o' Mammies!" She giggled again. Her thighs jittered with excitement.

Stefanus smiled again. Searching for words, he whispered, "Um, Nyla, I know you are very busy now with your colouring book..."

"She has a tail! Isn't that disgusting? At least I am notta fish!"

Stefanus could not help but laugh at the optimism. Five years old and mangled and she was cracking jokes. He absolutely adored the child and couldn't fathom a world where she had not been found, rushed to this hospital and saved. "No, but Nyla when you are not busy perhaps I can come talk to you more. Maybe visit you every day? Take you on trips around the hospital? You know I work here. Would you like that?"

"Yap! That be nice. OK see you tomorrow! Night night!"

Baffled by the child's dismissive confidence, Stefanus struggled to find a reply.

"Umm okay, see you tomorrow Nyla. Sleep tight little one. Don't let the bed bugs bite."

"You can help wit that!"

"I can? How?"

"You unknot my mozzy net. Is too high up. I tried to stand up, but it hurts."

"Jesus, of course..." He couldn't believe the nurses had forgotten to assist the child. This city was a malaria haven. Stefanus unknotted the baby's net and tucked its ends underneath her mattress so that it would stay put and protect her from further harm.

"Thanks!"

"Pleasure, my child. Now, lights out. Sleep tight. See you tomorrow."

She flipped the switch of her torch and sighed sweetly. He could tell from her breath that she at least felt safe. Knowing this gave him a rare spark of comfort. Leaving the room and his angel behind him, he realized that tomorrow was Saturday, but he would come and see her anyway.

He was in love.

Outside, Shalini and Mandeep were leaning against the buckie and on one another. Stefanus came running down the steps shouting, "I want to take her home. I'll see her every day until she gets used to me. I'll change my office at home into a room for her ... unless you were going to take her, Shalini?"

"No ... I have too many children. Also, the children at the orphanage wouldn't know what to make of her. I'm afraid she would be cast out or bullied. The thing is, she's the first of her kind. We know there will be more, but we just don't have a place yet for the ones like her, and she can't stay in there." Shalini pointed at Princess Marina. By night, the outside had a sadness about it. Its white walls stood dull against the dark and its gables drooped with melancholy beneath the dark sky.

"No. She can't. She's too special. I want her. What is the paperwork like?"

"Paperwork?" Shalini let out a sarcastic scoff. "Stefanus, this is Nkosi. If you want to look after the child, you can."

"But I'm a single man – won't people talk?"

"Pedophilia is not something these people have the luxury of worrying about. You are doing a good thing, Stefanus."

Beaming at the two of them, he told them a little secret. "She calls me Steffi! Imagine that ... Steffi!" He picked up his bike and rolled it past them.

"You don't want a ride?"

"No thank you, I really want to cycle. I need to feel the wind or something. You know what I mean?"

They smiled back at their friend, sharing in his elation. "Yes, we understand. Good night, Stefanus."

"Night!"

He rode out of the gates feeling liberated, free, ready for everything that was surely to come. Goodness, bleakness, helplessness.

THE BRANDING

Doornbos Preparatory
Late September 2008

The boys had been training in the camp for a few months. They had seen the older soldiers come and go. Groups rotated, and when new ones arrived, so came with them more stolen supplies – and children, thieved from villages that had been pillaged to keep Doornbos in business.

Severin took his spot on one of the old sports bleachers, AK between his knees, elbows on the step behind him. He leaned back and watched these new 'recruits' swarm the courtyard. Their lost faces searched their new surroundings for familiarity. He paid special attention to the ones who held hands and whispered into each other's ears. He concentrated on the structure of their features and seared their appearance into his brain so that he would remember to leave those kiddies alone. It was hard though. He broke out into moments of anger and found himself blaming the newcomers for things that couldn't have been their fault. Last week, he hammered the butt of his gun into the temple of a child while he was messed off his face. He didn't like the white stuff – it made him feel wildly fuzzy – but he hated the brown brown[22] more because it made him do things he

---

[22] Cocaine mixed with gunpowder.

did not like to do. The problem was, though, that by snorting or eating the stuff, time went by faster than usual. It made life fast forward, and before one knew it night had settled over them, and they could go to sleep. Also, it helped him forget that he was all alone now. That he had been stolen from his family, that his sister was probably dead and that he no longer had a partner in crime.

Dorian and Severin had drifted, and though Severin still loved Dorian lots, it hurt him when they got to play soccer and Dodo would choose to play on the other team. Severin knew that the choice was malicious. His friend had turned in the last couple of months, and though Severin could feel a shift within himself as well, Dorian had become faulty, menacing, dangerous. He was playing a lot with the older boys – the ones who had already fought in battle, who had already stolen food and, with it, lives. They would offer Dorian the white stuff all the time, which he would dip his finger into and rub into his gums. Severin had watched the deterioration from his bleacher over the last few months. Dorian's eyes would widen and his lips would part, revealing a playful grin and tight dimples. He'd dance around laughing, and when he slipped slightly from the white stuff's spell he would sit inside the big boys' classroom, where they had made a comfortable home out of blankets that had been taken from various villages. Here, he would listen to them boasting about their adventures. Severin would stand outside the door as Dorian denied him entrance and watch his friend as he welcomed the older boys' battle stories into his imagination.

Dorian had found new friends and had left his best one behind. The protector had become the bullied. Seve felt lonely. He did not want to make new friends or even keep up friendships with the other kids from his village that had also survived the first months of training. Many of the older boys from home had not lasted. It had been too demanding on them. Having spent the last few years as shepherds, they were not used to carrying heavy loads for long periods of time. So when they collapsed on training excursions from exhaustion and thirst, the commanders had left them there for the vultures' dinner. Luckily for Severin and Dorian, who had been running to and from the jungle with sticks on their backs for as long as they could remember, they had never keeled over. Their strength and nimbleness had caught the eye of the older soldiers, who had passed their observations on to Mr. Zaza.

It was on one of the days when Severin was milling about in loneliness that Anthony approached him. The commander took the boy by the shoulder and led him to the bleachers where they sat down. They watched the camp together. Once Anthony sensed Severin had settled, he began.

"Son, may I speak with you?"

"Yes Sah."

The commander smiled broadly at him. Severin felt warmed by the gesture of friendliness, and the thought of his father sunk into the pit of quicksand that hid in the bottom back corner of his little skull.

"It has been brought to my attention that you are quite the foot soldier."

"I think so, Sah."

"Yes, you are fast, you are strong and you enjoy completing a task."

"Yes Sah. Dorian is the same though."

"I know. The big boys say that when you two are on the same team during drills, you are unbeatable. They say that the two of you speak without speaking."

Severin tightened his fists around the barrel of his gun, trying to pull the emotions of longing back inside of himself. He blinked back tears and softly managed another "Yes Sah," and further, "I think it is because we have known each other for a very long time, Sah. We used to be very best friends you know."

Severin sought some comfort from the man, but received none. Instead, the man remarked, "This is very lucky for our movement, son. I think we will use you two as group leaders on your first raid. How would you like that?"

"I don't know, Mr. Zaza. I think I would like to have someone more experienced lead me the first time around."

"Don't be silly, boy! You are strong! You will be a good fighter."

"Maybe, Sah."

"Surely."

The two sat quietly for a while. The sex slaves walked past with water in big clay pots upon their heads. They were clad in beautiful prints and had clanking bangles adorning their emaciated wrists. The girls, no older than sixteen, had babies on their backs that slept quietly in the afternoon heat. For the first time, Severin realized that this school was a village! It had its women who cooked and cared for the men. It had goats, it had a supply room where maize and blankets were kept for the wet season, it had a medicine man who made potions in the art class, it had a chief, who sat next to him, and it had warriors. Little Warriors.

Anthony laid his hand affectionately on the child's back and declared, "Right, I must go see the little missus. My lunch will be ready soon. Speaking of Helena, she is very worried about Dorian, and she is sad that he will not talk to her. I don't want to make him talk to her, so will you do me a favour and persuade him, son?"

"Yes Sah. I will tell him."

"Good boy. I will see you this evening for your group's branding. You have earned it. You are going to put up a good fight for your country boy ... a good fight indeed."

Severin wrung his barrel with his palms, "Thank you, Sah. See you at sundown, Sah."

The boy watched him go and then looked over to the soccer field where Dodo was playing by himself with a deflated ball. What a heavy burden to be cast upon a broken friendship. How would he manipulate his friend, or foe – he was not sure what shade of grey they were – to talk to the person he hated most in this world?

As Severin's feet burned their way over the cement of the courtyard, he couldn't help remembering his own sister and their afternoons together in the doorway of their hut. The memory was so overbearing that he had to stop and push the butt of his gun into the ground. He put all of his weight into the weapon so that it supported him while his chest heaved. There was nothing worse than the pain of her absence. He hated Dorian for not supporting Helena after what she had been through.

Severin often walked past her room, door ajar, and noticed her sitting, a broken bird, tweeting none, twitching none, staring hopelessly into the face of her next night. Severin would whisper her name. "Helena ... psssssst! Helena!" Her eyes would seek out his myopically, and there she'd find him and gulp down her pain. He'd lean against the doorway and stay with her a while, saying nothing. Saying everything in silence. Just being there was enough. It was painful for him too. He was used to her being a lioness, but now she was the prey. Sadness would overcome him as he watched her try to distract herself. Stroking her mat, she'd pick at its loose ends, or she'd examine the lines of her hands, all the while breathing shallow, unnourishing breaths. When he stood there with her, he gave thanks that his sister was at least not living this. If she was alive at all.

Severin picked himself off his gun and continued towards the soccer field. He came up beside his one-time friend.

Dorian hardened and growled, "What you want?"

Severin, at a loss, retorted, "Zaza says he'll kill you if you don't talk to his wife. So enjoy death, scaredy cat."

Severin turned on his hole-toed takkies[23] and began to walk away. Dorian kicked the ball up into his hands and threw it at the back of his friend's head. "Did that hurt? Huh, did that hurt?"

---

[23] Takkies are cheap running shoes.

Looking back, Severin stung Dorian with his reply. "No, you pussy. It didn't hurt. You throw like a girl."

Severin left the lost boy in the middle of the field. Dorian, in a fit of rage, began to cry.

The tearful rage started to bring Dorian down from a loose cannon of a high. He had been flying confidently all morning, marveling at the light that washed the sky. He had felt it clean his dirty mind; he had enjoyed the liberation from agony that the white stuff had provided him, but now ... now it was all coming to an end, just as it always did. He sat tearing at the grass. Frantically, he uprooted the blades. He attacked the earth, but soon tired, for the destruction could not cure him.

"Why, Mammi? Why are you gone, Mammi?"

The child fell back onto the tattered pitch. He held himself as he choked on his own misery as it slipped through his veins and tightened his heart. The midday sunburned his retinas. The world swam red through tears. Conceding to reality, the child sat up and took in the school. Its beautiful Dutch gables rose up from its dusty grounds. The tennis courts lay messy, unkempt – gardens more than courts. The jungle gym stood rickety and dangerous, an apparatus that constantly drew blood, leaving the boys and girls scabby and resentful.

Dorian picked softly at the grass around him. He found a thick blade. He placed it between his thumbs as they used to in the jungle, on those shaded days so many months ago. He licked the skin of his thumbs and lubricated the grass. He placed his lips against them and blew. Bzzzzzzzzz! The grass tickled his lips. The practice was cathartic and reminded him of Severin, whom he missed a great deal. Dorian let the grass fall from his thumbs. Lost in his own helplessness he studied the blade in his lap. How would Severin ever be his friend again?

The boy squinted towards the sky. "Mammi, will Seve ever love me again?"

An iridescent cloud moved softly above him. She was not there.

Dorian faltered a little as he stood up. His head rushed. His heart pulled. He made his way across the field. A soft breeze carried voices of kids on the jungle gym. As he moved past them, he felt his toes sinking into the sand. The granules rose up around the soles of his feet, capturing every one of his creases, every one of his callouses as he moved on.

Time took a beating in his drug-wracked blur. The playing kids moved in slow motion. Their smiles grew and fell as slowly as their shapes changed, stretching out over seconds. The metamorphosis was slow enough for him to make out the fear in their eyes as they vomited out forced laughter. Their eerie echoes ruined the silence in his head.

Feeling as though he was moving through quicksand, the boy pulled himself towards her and at last arrived at Helena and Zaza's room. It was an abysmal sight. Helena sat morosely, chewing nervously at her lips and rubbing her fingers together as if she was trying to get something off them. Dorian's throat swelled. His heart moved heavily against his sternum.

"Helena?"

The girl looked up at her younger brother. The light in her eyes no longer burned. They were dull – the colour of stone. The boy asked again because, uncertain that this sorry sight was even his sister. "Helena?" In her head, she asked him, 'Dodo, pull me up from the ground.' For Dorian, there was only heart-wrenching silence. "Helena, what are you thinking about?"

She dropped her eyes. Her soft, slow speech was a startling contrast to the frantic wringing of her hands. "Nyla. I'm thinking of our little Nyla. I am hoping she is not trapped like me."

The last walls around Dorian's heart crumbled. He wanted to rush to her, to hold her, to squeeze her hard enough so that he might erase all of her pain, but he could not move to her. He did not know how.

A familiar voice pulled him from her and the goose bumps rose on his skin, traveling from his neck down to his fingers. Cigarette burning between his lips, the soldier who cut off Nyla's shins walked by with several other grown-up soldiers. Their belligerent voices echoed off the caverns of Dorian's memory. The boy fantasized about running to the art class, grabbing a machete, surprising the commander from behind and hacking him to bits the way the bastard had done with their little Nyla.

Fantasy spurred him to action. Without saying goodbye to his sister, Dorian pulled himself off the wall. He pushed his bare feet into the sand beneath him and crossed the dusty playground. Skidding to a halt by the art class, he saw the weapons scattered upon the floor. Quickly, he rummaged through them to find the sharpest of the lot. He instinctively knew that he could not take chances. The blow would have to be quick and fatal. As he was digging for his weapon, he realized he may have to slash the other soldiers as well if they attacked him in defence. That was fine with him. He would do anything at this point.

Finding his piece, the boy geared himself for the task. He bolted out of the dark room into the glare of midday. The soldiers were now sitting around a small fire by the bleachers. They sat on milk crates and cinder blocks. The soldier's cigarette was still burning. As Dorian ran he thought to himself, 'I will come in from the top.' He held the blade high above him and as he closed in on his victim, his mouth involuntarily opened and released a guttural call. It alarmed the soldier who turned to find Dorian flying towards him. The cigarette fell from his mouth.

The scrap lasted mere seconds, but the boy fought with every fibre of his broken heart. Because of this, he put up a powerful fight. A child is only so powerful, however, and soon he was pinned to the ground with the end of a handgun pressed into his chubby cheek. Dorian squirmed for a release from all of the soldiers' grips, but it was futile. He was not able to escape them. Severin, having seen the attempt from his bleacher, rushed in without thinking. There he was on the backs of soldiers, pulling ears and biting necks to get them off his best friend. The mass of soldiers, big and small, squabbled, pushed and pulled.

Desperate, Severin screamed, "Let him go!"

"You killed our Nyla!" spat Dorian.

"Let Dodo go! I'll kill you! Watch me kill you while you sleep!" screamed Severin.

"I'm gonna put a bullet in your head you little shit! You try and cut me! Just you wait! This gun's gonna go bang!" one of the soldiers was screaming at Severin as the boy continued to fight.

Dorian screamed for breath beneath the struggling mass. Wakened from her stupour, Helena came rushing to the scene. She added her voice to the fray. "Leave him! Leave my brother alone!"

And then a shot rang out and the wild crowd dispersed. Dorian lay panting in the dirt, his eyes wild with fury. Still holding his machete, he came up to his elbows to find Helena, Severin and the crowd of older and angered soldiers.

Dodo then rolled onto his stomach to find a smiling Zaza who lifted him into his arms in one swoop. He dusted the sand off of Dorian's face. "What are you up to little one?"

Pouting, the boy pointed his finger. "That guy is a baddy! I don't like him! Simple as that."

"Why is he a baddy, Dodo?"

"Because he chopped off Nyla's legs, and ... and ... and ... and I want him dead!"

The soldier who usually sported a dangling cigarette lurched forward as if wanting to smack Dorian out of Zaza's arms. Zaza raised his hand. The soldier froze.

"How about you kill some other people instead, Dorian? Ones who really deserve it? This one ... this one cannot help it ... he is too stupid to know any better."

The soldier's lips grew tight at this comment, and he huffed as Zaza continued to speak. "You are a very good little soldier to take on four big men! I am very proud of you, but remember that they are on your side. They are your brothers also." Zaza collected his thoughts before adding, "I think you are the right one Dorian. Will you lead your group next week?"

Dorian turned to look at the idiot soldier. He still hated him and wanted him dead, but felt himself complying with Zaza's request. "OK, but only if Seve's on my team."

"How about you boys do it together and make Pappi Zaza proud?" A grin crossed the man's face.

Dorian did not know why, but his smile made him uncomfortable. He gestured that he wanted to be put down, and so Zaza placed him on his feet. "Thank you Sah. Whatever you wish Sah."

Dorian took Severin's hand and together they ran past his sister. He did not have the nerve to look her in the eyes as he went. She turned and watched him go, all the while wondering when she would know him again ... when she would hold him again. She was proud of his fearlessness, of his taste for revenge and of his unwavering loyal love for those that were no longer there to protect. 'He is a true warrior,' she thought. 'Just like Pappi.'

. . . .

The sun was coming down behind the jungle gym. The children sat in a semi-circle around a smouldering metal trashcan. The fire leapt up and licked at the mirages that played in the pockets of hot air.

The kids were simultaneously nervous and excited. They were finally going to become part of the team, of the Militia for Minerals family. Getting branded meant that they were worthy of being fed and sheltered. It also meant that they had survived the last three months of training. They had run drills, they had learned how to aim and they had learned scare tactics. Some of them had killed close friends or family to prove they were as earnest and reliable as Rambo. They had cried themselves to sleep night after night and – despite their living nightmares – had survived. The only things left to do to be considered a real warrior was to take the heat of the iron and then, if they hadn't already, make their first kill.

The big boys passed around a plastic bag of cocaine. The kids sucked their index fingers for the dip, and tried to make as big a mountain as possible on their tips. They put the powder in their mouths and rubbed it into their gums. Anthony Zaza stood over them, reminding them that the cocaine was a magic powder made by the medicine man. He told them it would make them strong so the burn would not hurt too much.

Then, one by one, they stood up and presented their right arms to the leader, who drew a long pole out of the flaming can. With a cigarette fuming between his teeth, he pressed the hot end of the pole into their flesh. Two capital Ms sizzled into their arms. The children cringed at the scalding and then held their new burns, their new mutilation. Suffering, they cried out, "Owy owy owy owy!"

The sun set with the last of the boys hobbling away from Zaza. He threw the pole into the can and directed one of the commanders to put out the flames. He walked over to the headmaster's office and peered in through the door. Sitting on the bed was a lost child. Helena looked up at him and studied his eyes. He flicked the switch. The room illuminated.

"I want to see you tonight," he said as he walked through the doorway and closed the door behind him.

. . . .

Paris was sitting on the bleachers with Severin and Dorian. He poured cold water over the children's ugly scars. He shot several glances over to the room where Zaza was taking Helena. Dorian sat quietly, unwilling to participate in the conversation. Severin, on the other hand, felt comfortable enough now with Paris to open up.

"Do you love her?" he asked.

"I don't know what love is Seve, but I worry about her."

"Me too. I worry about her a lot. She was my Mammi when I lived in the village. Paris, I have these dreams..."

"We all have dreams, boy."

"No, I have dreams about Nyla."

"Your sister?"

"Yes, I think she is still alive."

Paris looked at the hope in the boy's eyes as he cleaned Severin's arm. He could not be the murderer of this boy's longing, so he simply nodded his head. He felt safe with Severin, and thought about telling him that he dreams of slicing Zaza's throat. However, he did not know where the boy's loyalty lay quite yet, so thought better of it. Then, thinking he should say something affirming, remarked, "Maybe she is."

Severin smiled at Paris, bearing all his teeth. He was missing an eye tooth. Paris, excited, pointed at his mouth, "Seve, are all your baby teeth gone?"

"Yup! I'm a big boy now! Helena noticed. She put a little chocolate under my pillow."

"That's really sweet of her. Wait, but how do you know it was her?"

"Well, because she always did that for Nyla and me. My Pappi was never there. He works in the mines. Not here in Nkosi, because the Militia for Minerals have the mines ... I mean, we have the mines. My Pappi works at the mines over the border."

Paris continued to clean Severin's wound. "I don't have any parents," he said.

Severin shrugged his shoulders. "I guess none of us do? Do you want to know more about Dorian's sister, Paris?" Watching the room and wishing he were inside of it squeezing the last breath from the man who raised him, Paris answered, "Yes please."

A NEW HOME

The orphanage at Princess Marina Hospital, Baobab
October 2008

Shalini heard the trap shut. She looked at the drop-off box and sighed. She moved towards it dejectedly and then braced herself against the wall. She stayed there a while before opening the small cupboard in the wall – a cabinet where young girls leave their babies when they are incapable of taking care of them.

The process is completely anonymous. Though it may ease their humiliation, it cannot possibly relax their anxiety. Shalini could feel the young mother on the other side of the orphanage's wall. Though the room behind her buzzed with children at play, scolding volunteers and shouting from the playground beyond the back stoop, all of these sounds faded into silence. They could not compete with the remorse that cried out from the other side of the wall. Shalini placed her forehead against the cool cement. A sponge, she soaked in the vibrations of the mother's pain. A tear slipped as she clasped the inside handle. It felt cold in her fist. She held her breath as she opened it. There, wrapped in a traditional dulla[24] of colourful prints, slept an unperturbed child. Deep

---

[24] Baby blanket.

in slumber, it would never come to know the person who had brought it into this godforsaken world.

The perfection of the baby swelled Shalini's heart. The baby breathed easily. Its bushy lashes fluttered from sweet dreams, and its chocolate skin was dewy and healthy.

Shalini found a note next to the resting child. Written in scribbled pencil was the name of the Mammi with a message: "Primrose loves you." Around the child's wrist was a small copper band – placed there with love and a mother's longing for an entirely different world. A world that could enable her to care for her bastard of a child. Shalini took a deep breath before gathering the baby into her arms. She cuddled it close to her, inhaling its sweet African scent of dust and lilies.

She closed the drop-off box and walked gently over to the stoop to not wake the infant. There she watched little Nyla wagging her stubby thighs. The child was studying the girls who skipped in the playground. They were chiming their skipping song as the rope whipped round and slapped down, round and down.

"One, two, three, four – lamore, lamore, lamore!"

Shalini could tell that there was a great longing in this maimed child. She knew Nyla wished she could move, play, express. She longed to encourage the child, but she needed to tend to this baby first. She brought the new baby to an O'Mammi,[25] who reached for her, cooing. Shalini petted the baby's head as if to say, "Goodbye," and then walked over to the little girl on the stoop.

"Nyla, child ... are you ready to go?"

The little girl swivelled round and looked up at her with huge eyes. "Maybe be ready?"

Kneeling down beside her, Shalini asked, "Are you nervous, little one?"

---

[25] Grandmother.

The girl nodded and turned her attention back to the skipping girls.

Placing her arm around the child, she hugged Nyla's nervousness away.

"It will be so great to have a room of your own and a Pappi who loves you! Why are you all of a sudden so afraid when you are usually so brave, little one?"

Nyla shuddered before asking, "What if Steffi wants to give me back? What if he doesn't want me in the end because me don't skip?"

Shalini, stunned by Nyla's sudden self-doubt, tried to make her understand. "Oh, little one! You don't need to have feet to be perfect! Feet are often overrated. They sometimes have minds of their own and take people places they ought not go to. Consider yourself lucky. Little one, you have a big, beautiful heart and determination. Steffi fell in love with you instantly. I can promise you ... he will never ever want to give you back. The thought won't even cross his mind for a millisecond."

The little girl's eyes stayed fixed on Shalini. She did not say a word. She definitely didn't know what a millisecond was, but finally nodded and said, "OK, me be ready."

Shalini lifted Nyla onto her hip and carried her back through the orphanage's crèche. The great room swarmed with action. Toddlers played with blocks. Young boys fought over G.I. Joes. Little girls played with dollies. Nyla's heart sunk at the sight of them. She wished she had a dolly she could spend her days with.

Outside, Nyla was placed lovingly in the passenger seat. Shalini drew the safety belt across the girl's belly and fastened the lock.

"What's this for?" Nyla puzzled over the safety belt.

Shalini replied, "It's for your protection. It's in case I crash the buckie. It will keep you safe."

Nyla nodded and then looked out over the courtyard as Shalini walked around the vehicle and placed herself in the driver's seat. The first and last time Nyla had been in a car was when the NAP men rushed her unconscious to Princess Marina. Alert now, Nyla got a fright when the engine started and then, once she recognized its roaring was normal, laughed at herself. They pulled out through the courtyard, passing the older victims as they went. Nyla watched women with no noses, men with no hands or feet, grandpas with no arms and grandmas with missing fingers.

She looked up to Shalini and asked, "They'll be okay without me, won't they?"

"You will be missed, little Nyla, that is for sure. You are very good at making them all laugh, but you will be back to visit lots!"

"Good. Me like it here."

The hot sun lulled the girl into tranquillity, and by the time they had reached the end of Jacaranda Drive, the rolling of the wheels had put her to sleep. Waking up fifteen minutes later as the buckie rolled to a stop, Nyla opened her eyes, and through her grogginess saw Stefanus waving at her from the front door of a big brick house.

Shalini reached over and unclipped Nyla's safety belt. "You're home!"

Nyla cried out, and her heart began to beat a little harder as Stefanus ran down the steps, waving enthusiastically at her through the windscreen. He opened her door and pulled her out. All of her fears melted as he wrapped himself around her. Lifting her up, Stefanus walked up the stairs and through the door. Shalini followed. They stepped into a large lounge with solid wood furniture and walls lined with paintings. They moved deeper into the home. In the hallway was a large photograph of a cobblestone street. Nyla seemed to be staring at it intently, so Stefanus decided to talk about it.

"That was taken in Amsterdam, the city I am from."

They came to a closed door. Shalini asked, "Are you ready, Nyla? This is going to be your bedroom."

Nyla put her thumb in her mouth and nodded. Stefanus pushed the door open. Light poured in through a big window over a lilac-coloured room. The sun cast a warm glow over a small twin bed dressed with plush pillows and – to Nyla's wonderment – a little black dolly.

"Do you like it, Nyla?" asked Steffi.

Reaching for the bed, she giggled and wiggled her thighs. Stefanus walked in and placed her down on the little bed. She grabbed ahold of her new best friend, her first dolly. Squeezing her, she asked, "Can I call her Thandi?"

Stefanus nodded. Nyla squealed. She played with Thandi's hair and placed her fingertip on its nose. She looked up over the doll's forehead. Across from her was a closet and inside hung several dresses and a couple of frilly cardigans.

She looked up at Steffi who beamed down upon his excited daughter. "Are those for me Steffi?"

"Yes, little one, they are all yours. So is that little desk in the corner, so are the colouring books and crayons, so is that box of toys and so is that little dolls' house."

Nyla lay down upon her bed and cuddled Thandi. She breathed easily against her. Stefanus and Shalini softly backed out of the room, leaving the little one to have her afternoon nap. When they were gone, Nyla momentarily thought of her father – but those thoughts soon faded away forever. As she drifted into sleep, a hope flickered through her: that Severin was in a safe place like she was.

THE INTRUDER

The soccer pitch at Doornbos Academy
Late November 2008

The kids had a few weeks until they launched their first invasion. The target had been scouted out by some of the bigger boys: a small, well-stocked village in the thick of the jungle. Doornbos was running low on supplies. The boys needed to pillage for food. The kids knew this, but their morale was low. They were scared. Buried deep within them was unbearable fear, though no one dared to admit it. In solitary moments, the sheer idea of it gnawed at them with sharp teeth. Thoughts of massacre ruptured their innocence. It bled out of them as night sweats, as hammering hearts, as nervous twitches or as the grinding of teeth. The only consolation was there would be no counterattack.

The village they were going to take was secluded. They would overcome it at a time when the villagers were congregated in one place where no one could escape. Their bullets could pummel everybody at once, and when the villagers were all dead, the boys could steal the relics of the people's lives.

After their morning drills, the afternoons ticked slowly away. They filled the hours by distracting themselves with nonsense. On one of these waiting-days, the boys found an ancient ant hill on the other side of the soccer pitch. Its history was written on its thickly built walls – fortifications that had been industriously constructed by forgotten dynasties. There was evidence of erosion against the main hub. It had weathered many a wet season and undergone rebuilding during the dry seasons.

Uncontained, the colony sprawled into mini-mounds – suburbia – that stretched out to the north and south, to the east and west. The boys had set this epic ant-city on fire and gleefully cheered as its inhabitants fled. A world in miniature disintegrated. Entertained by death, they were hyenas on their backs, jiggling their calves.

It was there at the soccer pitch that Paris first noticed the child. Yes, there were hundreds of them at Doornbos, but he knew he had never seen this boy's face with its chiselled, high cheekbones and startling slanted eyes. His features bore more likeness to a girl than to a boy. One could even call him striking. A face of such distinction would not have gone unnoticed.

An unusual suspect, Paris approached him and asked for the pretty boy's name.

"Joshua."

Intrigued with the interaction between Paris and this unfamiliar boy, the others stopped their tomfoolery and settled down to take it in. Dark smoke and ashes from their burning city puffed upwards behind them. Sizzling ants squealed in the grass. The boys bore their eyes into this Joshua.

"How long have you been here?"

Joshua shifted before replying, "About a month, I think?"

"What classroom do you sleep in?"

Joshua's eyes darted from Paris', to Severin's, to the other boys and to the guns settled in the grass. He pointed across the field, past the bleacher and to the headmaster's office where Helena and Zaza slept, "That one."

"Oh, okay." Paris feigned agreeability before swiftly grabbing Joshua's right shoulder. He looked for the marking and found none. The other boys noticed this too and began making apish sounds as they got to their feet. "Hu hu hu hu hu!"

Moving grotesquely and as one, they surrounded him.

Paris threw Joshua's head down. After a short wrestle, he read aloud the letters on the back of the boy's neck. " LLLS!"

The boys made for their guns that lay scattered in the grass, but they were not fast enough. Out of Joshua's pants came a handgun and with its Crack! Came a shrill sensation in Paris' shoulder. Severin and the hyenas wrestled Joshua to the ground. The boy struggled hard and begged for release, but the MM boys were trained to work as a team. They seized his gun before another shot could be fired.

Paris stumbled backwards before falling to the ground. Staring up at the sky, it all became clear to him. The games they were playing, these wars in the jungle, were one day going to kill him. He held his arm. Too shocked to feel the aching, he bled for the first time.

Dorian and a few others dragged Joshua towards the courtyard while Severin picked Paris up and carried him across the field towards Helena, who was running towards them. With a fearful heart, she took Paris in her arms. He fell into her like a dream. They gazed at each other before his eyes flickered and he fell away into a numb abyss.

And though he reached out for her, he could not find the girl who could save him from drowning. He called for her to pull him out. He begged for her to come and find him because he was struggling to breathe, but no one came. He got lost in the whirling winds of the middle of nowhere and its current swept him adrift.

. . . .

Dorian sat in the classroom, grimacing to the sounds of Joshua's beating. He turned his head away, taking in the moving shadows on the wall as the older soldiers thrashed Joshua to tear open his skin. Then Dorian, commanded to turn back his head and watch, stood witness to the breaking of Joshua as he was bludgeoned with a traditional warrior club. The boys' bones crumbled. Joshua's regression from a soldier into a child first became clear through the watering of his eyes, then through his high-pitched cries and finally with the breaking of his back. By the end, faint whisperings for his mother escaped his bloodied lips. Dorian felt his eyes well up with tears. No matter how hard he tried to be angry with the intruder, empathy grew hotly within him. All he wanted was for Joshua to die already so he could go hide under the bleachers and try very hard to forget about him.

After they had beaten him, the older soldiers sprawled Joshua over a desk. They encircled him, taunting and belittling him. A knife emerged into the fray. Dorian stiffened as he watched Joshua mouth the words, "But I told you ... I told you where the LLLS are."

Unable to bear any more, Dorian quietly withdrew and stood outside. He unscrewed the bullet casing that hung around his neck. He inhaled the stash of brown brown he kept hidden there for 'times like these.' And finally the ether withdrew itself from the stale light that hung lowly over Doornbos Academy.

Dorian let some tears slip as Joshua's cries crept along his skin.

After the brutal torture administered by the older soldiers during questioning, they dragged the intruder to the burned anthill where Dorian was standing, wringing the neck of his AK with his fists. They pushed the bloodied Joshua to his knees.

The child stared up at Dodo and then at the weapon. Dodo took in the boy's face - flaccid with defeat. No fear was written there, nor anger. This LLLS scouter understood what his punishment would be, and understood that it had to be.

Dorian raised his weapon with a speedy heart. As he took aim on Joshua, Dorian's drugged mind tricked him and for one harrowing moment, he saw himself on the other end of the barrel.

Dodo squeezed his eyes shut and then refocused on the intruder.

'He is me and I am him,' thought Dorian, but he rejected the sentiment as soon as it surfaced. His finger twitched, and then he pulled the trigger.

After the bang, Dorian stumbled backwards. Joshua, too, fell away and then bled out upon the grass. Those ants that had survived the burning of their garrison now drowned in a Dead Sea of blood. Dorian looked on the lifeless boy and concluded Joshua's age. He couldn't have been more than thirteen wet seasons.

Dodo's friends laughed and cheered. He felt strange. Guilt, remorse, sickness: none of these likely feelings overcame him. Rather, he noticed how simple it was, after a short emotional battle, to fire the AK and for it to actually hit flesh and bone. He experienced how it felt to be someone's master. Dorian turned to wishing that he himself had been shot and killed, that perhaps Joshua was the lucky one. In order to distract himself from his emotional strain, he slung his AK over his shoulder, knelt down and removed Joshua's takkies. They looked about the right size for Paris.

Feigning pride, he grinned widely and gave the boys high fives before turning away from them and seeking out Severin. He was desperate to cry on his friend's shoulder.

. . . .

Paris woke up to the sound of her breath. It was soft against him. She placed her hand on his sweating head and transmitted all her love into him. The urgency sent her calling for the spirit of her mother, who came and wrapped herself around the two children. The warmth of the two women kept him awake, kept him treading in the warming water of their spirits.

Vitalized by their energies, he resolved not to slip back into the coma. He stayed with them and listened to their voices encourage his weak heart.

The girl whispered, "My mother says she will not let you leave me."

Her nose came down to his cheek. He felt her sweet tears moisten his chapped skin. Protected by her, he felt safe enough to fully emerge from shock. As the moments drew on, her light melted the darkness upon him. He rolled his head to look at her. Their noses touched, and he allowed himself to finally accept that Helena returned his love.

It had all happened so suddenly. No sign of her affection and then this moment all at once, when they softened into one another. They moved house within themselves. Their new meaning for life became clear. He smiled and chuckled in spite of his pain.

"It's not funny Paris."

"Yes, it is. It took a shot to the arm to get this close to you."

Luckily, the bullet had gone cleanly and completely through his shoulder. Now all was calm, and his body was succumbing to the task of recuperation.

When Paris was breathing normally again, Helena threaded her needle, burned its end, and kissed his forehead before she began to sew him up. Paris winced against her picking and toiling, but the sound of her breathing eased him.

He suffered nothing in the conscripts of her attempts to heal him.

Periodically, she smiled at him, and he managed to wanly smile back. Sweet serenity settled over the two. They revelled in their togetherness. Each time her fingertips reached his skin, his nipples would grow hard and his hair would lift away from himself. When she caressed a millimeter to the left or to the right of his wound, she'd feel warm and giving and – finally – whole.

Together, while she tended to him upon the defiled bed
she usually shared with Zaza, they dreamed that one day
they would share a bed. He strained to lift his head and raise
himself to his elbows. He released his hurt arm quickly, as it
did not bend that way just yet. Tenaciously, he reached his
nose out to hers and smiled. She met him in the middle and
settled hers against his.

Interrupting, Severin came in and tinkered about with the
bowl that was filled with rags sullied by Paris' blood.
Keeping himself busy, and out of their way, he began to
mop up the floor with dirty old towels he had found on the
laundry line. Finally leaving them in peace, he lifted the
towels and carried them outside. He then put them in the
middle of the courtyard, pulled out some matches and set
them on fire. Severin took his spot on the bleachers and
watched the flames. Hypnotized by the heat, he grew tired
and fell asleep.

Dorian sat down next to him, shaking.

"I have killed Joshua, Severin." His lip began to quiver,
and he whispered. "Severin ... Seve, please say something."

Severin did not awaken as Dorian's tears began to fall, so
he did put his hand on his friend's breast and felt Severin's
heaving chest rise and fall.

"Never let anyone kill you, Seve."

Dorian stayed crying by Severin's side. By the time
Severin woke up, Dorian had stopped crying – but the
evidence of remorse was written on his face.

Severin blinked away his sleepiness, "Are you okay,
Dodo?"

Dorian nodded.

"No, you're not! What's wrong?"

Dorian, trembling, shuddered out more tears. Fearful that
the older soldiers would see Dorian crying, Severin got up
and pulled Dorian from the bleachers. He held his friend's
hand tightly as he guided him into a hiding spot beneath the
bleachers. It was a place he went to cry when he missed
Nyla. Once they were tucked away from plain sight, he

cradled the snivelling Dodo.   Staying strong, Severin made
Dorian a promise. "Dorian I love you, and I promise that I
will always keep you safe, okay? I will keep you as safe, as
your father would have kept you. I promise. I promise. I
promise."

Severin felt his friend's head nod in thanks against his
chest as he continued to cry.

. . . .

At dinner that night as the kids gorged on millies[26] and
small portions of goat stew, the chief gave a speech to his
Little Warriors. "I know all of you are concerned about our
boy Paris. Know that he is healing. I would not be surprised
if he is up and about by this time tomorrow. Why is he alive?
Why is he not with the ancestors? This is because the
ancestors know he has work to do in this life. They believe in
our cause and want the best servers to stay to fight the good
fight.

"He is invincible, and so are all of you. Paris did a
courageous thing. He followed his instincts and took a bullet
so that you may be safe from the LLLS – the demons that
want to take your land from you, and keep its profits for
themselves! So as you fall asleep tonight, I want you to
imagine yourselves acting with the same kind of courage as
your big brother Paris. Thanks to our intruder we now have
Intel of an LLLS camp a few days' walk from here. We will
beat them with our MM power after our next raid. We will
ruin their advancement on the Nothingness because we all
know what is beyond the Nothingness, boys – our mines!
And I'll be damned if I let them take our mines. Instead, we
will overcome their forces and steal their soldiers to forge an
enormous army. Right, eat up! You have a week to prepare

---

[26] Corn.

for the MM's next raid. For those of you who have never
taken part in one before, it will be good practice for the
battle that is upon us."

Those children who had never raided before felt
unconvinced and terrified. They let their food grow cold.
Some stared at their plates, refusing to make eye contact
with others. Others watched their feet. Still others stared at
the walls. They understood nothing beyond what was
expected of them and the futility of trying to escape those
expectations. Stuck. That's what they were. Stuck in a way of
killing. And many of them could not recall how this came to
be, where they came from or how long they were going to be
here for.

THE LITTLE RUNNER

The Mines at the mouth of the Crocodile River
Early December 2008

He had been enslaved for a very long time. He barely remembered the beginning, and he could not imagine an ending.

The MM took him from his family when he was four. He was a tiny child, so they knew exactly what to do with him. They brought him to their mines in the plateau where they put chains around his ankles and a lamp on his head. They put a pick in his hand and sent him down a narrow chute into a black cave, and that is where he spent his days, digging at the dirt.

He did not learn how to read or write. His first lesson was on Coltan instead of the ABCs, a highly demanded mineral used to build electronics like computers and cell phones. He knew nothing of where it went or what it was used for after his bruised fingers had dug it out from the walls of the mines. He learned quickly how to master those walls. He had to, as the punishing whip that lashed about in the blackness of the lair brought with it a menacing sound and an unbearable sting if he worked too slowly.

At night, after spending all day chipping away, the MM slave drivers would bring the little ones up for air and for their daily feed. If the children were lucky, they'd be brought up before sundown. At lights out, they'd each get locked up in a little chicken cage. The first few times he experienced this, he was miserable. He missed his Mammi and Pappi and little puppy. He would cry a lot, unable to sleep, but he soon learned that all the crying and no sleeping would make him too tired to mine for Coltan the following day. No sleep meant more whips, so he soon chose sleeping over whipping. Finally a day arrived when he entirely forgot why and for whom he had ever lost sleep over at all.

During the beginning, he used to allow himself friends, but that too was a luxury with harmful consequences. They were costs too cruel for the little Babba to bear. Children died off. They were taken by exhaustion, consumption, diphtheria, polio, malaria or tuberculosis, so little Babba stopped friend-making. Having friends meant losing them. So he simply stopped loving and continued mining.

Then one night at bedtime, after mining for far too long, the guard forgot to lock his cage.

The boy's fingers stretched through the square spaces between the wires. He called out after the guard to show how he had not been locked up, but since he had not used his voice for a very long time, only a faint squeak passed through his lips. The guard left the room where the children in cages were kept.

The boy clambered around the wire and shook his gate. It was loose. His fingers were short and he had to force his knuckles through the holes in the wire so that his stubby fingers could struggle with the latch. After some grunting and manipulating, the cage door swung open. Gasps from his fellow captors let out around the pen.

The room was pitch black, but he could feel his comrades staring in anticipation. With a heart readying itself for disappointment, he reached his hand to where the cage door usually was. Instead of touching metal, the child found himself waving freely with his outstretched arm. Excitement pattered within his chest. As he thrust his arm into the blackness, he noticed something very strange happening to his face. It was smiling!

Babba brought his hand back into his metal home and touched his lips – miraculously curled skyward. He could barely fathom their shape. His cheeks were puffed like an adder's neck and his teeth were squeaky against his fingertips like a lizard's skin.

Uncertain about his next move, Babba sat, staring into the darkness. From below came a strangled question. "Did the guard forget to lock your cage?" Babba couldn't find his voice to give an answer. Instead of speaking, he continued listening to the boy's hushed words. The boy was guiding him through his escape, directing his way to freedom. All the while, the other captives murmured and whimpered to one another, devastated that their cages were securely locked.

The boy from below gave steady advice. "Take your headlamp and climb down from your cage. Grip the cages with your toes, just like a monkey would. You have climbed down that cage a million times. You know how!" Babba did as directed.

"Now, walk over to the window and open it slowly so it does not creak."

Again, little Babba did as he was told.

"Climb out and jump into the bushes. Make sure you can't hear any voices. Take your time to make sure it is safe. When you are sure you are alone, run boy ... run boy ... run!"

So the little boy did. With his head light guiding him, he ran, and he ran, and he ran. He whacked his way through the bushes and journeyed deeper into the jungle. He ran barefooted towards nowhere and with nothing, certain that he would meet that thing everyone calls death. However, this did not stop him – he did not care. Proudly, he ran towards the very end of his life, wearing a very handsome smile.

THE LITTLE LORDS

In the Nobody-Knows-How-Vast-Jungle of Nkosi
25 December 2008

The little army had spent two days and one night closing in. They hunted through the jungle for the chosen village that was hiding in the faraway thickness. Innate trackers from their childhood chores of gathering, these kids listened to the calling of their guides to figure out their whereabouts. The sweet call of a kingfisher meant that they had headed too far south. The whirl of a lilac-breasted roller meant that they were dead on, and the eerie harping from a kite meant they were too close to the jungle's skin.

The boys and girls slugged their way through the sloppy floor of the forest as they headed for their doomed destination. Mud sucked on their bare feet as they waded, guns and arms high above their heads, through serpent infested pools. Machetes cut at the night. Sharp whistles aggravated small ears as the tools' edges caught on vines that first snapped as they broke and then moaned as they fell. The soldiers' small throats swallowed hard against their fatigued fear as they pressed on into the unforgiving mugginess of the night. It would rain ... they all knew it. They could feel it in their exhausted bones. At times, their brilliant eyes looked upwards in search of the first few droplets. They waited for the inevitable purging of the clouds, and with it the heavy pouring of its guilt. Guilt that was wet, like the inside of a crocodile's bite. Those eyes found towering trees, and between mangled branches, caught the glimmering of the intrepid night. The innocence of the sparkling sight triggered their nagging nerves. No rain ... at least not yet.

The children sucked and chewed on their lips as they swatted at buzzing insects – insects that delighted on the sweet delicacy of young blood. Deadly bites itched at their skin. Severin kept telling himself that these would be the only animals to claim his blood in the coming hours. Their task, once they reached the hiding village, was to rampage. Pillage. Maraud. Zaza had forecast no defence. This gave the boy some solace. He himself would not die. Nor would any of his group. He could keep on dreaming of a day when he might see her again.

By dawn they found themselves at their destination and ready for sleep at the flora's edge. Beyond them they beheld a little white chapel. The poor, unassuming house of God sat in a clearing, barely visible in the dark blue early hours. Chests sunk and guts wrung as they came to terms with the fact that this was where their ammunition would rattle against the quiet morning. Severin and Dorian, the two leaders of this group of AK-wielding mini warriors, perched themselves on a rock and against a tree trunk. Their soldiers were small enough to nicely nestle themselves between the ancient roots of blue gum, banana and lychee trees.

Dorian looked above him to find a bushel of bananas and smiled excitedly. "Look! Breakfast!"

No one seemed to care. No one felt hungry.

Giving up, he settled back into his trunk and held his knees. He surveyed the chapel. He had never seen one before. At first glance, it was just a simple white building with a steeple. Further scrutiny of its sheer hue grounded Dorian in a curious tranquility. Its patient bones gave Dorian the sense the building had its own raison d'être. The young warrior felt the chapel lull him into an uncommon ease. Its beautiful teak doors were dark and bold – heavy and weighted in goodness. Given its quaint exterior, he wondered what was on the inside.

At that moment, Dorian made an impossible wish – that he could freely walk up to the little chapel, push the door ajar and enter. He wanted to wrap himself inside that marvellous white building and close those big doors behind him. He wanted to lock himself in and everything else out. Confused by his own imaginings, he willed himself back to reality and said what they were all thinking.

"It is not what I thought it would look like."

The other kids nodded soundlessly. To himself, he added, 'It is not what I thought it would feel like.'

The group sat in silence and listened to the morning. No foggier than any other, yet thickened with fate, the seconds wound on with the rising of the sun. Its fiery orange kissed the top of the mountains to the east, illuminating a thin platinum meniscus between the earth and the sky. Witnessing this incredible beauty sent Dorian shuddering into a state of panic. His hand, not trusting his weapon, felt hot against the metal. His forehead perspired and his stomach knotted. The distressed little boy sunk into a sticky tar of melancholy. Helplessly, he looked up at his best friend and wished that they were not there about to do what they were, indeed, about to do.

Severin noticed the shift in Dorian's disposition. "Try to sleep Dodo. I'll wake you up when it's time."

Dorian begged back with his eyes as if to say, 'Please don't wake me up.'

He rested his gun upon his chest and leaned back against a tree. He drew air into the pit of his stomach and made big, infantile belly breaths. Seve watched Dorian take himself to another place – home perhaps – before turning his focus to the little white church. It was remarkably simple: one entrance, which was also the only exit. The orders were to wait until the entire village had entered and the congregation had begun to sing. Then they would storm the church. Dorian was supposed to lead and fire the first shot.

They were then to join in and kill all the traitors inside. At that moment, the Little Warriors' job would be done. They were told they could sit outside in the sun while the big boys ransacked the village, and then, after all was shot and done; the Little Warriors would then have to carry what was pillaged back to the camp. 'Simple enough,' thought Severin.

He looked at the boys and girls under Dorian's and his command. Every one of them bore faces of concentration. He knew they were as tired as he was. They looked tarnished and emaciated. They were drowning in their army fatigues. He giggled at the youngest, Nelson, who was only seven wet seasons old. Nelson was adorable in his little outfit. Severin chuckled over the absurdity of it all.

The sounds of his own amusement sent Severin's mind to a recollection of his little sister. Giggles always reminded him of her. In his imagination, she was dressed up like a soldier with plaits in her hair, and she held a gun in her hands. This image made Seve's stomach hollow and his heartache. 'She would never do this,' he thought. 'She would never, after knowing what a gun was capable of, hold one. She would rather die than survive, given the option.' He hung his head and tried to shake Nyla's morality from his imagination.

"Go away," he whimpered aloud.

Dodo woke up. "What?"

"Nothing. Everything is fine. Just a mosquito."

"Ah," said Dodo. In his own agony, he failed to comprehend his friend's suffering at that moment. Oblivious, he dropped his head back upon the tree to wallow in his own torment.

Dawn dragged on. The children's regret for choosing life over death was palpable. It hung in the air as meat on hooks in butcher shops. Severin wished Paris were there to instill the courage necessary for the undertaking. He turned his nose to the radiating morning, and upon doing so he heard the first conversation between of his prey. Time seized. Two girls wearing white sundresses waded through the softly lit mist, chattering delicately as they swung baskets by their sides. The Little Warriors watched them.

Severin's heart beat. It beat and beat and beat. And then, from pure exhaustion, it numbed within him. Like a young lion that peers through tall, long grass, he watched them. Between his hungry breaths, the girls performed their ritual: They scattered petals of hibiscus flower, bougainvillea and lilies in front of the chapel's teak doors.

Petals and angel voices fluttered.

Severin's eyes pierced his prey.

The girls twirled, revealing the bones in their backs where supple skin moved over muscles.

Severin imagined a killing. He looked for a sweet spot for a shot.

One of the girls lifted her basket high in the air and giggled, "All empty!" Holding her hands above her, she exposed the back lines of her body.

Casting his eyes down over her neck and shoulder he found the nape of her scapular. 'A beautiful place for a bullet,' he thought. 'A graceful place for a hole in a woman.'

He corrected himself, 'In a girl.'

Instantly embarrassed by his musings, the boy darted his eyes nervously around his group, worried that they may have been able to perceive his revolting daydream.

Luckily, the other children were lost in their own contemplation. Severin turned his attention to watch them.

One of the younger girls blinked heavily as she watched the church. Severin could not decide if she was physically or emotionally exhausted, but he was worried she would not make it through the morning. She was one of those kids that needed a nap even at ten years old. She was like a baby that never grew up. She started inhaling deeply and exhaling cautiously and lightly, determined to stay awake.

One of the boys clouded his world with his shoulders. He suffered through uneven breaths and moved his eyes around apprehensively, unable to look at anyone. He shifted a lot, trying to use his body as a means for his mind to escape. His anxiety coursed down his arms and into fingertips that drummed out on his knees. It worried into his brow, which scrunched and pulled at his anxious almond eyes.

Another lay back with his hands folded on top of one another upon his chest. He sniveled quietly. Soft tears tracked down his face, slipped over his chin and carved down and around the back of his neck. The rest of the kids in Seve and Dodo's group were variations of these three.

Severin remembered he did have one thing on him that would help. He dug into his pocket and pulled out a plastic bag of brown brown. He snuffed some himself and then passed the packet around.

A rushing expanded his brain.

The rain began pelting down as the village people rushed from the far side of the clearing into the chapel. The beautiful teak doors closed behind them, barring them in. The chapel was silent for quite some time, a stark contrast to the relentless noise in the Little Warriors' heads.

Then, and unfortunately, the singing began. The villagers in the church joined their voices in a merry song. The sweet sound of joy played with the rain.

With Dorian and Severin in the lead, the group of Little Warriors stalked the church. The death-smiths, padding softly towards its entrance, were blinded by a wash of falling water. The falling droplets pelted their suffering skin as the villagers' joyous chanting rose up into the weeping sky. The voices called out to their spiritual father on that Christmas morning, though none of the stalkers knew the date or its significance. Nor would knowledge have made a difference as the rain-drenched morning castrated the innocence of these Little Warriors.

Eyes shot down AK shafts as seven groups of twelve closed in on one of God's holy dominions. Dorian and Severin's group met up with four others at its lovely doors. The remaining parties surrounded the church, guarding its windows, the only other possible exits.

Dorian nestled the butt of his AK nicely in the nook of his shoulder. Its barrel poked itself into the door, searching for something that, if released upon, would suffer a bloody hole. Dorian's hand reached out for the teak. He felt the wood beneath his palm and pushed all of his weight into its solidness until it finally gave way and moaned ajar.

The entire congregation pivoted to welcome the unexpected latecomer who, to their surprise, was toting a handy weapon. The village of carollers' voices sunk into premonition as they met eyes with Dorian, the fiercest of baby boys. Behind this angry child was another, Severin. Together, they breathed hotly, like hunting cats. And then the congregation watched woefully as the whole host of Little Warriors closed in on them.

The people murmured nervously to one another as one of the child soldiers closed the doors of the chapel behind him. Dorian's heart raced at the sound of the latch hooking into place. His fingers numbed, forgetting how to pull the trigger. Severin, too, couldn't make his hand work. Eventually, after what seemed like endless moments of uncertainty, one of the boys from the back took the lead and fired a shot into the worshippers.

The villagers punctuated the dusty glow of the chapel with their panicked voices, "Nkosi! Nkosi!"

And so the young kids wrote it, inscribing inhumanity with the unleashing of their bullets. The Little Warriors squeezed their triggers. Their AKs killed every parishioner in the white chapel behind closed teak doors.

Walking back out into the rain, they dropped their guns. They watched the ground surge with red mud. As if falling into a thrashing sea, they tumbled into puddles. Water and blood splashed about them. Their hearts whined for the silenced voices that now lay mute and still. They worked their way back to their hiding place. Many of the children fell asleep, exhausted from the trauma. Others, those of whom were too hopped up on brown brown to relax, quivered and chewed their lips while concentrating on life's greatest ailment: regret. There they sat, in the gloomy rain, drowning under silence and remorse as the older boys rushed past them towards the village in to steal everything in it.

. . . .

Dodo awoke when the rain stopped spitting. He looked up into a mist as thick as budding cotton. It was a quiet time of day, though in his disorientation, he could not quite make out how old it was. Was it dawn or was it dusk? He sat up to gauge his whereabouts. He found he was in the clearing where he had passed out after the rampage of the church. He was all alone. Everyone had left him. Turning to find the church, he felt relieved to be by himself. He got to his feet and watched the building. It inched towards him, growing bigger as it approached, until he was face to face with its doors. He pushed into them with all his weight, as he had done before the massacre.

The chapel was dark and soundless, quiet as the late, sleeping hours of nighttime. He stepped into wetness. An ankle-high pool swallowed his feet. The substance of which, in the darkness, he couldn't at first make out. Suddenly, the great room began to glow. Candles illuminated themselves along the walls and upon a chandelier overhead. He looked down to find his feet, and then he saw it ... a shallow sea of blood.

He heard the echo of a drip. He looked up to the end of the aisle.

Another droplet.

He screwed his up eyes to make out a female figure kneeling at the altar.

Drip.

He moved towards her. It took him forever to gain ground.

Drip.

Finally, he came close enough to see that it was a girl wearing a beautiful white dress. He could hear her soft whispers. She was praying. Above her hung a man on a cross – Dorian had never heard of Jesus – his drooping head adorned with thorns, his eyes saddened by the lunacy of humankind. The dripping echoed as blood slid off his makeshift crown and slipped passed his melancholic eyes. A single drop ran down his temple, over his cheek and cascaded great lengths to meet the blood beneath his crucified feet.

The girl whispered further prayers. Intrigued, Dorian softly asked, "Hello?"

The room went quiet as she slowly softened her chin towards her shoulder, turning her head just enough to reveal her profile. The candles shimmered against the girl's cheekbones, and he was able to make out her face.

"Helena? Helena? Are you okay?"

The girl raised her tiger eyes. They pleaded, glinting with fevered tears. "No, Dorian," she whispered. "No, please! No Dodo, please don't!"

"Don't do what, Helena?"

Ambling like a baby buck, she stumbled to her feet and tried to pull herself to safety. He noticed that she was shackled to the man on the cross with great chains that cuffed her wrists. Frantically, she looked around the room for a place to hide, but there was nowhere, nowhere for her to hide from her little brother. She tried to pull herself free. The sound of her clanking chains and frantic pleas angered his ears.

"Dodo! No! Stop it!"

"Helena, what? What mustn't I do? How did you get here? Who chained you up?"

Growing hysterical, she screamed at him, "Dorian get away from me! Dorian don't!"

He rushed for her in a motion of protection, but with no provocation his arm rose and pointed towards her. Dorian stopped dead, understanding that it was not his arm at all. It was his Kalashnikov, apparently raising itself.

He, too, started to scream. "Helena it's not me! What's happening to me? Helena! I can't stop it! It wants to fire! It wants to..."

Helena's pleading brow uncrumpled after the blow. Her lips parted, and through them, she sighed out her very last breath before collapsing into the red beneath her.

Dorian let himself cry because watching the blood paint her pretty dress hurt his heart. Only now did he understand her pain.

Drip.

He shot an angry look up at the man on the cross. Dorian's breath fell short. Hanging from the cross was a wickedly smiling Zaza, and from his dick dripped Helena's blood.

. . . .

"Dodo! Dodo! Dodo! Wake up!" Severin shook his sweating friend. "Dodo you're scaring me! Wake up!"

Dorian moaned a few times more before blinking away the blinding light. Coming to, he scrambled to grab onto his right arm, as a man tries to wake a sleeping limb. He squeezed it tightly. Rocking into his friend who tried to calm him with his weight, he cried. Severin held him close with his chin a top of Dodo's head.

"Tula child, tula."[27]

Beside himself, Dodo wailed, "Seve, I killed her! I killed her dead!"

"Tula Dodo ... who did you kill?"

"My sister. My beautiful sister!"

---

[27] 'Quiet' or 'Shhhh...' in Zulu, Tswana and Sutho.

"No ... Dodo. It was just a bad dream, Dods ... a nightmare. Tula. Helena is safe at home."

Dorian pushed Severin from him. He trembled furiously. Fuming, he resolutely replied, "She is not safe!"

The children breathed heavy, sorrow-filled breaths as they stared knowingly into one another. Their brows glistened from burden and with lips taut, they made a silent agreement, an agreement that was inevitable, incomparable, and inadmissible. They silently vowed they would save Helena.

ONE CAGE TO ANOTHER

Doornbos Preparatory
Early January 2009

Severin, Dorian and Paris were sunning themselves on the tennis courts. Old colonial boarding schools had their charms. There were racquets in the stock room and surely, if they rummaged around enough, they could find some tennis balls amongst the field hockey sticks and deflated rugby balls, but none of them knew how to play.

A rustle came from the bushes.

Dorian shot upright, peering into the brittle bushes, now alive with motion.

"It's a baby bush buck," Paris stated affirmatively. He resumed his repose, absorbing the warmth of the sun.

"How do you know?" snapped Dodo.

"Because I heard the same thing a couple of days ago and it was – low and behold – a baby bush buck! It was so cute. I love bushbucks. I think they're my favourite animal."

Severin nudged the sun soaker and grinned, "You love cute things..."

"Shut up, Severin!" Paris punched him in the arm. The boys rolled about on the court wrestling until they heard another a rustle. All three of them stopped and searched for its source.

Feeling assertive, Dodo exclaimed, "I'll bet you twenty-five bullets that thing out there is not baby bush buck."

Paris, accepting the challenge, insisting, "It is a bush buck ... you'll see."

Dorian stood up and walked over to the fence. "Hello ... pssst ... pssst ... cou cou!"

Severin and Paris stared intensely at the bush as Dorian surveyed the greenery. After a few moments, he noticed a chocolate stain. "I thought bush bucks had hide, not skin like you or me, Paris."

Paris stood up and joined Dorian at the fence. "Hey! Hey! You! Come out!"

Between the bushes the boys found two bewildered eyes glinting inside a frightened face.

The little boy had no other option than to reveal himself. If he ran, they would chase and catch him. They were big and strong and seemed eager for a hunt. He was exhausted and had seen a pack of hyenas take down a baby wildebeest the day before. He did not want to be dealt a similar blow after all this walking. So, he braced himself for the unveiling.

The baby boy emerged from the bushes and arranged his face to plead mercy.

Severin, moved by the child's fear, thought on the little boys he'd been forced to kill. Here was a boy he could save. His nearly hardened heart softened. How could it not when a tiny, lost little boy stood alone before them? Fatigue drooped around the young child's eyes as his bottom lip, lazy from malnutrition, relaxed towards the ground. The Little Warriors knew that look well ... they themselves of course, had worn that look before. Empathy rose within them.

Severin, who was especially moved by the boy, stood up and walked towards the court's gate, lifted its hinge and swung it open. He purposefully left his gun leaning against the fence and slowly approached the young'un, a boy whose vulnerability reminded Severin of that girl he hid in the southern chamber of his heart – the chamber that ached as he slept and dreamt of her. As Severin approached the child, he noticed the little boy's eyes were red hot, stinging with tears. He had forgotten what tears felt like. Crying was a luxury he could no longer afford now that he was a leader of a pack. Now that he gave orders to kill. Now that he made strategies to destroy entire villages, to harm, to hurt. To annihilate.

Seve unclipped his canteen from his waist, untwisted the top and handed it to the child. It was too big for the child to hold with one hand, so he held it with two. Still, it was difficult to steady the water's shifting weight. The boy struggled with it for a while, so Severin balanced it for him. The boy took a long gulp. The cool water caressed his throat. Gratitude overcame him. Tears slipped hotly down his dirty cheeks, forging thin rivers in the film of sweat and dust that caked his face.

Severin studied the tiny drinker and asked, "Where did you come from?"

The child stopped drinking. He looked from one face to another. Since he had no answer, he stretched his hand out behind him and pointed into the jungle. The child soldiers understood. This little boy was from nowhere.

"What is your name?" asked Severin.

Again the tiny child's eyes darted from one big boy's anxious face to another's. The baby buck's sharp shoulders shrugged up towards his ears. He had forgotten.

"It doesn't matter. Your village is not there anymore ... it is as lost, as you are," said Paris.

With unmoving eyes, the little boy put the water bottle back up to his lips and took another desperate swig. The heavy bottle tilted too far. Sacred water was lapped up hungrily by parched ground. Terrified that he would be punished for being wasteful, the child's stomach turned. Severin, not one to cry over spilled water, placed his hand around the boy's jagged ribs, calming the child instantly. "Are you hungry?" he asked.

The boy nodded. He was unutterably starving. On his month-long struggle from the plateau and through the jungle, he had kept himself alive on worms and stolen snake eggs. He had used sticks to spear small rodents and – not knowing how to make a fire – had eaten their meat raw. It had been a disgusting adventure for him. He had often asked himself if such a life was worth fighting for, but an innate will to live kept him going, kept him walking.

"Come with us, okay?"

After a stretch of hesitation, the big boys' continual urges prompted the lost one to follow. He used careful steps to move towards the fence, placing the entire soles of his feet upon the earth at once. He winced as he transferred his weight from one foot to the next. Finally, he made it to the gate. He surveyed the big cage around the tennis court. Severin stood at the entry and waved him through. The boy inhaled his nerves deep into his empty gut and took the painful step into Doornbos' tennis court.

With this single step, the child had unknowingly renounced his freedom for the second time in his young life. Paris noticed the boy's limping and so, effortlessly, lifted the child up onto his hip. The boy took in the sweet stench of puberty when he laid his hollow cheek upon Paris' shoulder. Paris softly took the boy's dangling foot. He curled his sole up to the sky to reveal tattered flesh. Sweet strain-filled squeaks came from the back of the boy's throat. Paris felt his heart twist in the same way that it did during those wakeful nights when he listened to Anthony grunting into Helena.

Dorian, too, had the same sensation of helpless sadness at the sight of the child's soles. Determined to do something, Dorian ran off to find his elder sister, forgetting in the moment of empathy, that they had not spoken directly since the day he tried to kill his arch nemesis, the smoking soldier.

He found her staring into the dark memories of her nights with the rest of the sex slaves. Her calloused hands pounded millet.

"Helena! Helena!"

Unheeding, the girl carried on peering into her emptiness, using all of her intelligence and attention to search for her life before Doornbos.

"HELENA!"

The girl startled, blinked herself back to reality. "What is it, Dorian?"

Her brother panted against the air. He had run all the way across the school grounds to her and now, facing the person whom he believed to have hurt him most, about to speak directly to her for the first time in months, he suddenly felt as if his body were aflame with the longing for his kin.

Dorian's words stammered forth. "There is a child. We found him – or – he found us! He is so little, Helena ... He has owies on his feet."

Helena saw a replay of her past. It was a simultaneously gratifying and disheartening vision: Dorian crying in her lap as he pointed at his scraped knee. She called it an 'owy' and kissed it better. He must have been only four wet seasons old. Now look at him. A man-child.

"Helena!"

"You need me, Dodo?" Her voice pleading with desperation.

"No, I don't need you," he lied – he knew damn well he needed her every moment of every day. "The lost boy needs you!" He took her by the arm and pulled her away from the other sex slaves. She reluctantly followed.

Meanwhile, the little boy tried to stave off sleep as Paris carried him, Severin in the lead, from the tennis courts to Severin's dormitory. There were several buildings, stoically clad about the grounds of Doornbos Preparatory, but Severin had chosen a dormitory hidden from the rest of the community. He had made himself a home in one of the cop rooms.[28] There were benefits to leading the pack of killer-children, and one of these benefits was well-earned privacy.

On their way to Severin's room, the child noticed groups of wild-eyed boys cleaning guns. They laughed loudly as

---

[28] A private dorm room where a prefect would sleep.

they sat in circles, telling stories. He was nervous of this place, but Paris' warmth made his surroundings a little more endurable.

Paris carried him into Severin's building. Team photographs of white boys streamed past him as they walked through the foyer. Forgotten history covered the walls of these orphans' home.

The three of them continued down a long, unlit corridor and into a room at the end of the hall. Inside was a desk that looked out onto a garden of weeds. Seve had etched his name into the desk with his knife, as all the boys who had lived in that room before him had done. Names like Wickus, Guillaume, François, Elric, Louis and Johan. Their names would be there, their legacies would remain ... until the camp needed firewood during the wet season. Then their names would curl up into themselves and be forgotten, consumed by hungry flames.

Upon the desk were the weapons Severin was laboriously studying: a machete, a handgun, and bullets. Severin lay his AK down with the rest of them. Even in the face of these death-devices, the little boy was no longer nervous. He was comfortably curled up in Paris' strong arms, feeling safe.

Paris placed him down on Severin's makeshift bed, which was a pile of blankets and clothes thieved from villages long since burned. Severin rummaged through the drawer of his desk and pulled out a Lunch Bar.[29] He peeled away the plastic to reveal chocolate. Generously, he handed his treasure to the child. Severin had been saving it for one of his miserable days, but when those arrived, as they cruelly had, he found he was no longer hungry. His stomach grew angry on days of missing her, when there was not any daga or cocaine to help him forget. Simply knowing the chocolate was there to make him feel better sent him into further anxiety because he knew that its taste would never

---

[29] A Cadbury chocolate popular in Southern Africa.

sweeten the sourness that swam in his mouth whenever he imagined the cutting of her legs. He was happy to be rid of it.

"Have you had chocolate before?" It was a stupid question – of course the little boy hadn't – but Severin didn't quite know what else to say or what to do. "The mess hall doesn't serve until six. The girls do a good job. Sometimes it tastes as good as if your own Mammi cooked it, you know? This chocolate will have to do until then."

The child accepted the gift with a gracious nod of his head. He brought it up to his nose, inhaled the sweetness of the bar, and took his first bite. The nourishment was a prize Seve had won on a dark and deathly day. It came from a village that was very far away now. It haunted Severin's memory; he would never forget how hot it felt, burning at his back.

Sin or not, stolen or not, chocolate, nuts and caramel melted between the little one's rotting teeth and in doing so, sent his lips curling upwards in an involuntary smile. Paris and Severin chuckled at the child's delight and wonder. The two of them leaned against the desk and watched him eat.

Helena and Dorian came through the door. Catching sight of her dream incarnate leaning against the desk, she stumbled backwards into her brother. Paris smiled at her and nodded toward the chocolate-smudged face on Severin's bed.

"Oh, babba!" she cooed at the tiny, sickly boy. Stunned by Helena's volume, the baby boy stared back at her with wide wooded eyes. A wave of sobriety came over Helena. Her attention shocked the three MM soldiers. She was not quite the lioness they remembered her to be, but this meeting had indeed suddenly changed her temperament. The boys smiled at one another, sharing the beautiful moment where Helena was nearly Helena again.

"My name is Helena. I once walked very far like you have. Your feet ... they need to be cared for. May I take a look?"

The child looked up at the boys for his answer. Dorian and Severin nodded back at him with reassurance, so he stretched out his short legs, showing off his shredded soles.

"Ay, little one! How long have you been running for?"

His look suggested he had been searching for somewhere safe for a very, very, very long time.

"OK, we clean these first, and then after dinner we give you a bath because you are very smelly, and then we'll clean them again okay?"

He shied away from her, turning his chin into his armpit.

"Oh don't worry little man. We have all been on a journey like you. We understand. In fact, we were all a lot dirtier than you by the end of it."

Watching her now, Dorian had an image of the day Zaza drove her off into the jungle. He remembered how she had sat proudly, her nose held high even though she knew where she was heading. For the first time, he imagined how that must have felt for her. He realized now what he should have felt then, instead of stubbornness and hatred. Her task had been one of dreadful obligation and the horror of it now stung at his nose. His chest ached. He began to cry quietly. Only Severin noticed. He put a hand on his friend's shoulder and squeezed it warmly. Dodo had missed her and was glad to be in her company again. His sister cleaned the babba's feet with fermented cane juice, water and aloe leaves and then wrapped his wounds in banana leaves.

The boy was very brave through it all and did not fight or fuss as she worked. Finally, she lifted his banana-leaved limbs off her lap, pulled the little babba closer to her and laid his head upon her lap. She hummed a lullaby and petted his head. He marveled up at her beauty, as she sang, "Tula, sana, babba."[30]

Even though her melody was directed at the little child, each boy in the room felt the tenderness of her voice touch

[30] 'Quiet, little baby' in Zulu.

his own heart. The child was lulled into a very, very good sleep. He was stretched out in the lap of a makeshift mother, elated that he would never be sent back down into the mines again. Because he had escaped. Because he had survived. Because he had proved to be more powerful than all the evil in his world. For now.

. . . .

This is how Babba joined their team. He became the Little Warriors' assistant. He cleaned guns, he polished the commanders' boots and he carried food to Anthony Zaza. He became their Babba-helper. In return, he was fed, given a place to sleep in Severin's room and he was loved. Very much. For it was impossible not to love the unspeaking child. Though he said nothing, he managed to say everything that tinkered about within him through his expressive eyes. It was because of those eyes that Severin, Dorian, Helena and Paris knew when he was sleepy and needed his nap. They knew when he was thirsty and when to take him to the river to fill up his canteen. They knew when he was hot and took him down to the watering hole to dunk him in the mud. In Babba, they found their once-lost innocence. Consequently and protectively, they kept him naive. He did not know much of what happened outside of the camp, and he himself did not want to know, for he was safe, and he was sound, and he didn't have the strength to leave yet another family. He had lost too much already. So he performed his chores, loved them back and sometimes ... sometimes ... his big brothers and his big sister would say something or do something for him which made his tummy flouncy with joy, and he would smile. And they would smile back.

THE BOY

The Orphanage at Princess Marina Hospital, Baobab
2 February 2009

"Thanks for coming, Stefanus."

"Of course. What's the problem? You sounded quite distressed on the phone, Shalini."

She averted her eyes and tapped her desk with her pen, sucked in her breath and finally mustered the courage to come out with it. "A boy was brought to us."

"Aren't there lots of them brought you?"

"Not like this. He is the first of them to come."

"A soldier, you mean?"

"Yes, he escaped from the LLLS about three months ago. Supposedly trekked his way through the jungle all by himself. The kid's a machine. It's unbelievable. He finally made it to a village called Mokolodi, where the chief, horrified by his story, took him in and tried to care for him. Only he couldn't. The child's temper is wild and it flared too often. It made the wives nervous for their own children, and try as they might, they could not console him at night. He has night terrors, you see? So they gave up and sent him walking alone, here to Baobab. Deborah found him in the displacement camp. She brought him to me this morning." Shalini pressed her fingers into her forehead, trying to push away a headache.

"Jesus. The poor boy, what's his name?"

Her fingers dropped to her mouth as her eyes flashed over Stefanus. Her disposition made him feel uneasy.

"He says he can't remember, but the LLLS … they called him Scarface."

"Does he have scars on his face?"

Shalini smacked her lips nervously. "I wish it were that simple. Just a nickname." Trembling, she continued, "He told me he got it because he slashed the faces of people instead of killing them."

"Holy shit."

"Jesus, Stefanus. If we're going to be meeting more and more of these kids, you're going to have to work on your astonishment … and your vocabulary. They'll be feeling guilty enough without your responding to their stories with words like that."

Stefanus sunk himself into a chair opposite her desk. He stared down at his great palms. "I'm sorry Shalini."

His sincerity incited her own remorse. "No, I am," she returned, shaking her head. "I'm angry at myself for not knowing where to begin with him."

"May I meet him?"

"Please? Would you?"

Stefanus took in her worried face and answered, "I'm in this now, Shalini. I want to make this all go away. I need to learn how."

Shalini got up from her desk, patted down her dress, wiped away the residue of tears from her cheeks and murmured, "You're a good man Stefanus."

"No, I'm a stupid man. Stupid enough to have come to Africa in the first place."

"Weren't we all?" She laughed wryly. "Follow me. I've put him in the play room, hoping he'd take to the Lego."

He mocked her gently as they passed through the door. "Isn't he a bit old for Lego, Shalini?"

"No, I'd say he's about 9 or 10."

Stefanus' face fell flat. What type of child could do such cutting?

Noticing the sudden lump that had grown in his throat, "Oh Stefanus! I've upset you!"

"No, no you didn't. I just forget sometimes that children that young can... "

The two of them continued down the hallway in silence. They came to the playroom where Shalini and Stefanus peered through the glass portal in its door. Sitting on the floor beneath the window was a small boy. Lego was scattered all around. Evidence that he had been trying to find pleasure in building. A few piles of blocks stacked about him – nothing imaginative, but he had indeed tried. No cars, houses or spaceships – just monotonous square towers.

Behind the boy's cloud of misery was a stunning face fixed with sharp features, plush lips and a fine nose with wide nostrils. His feathered lashes fluttered intermittently. The boy sat frozen in a secretive moment. Stefanus felt as though he was not supposed to be watching. The boy sighed heavily and glanced up to find the golden haired man peering in at him.

Anger overtook the boy. What the hell did this guy want? What was he looking at? Defensively, Scarface threw his hands out and toppled his towers as if to say, "Get away from me!" The man in the window disappeared as the little lion huffed in solitude.

Scarface could hear a muffled conversation from the other side of the door, probably between the burly white man and the pretty woman who had welcomed him this morning. He had thought she was gentle upon meeting her, yet he had glared at her when she smiled down on him, and when she placed her gentle palm upon his shoulder he had shot back reproachful, icy eyes. At his glare, her countenance shifted from openness to despair. He hated when women gave him that look. Sometimes he wished that there weren't any women left in Nkosi to give it. It made him feel inadequate, though he did not understand why.

A creak from the door handle sent his eyes shooting through the portal. He could see the white man's furrowed brow as he passed into the playroom. Scarface grew livid. He anticipated a slew of questions he was too afraid to answer, having responded to them so many times before to the people of Mokolodi. He missed his family there but suffered the sting of their rejection. He was lonely for them, but he hated them for sending him out into the Jungle and over the Nothingness all by himself. At least at Princess Marina he didn't have to talk to all those children who couldn't understand why he didn't know how to smile, or why he had forgotten how to play, or why he sometimes refused to eat, or why he screamed in his sleep.

"Why are you so afraid, new boy? What do you see at night? Please tell us."

"No. Go away! You wouldn't understand! Leave me alone!"

And so they would back away, rejected and a little scared. Upon their departure, he could overhear them saying such things as, "There is something very wrong with that new boy."

Stefanus entered the room cautiously and closed the door behind him. Scarface could see the gentle woman watching over the two of them through the window. Knowing she was there made him feel safer, so he relaxed his puffed-out chest and let his face soften. Not too much, but just enough to calm his breathing. Stefanus sat down in a chair made for children. He looked a giant given the juxtaposition. Scarface let out a little chortle at the sheer absurdity of Stefanus' size. The man's wild hair and blue eyes made Scarface's lips part and reveal his teeth for a short moment before he gathered in his astonishment, remembering his Mammi's lesson that it was rude to stare. He shifted his scrutiny to his feet.

Stefanus sat quietly for a while so the boy could grow accustomed to his presence. He looked at the Lego pieces scattered all over the floor and decided to build some trust. Taking care to not make any sudden movements, he lowered himself to the floor to be with the child, collecting pieces and stacking them in the same way as the boy had done. Scarface soon joined him and they were building Lego together.

Stefanus plucked the courage to begin. "I like that one you built there. Bold colours."

The boy looked up at him but offered no response. Baby steps, thought Stefanus, and got up to leave. He would try again tomorrow. Once standing, the boy interrupted his departure. "I like colours."

Surprised, the white man stopped. "You do? Do you like to draw?"

"I don't know. I like to colour-in. I used to have colouring books that my Pappi would bring back from the mines."

Stefanus smiled down at the child. "Well, young man, I so happen to have a little girl who likes colouring very much as well, though you may have to teach her how to stay inside the lines. She doesn't listen to me when I tell her to, and everything turns out like a scribbly mess."

Scarface smiled hugely at the wild white man.

"Would you perhaps like me to bring her to you so the two of you can colour-in together?"

Scarface retracted slightly and nibbled his lip as he thought about all the questions she would ask. But the fact that she would bring colouring-in books and crayons outweighed how irritating she may be, so he allowed himself the pleasure. "OK big man."

Laughing pleasantly at the child, Stefanus explained, "It's Stefanus, though my little girl calls me Steffi. You may call me that too if you wish. It's easier to say."

"OK ... Steffi." The boy watched the white man go, and continued to play with his Lego, happier than before.

Finding a concerned Shalini outside, Stefanus put his hand on her shoulder and chuckled, "I'm bringing Nyla by in a few days to play with him. Seems like he doesn't like questions. Most boys don't, but this one is especially reluctant. However, he'll respond to simple statements. That's my advice to you."

Shalini's face brightened as he spoke. "Thank you, Steffi. Thank you!"

Stefanus was surprised at her use of Nyla's nickname for him. "Oh God, not you too now?" But then he had to admit, "Actually, I kind of like it ... or perhaps I only like it because she started calling me Steffi."

"That's probably it, but it suits you."

"She is rather perceptive."

"Notably so. Does she know where you are going next week?"

"No ... she's still a baby. Sometimes I feel we forget that. She doesn't need to know."

THE BLINDING

Doornbos Academy & the LLLS Camp
2 February 2009

Helena and Paris sat in the sun outside of the headmaster's office. They watched the quiet courtyard. No Little Warriors were playing there. Most of them, including Severin and Dodo, were on the front lines with Zaza, surprising an LLLS contingency.

"Did Dorian talk to you after their first raid, Paris?"

"A little bit. He seemed preoccupied. He didn't say much about it. Neither of them did."

"The sounds coming from the dormitories at night after the raid... they were horrible."

"The nightmares subside, but they come back to haunt the little ones now and again." The way he stressed the word, *they*, caught her attention.

"Who comes back?"

"The dead, Helena."

She sat cooling herself against the wall, taking in Paris' words; he stood in her doorway, watching her with unfailing admiration.

Helena wasn't sure she wanted to talk about the dead, so she returned to her original strain of thought. "So what did he say to you?"

"As I said, Dorian didn't say much. He has grunted a lot over the past two weeks whenever I tried to talk to him. Has he begun to talk to you Helena?"

Helena's eyes settled on her palms before looking up at the handsome young man and replying, "He looks at me differently now. I feel as though he is studying me."

Paris pulled his eyes from her, too nervous of her beauty, and continued, "Well I suppose that's better than him not studying you at all."

The school was quiet without the Little Warriors there. A couple of the grown-up soldiers lurked about, smoking ganga, drinking beers, playing cards and – when they had the energy – raping the girls and, sometimes, the boys.

The two settled into a comfortable silence. No one was around to watch them. For weeks they had been eyeing one another, unable to do anything more because of their proximity to Zaza. At night, Paris would wait in the courtyard. He'd watch the stars and pretend that Helena was gazing at them alongside him. 'That would be romantic,' he would think. 'One day, we will gaze upon them together.'

Anthony never stayed awake for more than a few moments after his orgasm. So, once he'd hear Anthony's last grunt, Paris would slowly make his way over to Helena's window to watch over her as she fell asleep.

Now, finally alone, they were too nervous to make much conversation. Helena finally thought of something to add. "Paris, will you take us girls down to the river to swim? It's so hot today and the younger kids won't be playing in it. I don't think the girls would like to be there by themselves."

"What would you be scared of? How could the river be scarier than here?"

"Well ... I don't know. What if we were stolen by the LLLS?"

"The LLLS is probably the same as Doornboss Helena."

"Well, you wouldn't be there would you?"

Flattered, Paris giggled to himself. "Sure. OK. Let's go."

Paris took his AK and led eleven slaves to the watering hole. He could feel them nudging Helena behind him. They teased her as they walked for being consumed by the kind of abandon found in teenage girls in love all over the world. Helena pretended to shun their attention.

She watched him move, shirtless, adorned only by a gun slung over his back. She took in the muscles that slid over his bones. Her heart and vagina surged. She tried to squeeze her excitement into her fists to expel the energy, but the feeling would not subside. And, after all, why should she want it to? Paris flirtatiously smiled back at the girls. This sent them stumbling, laughing gigantically.

One of the girls whispered into Helena's ear, "God he's beautiful Helena! You are so lucky!" As the girl spoke, her breath tickled Helena's neck. The sensation tightened Helena's nipples and rolled her eyes backwards from the bliss. For the first time in her life, she was aroused. Helena walked on, a fire ablaze between her legs, toward the watering hole.

Paris placed himself on a rock overlooking the lagoon. He lay back with his hands behind his head and cooked in the sun. He was truly happy with how the day was going. He wished every day could be like this. No kids. No Zaza. Just him and his beautiful Helena. He turned to watch her undress. She pulled her T-shirt over her head, stretching out her taut stomach. Above her ribs were two sweet breasts. His breath slowed as his penis swelled. She pulled down her skirt and stood glimmering, naked, next to the water. Her stomach flexed as she laughed at the girls splashing about in the water. They were also bare, but none interested the boy as she did. She noticed he was watching. Flirtatiously she covered the hair between her legs and found that she did not mind when Paris had 'that' look on his face. It was so different from Zaza's lustful expression. The younger man's eyes were hungry but not threatening. She found herself hoping he was thinking of touching her.

A shriek rang out, interrupting their infatuation. One of the girls had been pulled under. Her hands scrambled for help and, like mercury in water, blood drifted from her as a crocodile fed. Her screams exploded inside the muggy water and travelled upwards, bubbling pathetically on the water's surface.

There was nothing any of the others could do but whimper and call to her. They wailed, "Wayayayayaya!"

Paris stood up and fired two shots into the hole. The thrashing animal slowed and, weighed down by the water, the sound of its snapping hollowed. What was left of the girl floated to the surface. Paris kept his gun at attention and stepped into the hole. He made his way to the tethered prey, and with his finger still on the trigger, ready for a resurgence from the aged beast, took hold of her body and towed the dead along with him as he backed out of the water. He pulled her up on the bank. The girls crowded round, tearfully gawking over her lost limbs and face.

Paris looked into her brain and then down to her breasts that had nipples very much like Helena's. He realized this girl could just as easily have been Helena, and he felt sick at the thought. Instinctively, he reached for his beloved and pulled her naked body into him. He held her tightly and burrowed his nose into her neck, whispering against her skin, "Tula, tula."

Still holding Helena, he looked up at the rest of the girls and told them, "We are to not speak of this ever again. Do not tell a soul. The boys enjoy playing here. The water makes them happy, and you know that they are rarely happy. You are not to tell your husbands. If anyone asks where she is, just say you don't know."

Helena looked up at him and objected, "But Paris, they will go looking for her."

He whispered into her ear, "Exactly, we need the diversion."

She pulled away slightly and stared into him, trying to understand what he meant.

"You will see. Trust me."

Crying, she released herself from his embrace and collected her clothes.

. . . .

Surrounding the LLLS Camp that the intruder, Joshua, had come from, the boys twitched and raged in anticipation. They hid in camouflage and muttered angrily about the LLLS.

"Stupid assholes," spat one of the boys under Seve's command. He repeated the curse and carried on with his train of thought. "Stupid assholes. Who do they think they are? We're going to tear them apart, aren't we Seve?"

Severin said nothing; he silently pulled the packet of cocaine from the boys' sweating palms and took a pinch for himself before he handed the rest to Dorian, who greedily grabbed at it, muttering, "Shit, we could die today."

"Don't think about that, Dods. You're good with your eyes. You'll be ok." Severin paused here to look at the mountains of cocaine that Dorian was organizing before adding, "Well, unless you carry on with that stuff. Then you won't be able to see."

"That's my plan, Seve. I don't wanna feel death coming."

The boy who had just finished cursing indignantly piped up again. "We can't die! We're the Freedom Fighters! We're like Rambo! Invincible!"

Dorian, annoyed, snapped, "Whatever. We're flesh and bone just like the LLLS."

The boy chewed his lips. He looked back and forth between Severin and Dorian, waiting for one of them to tell him Dorian was just playing, but neither of them said a word. Instead they both lay back in the mud and gazed up at the rustling trees, leaving him to worry.

The two of them began to smile as the cocaine travelled further into their systems. Their perceptions were heightened and the world became overexposed. Dorian revelled in how spectacularly powerful his senses were when he was high. He could hear everyone and everything around him so clearly. People's breaths and their whispered conversations were magnified. He could even read Severin's mind. He was sure of it. He had always, of course, been able to read his friend's mind if he was looking directly at him, by reading his face and body language, but now he just knew. Knew without looking. In Dorian's coked-up world, Severin was, as always, planning: 'First: Stay alive. Second: Come back for Dorian because he's too high to make it through. Third: As soon as this LLLS raid is done, we two cannot risk fighting in another battle. So, Dorian will talk to Paris and persuade him to make a move. Paris would risk anything for Helena, so he'll agree, even if it means they risk being beaten till they are hung in the courtyard with barbed wire for desertion. We can flee the next week. We'll have to hurry, as the weather is turning, and it is the perfect time to go. It will be hot during our first few days while we are trekking through the jungle. Luckily, there will be shaded stretches, and by the time we reach the Nothingness and have to cross it, we will have collected enough fruit to survive. The wet season will have set in full force by then, so we'll be able to set out our canteens at night and collect some rain water to drink for the days...'

Dorian was distracted from his mind reading when Seve's kid picked up the packet of cocaine.

"Christ, kid that's enough! Give it back." Dodo swiped it from the boy and took another pinch for himself, snuffing it up his nose. At this, the greenery grew greener than it had ever been. The light was brighter, and suddenly amidst the glories of the morning, Dorian sensed he was missing something. His fear.

Dorian turned to Severin and pulled him up. The two of them were shaking as they stood like two kids hopped up on too much pop and candy. They scrunched their noses, laughed and hugged one another and started to dance, in the mud, to their own inner rhythms. They shook their shoulders and flapped their hands. They giggled their way through the time spent waiting for the whistle to blow. When it did, they called the other kids, who were just as high, and nonchalantly waved towards the LLLS camp. It was the middle of the afternoon. The LLLS boys would be playing cards or cleaning their guns. The commanders would be raping their wives or sleeping in hammocks. It was the perfect time to go in for the kill.

They swarmed the camp pulling their triggers and watching bodies fly. They danced around corners, and slipped, laughing, in mud. They played with their machetes, slicing up tummies. They pulled the pins from hand grenades with their teeth and flung them into tents, mimicking Rambo's heroic artistry. Explosions sent limbs shooting like fireworks into the daylight. They played ninja, kicking boys they did not know, but recognized all too well. They pulled the hair of girls and pressed the ends of handguns into their cheeks. They shouted at them and threatened them. They called them whores and sluts, echoing the words their commanders used on the girls back at the MM camp.

And then the whistle blew again, and the boys' momentum slowed until some were lighting cigarettes, trying to act cool like their elder commanders.

The only sounds were from the whimpers of the girl Zaza was raping in the mud. Through the haze of Dorian's come-down, he watched her hands clawing at the earth. She was on her stomach. Zaza pressed her face into the ground as he thrust into her. Dorian noticed how big his penis was and grimaced as the man forced all of it into the girl, who howled like a puppy with no Mammi. Dodo felt dizzy. An iota of pain tickled his side. He looked down to find his uniform torn. He dropped his gun and scrambled at his abdomen with his already bloodied hands. A great gash ran from his hip to his belly button. It bellowed with blood. "Help me!"

Dodo fell to his knees and then face-forward into the mud. His mind slowed as he lost himself in deluded thoughts much like those that taunted him before sleep. He re-dreamt the raping of the girl in the mud; only this time she had

Helena's face. Then, everything went black. The only sound was Severin's screeching, "Dodo's been cut! Dodo's been cut! Someone help me! HELP ME!" But no one moved an inch. They drew on their cigarettes and concentrated on their own mourning.

THE COLOURING-IN BOOK

The orphanage at Princess Marina Hospital
7 February 2009

Scarface sat waiting at one of the tables in the playroom.
There were lots of other orphans in the building and they
had not questioned him like the children of Mokolodi. In
fact, their own loneliness made him feel safe, as one does in
numbers. This sense of belonging had reduced his social
anxieties. The little man looked at the children's paintings
pinned up on the walls. He pinched himself like his Mammi
used to tell him to do whenever he thought he was
dreaming. He had not thought of his mother for a long time:
a forced forgetting of her existence, but here she was again
in his mind's eye, beautiful and giving. His heart heaved.
Remembering her brought back the horrible knowledge that
he would never feel his mother again. Unbeatable sadness
ensued as he recalled why he'd chosen to suppress
recollections of her those many months ago. Grieving was
too horrible and exhausting a thing.

The gentle lady, Shalini, had said that all the children in
this part of the hospital, the section they called 'The
Orphanage,' were parentless as well. He liked this about
them, and though he did not play with them, it didn't hurt
to watch them have fun. The knowledge that they were no
better off than he, kept his jealousy at bay. No Mammies or
Pappies to tell of what they had seen, heard or learned. They
had no one to be proud of them, to kiss their boo boos, or to

tickle their backs and help them fall asleep when they were scared.

And then, sitting there, something dawned on him, slowly and terribly. He had taken their parents away from them. Scarface fidgeted with his fingers. He watched himself squeeze them tighter together as his anxiety rose in his chest. He felt remorse for using his hands to take other kids' Mammies and Pappies away. Guilt. Another thing he preferred to repress.

A knock at the door interrupted his painful musings. He looked up to find the white man beaming through the portal. Steffi disappeared, bending down to pick something up. From the bottom of the window rising up came a head of braids, an inquisitive forehead, enormous planets for eyes, and then, a semi-toothed grin. The white man held up a giddy child who searched through the window for her new friend. Stefanus pointed him out to her. The little girl waved at him through the window. She was so cheerful, and Scarface found himself thinking, 'She can't tell I am a murderer.'

Her muffled giggles gently passed through the glass. Their sounds settled nicely on his skin, and numbed his fingertips, relaxing him. His hands softened in his lap. Steffi turned the handle of the door. The sweetness of her happy voice filled the room and calmed the boy further. The little girl was on Steffi's hip. She held onto some colouring-in books and a big box of Crayola crayons. Scarface's cheek muscles were weak from lack of use. As the two entered, he felt them finally work again. The glorious ache of curving lips crept up behind his ears. His muscles squeezed in a way that they hadn't for a long time, and his face opened into a smile to welcome his visitors.

Then, with temples aflame, he confronted her squirming, hacked-up legs, and his happiness vanished. His face dropped at the sight of the knotted-together skin at the tips of Nyla's thighs. He had been born in a time of war. He had participated in war. He had hacked. He had killed. He could very well have taken this beautiful little girl's legs.

In one unhappy instant, his memories usurped what had started out as a pleasant moment.

Scarface sulked away from Stefanus and Nyla, squeezing himself into the back corner of the room where he buried his head in his knees. The boy cried tears that had been pooling in his ducts, waiting to pour since he had taken life for the very first time. The child shuddered and wailed, his voice an instrument of helplessness.

Stefanus, stunned by his own stupidity, gently placed his daughter on a beanbag and rushed for the wreckage in the corner. He sat down next to the troubled child and pulled him onto his lap, drawing the boy into his burly self. The boy tried to kick and battle his way out, but Stefanus managed to lock his arms with one hand as he hugged him in harder. Putting him in a grip, he tenderly squeezed away Scarface's will to fight.

Finally, after a very loud tantrum, Scarface gave in and melted into Stefanus' chest. The child cried and cried and cried while Stefanus rocked him and whispered into his ear, "Tula, child, tula."

Regret-filled whimpers escaped the boy's mouth.

"It's not your fault," cooed Stefanus.

The boy could not stop heaving. He was indeed very sorry, for himself and for Nyla, and for all the other kids at the orphanage who didn't have any Mammies or Pappies anymore.

Little Nyla rolled off the beanbag and crawled towards the two holding onto the end of the other's nerves in the corner. Both lost now.

They watched her approach, her powerful arms deftly drawing herself towards them. She struggled her way closer with her crayons and colouring books in one hand. As though unaware of the trauma unfolding in the child's mind, she simply remarked, "Steffi, he's beautiful."

The boy exhaled short breaths through his nose. He
looked at her with simultaneous hatred and love.

"Can you feel that? He's hot like a bush-cat!"

Stefanus nodded.

She spoke directly to Scarface. "You look like my big
brother."

This statement startled Stefanus. Nyla had never spoken
of a brother. How selfish of him to not have asked.

Nyla continued to soothe Scarface. "You handsome like a
lion too ... I'll call you Leoson. OK?"

Leoson nodded, and licked away the snot hanging on his
philtrum. Nyla handed him a Ninja Turtle colouring book
she had picked out especially for him. He took it and
hugged it into his chest.

Then, the little girl with braids in her hair opened up her
box of crayons and scattered them over the floor. She leafed
through her own book until coming to find her present
masterpiece, My Little Ponies. Leoson watched her ruin the
page with her scribbles and rested his head on Stefanus'
shoulder. Though he had momentarily managed to rescue
himself from his past, it would forever be a part of him. His
memory was tattooed. He was not excited to remember the
rest of what he had stuffed away inside of himself, though
he knew one's history always rears its ugly head. After a few
long breaths against the warm wild man, Leoson reached for
a crayon.

. . . .

Stefanus pulled on a cold Castle and watched his little
girl from the doorway of the kitchen. She was lying on the
couch. Her eyelids kept failing her. They had spent a very
long day colouring-in with their new friend, Leoson. Try as
she might, she could not stay awake to see the end of her
favourite movie. "Hakuna Matata" sang in the background.
Suddenly she slapped herself on the cheek. Her eyes shot
open. She looked proud for waking herself up. Beer stung

Stefanus' nose as he laughed at her. He placed his Castle on the coffee table and picked her up.

"Time for beddy byes baby."

"Noooooooo," she whined.

"Yeeeeeees," he insisted.

Giving up her pout, Nyla wrapped her arms around her father. He carried her down the hall, into her room and settled her as lightly as he could into her bed. This was always difficult, as her bed was only shin-high. It was a long way down for him, but it needed to be just in case she needed to leave it in the middle of the night.

Once in bed, Nyla held out her arms. He reached over to her basket of toys and pulled out her dolly. He handed it to her before giving her a gentle kiss on the forehead. He left a trace of sticky spit. She felt lucky for it.

He sat down next to her bed and began to tickle her face with his fingertip to help her fall asleep. He thought this might ensure that she had good dreams since she often awoke in the middle of the night screaming. He ran his finger over her forehead, down her nose and over her cheekbones.

Stefanus wondered about her family, and guilt pressed against his gut for never having asked about them. He had been selfish, pretending to himself that they had never existed.

He lifted his finger away from her face. "Don't stop Steffi," she demanded with eyes closed.

"Nyla..." Stefanus struggled to begin. "...I'm sorry for not asking about your family. Would you like to tell me about them?"

Her eyes stayed closed as she answered. She felt around the bed for his hand, extended his index finger and brought it down to her nose so he would continue to caress her face.

"I have no Mammi or Pappi. I have one brother named Severin. I love him lots. He is somewhere ... somewhere out there."

Out there.

"You would like him because he taught me how to do things. Well, him and Dorian. I miss Dorian too."

"Who is Dorian, my love?"

"Another boy that went away."

Steffi squeezed her little hand and got up to leave, too overwhelmed to hear more of her life-lost. He made it to the door and switched off her light, thinking of where the boys might be, if they were still alive. His heart melted when he turned to find his little girl's moon-like eyes illuminate the dark room.

"Pappi? … Do you ever think they'll come here?"

Stefanus choked on air. To be called Pappi was at once a terrifying and beautiful thing. He caught onto his breath and responded, "Who, sweetheart? Your brother and your friend Dorian? I am quite sure they are looking for you, but they're stuck where Leoson was stuck. I promise you your brother is loving you, and missing you."

"I know," said the child affirmatively. "But will they come here?" Her voice grew deep with concern.

"Oh. Who are they?"

"The baddies that came to my village."

"No, Nyla." Stefanus summoned up courage. "Those baddies are afraid of the city," he uttered, trying to sound confident. He was unsure of how it would all end. Would the LLLS or the MM ever have the guts to come here? Would they have the gall to take the city and ruin what was left of the Republic?

Nyla believed her Steffi, as all children believe their Pappies. "Ok … good."

"Good night, Nyla."

"Good night, Pappi."

Stefanus tapped the doorframe a couple of times in response. He walked down the hallway into the TV room, picked up his beer and found his keys on the kitchen counter. He walked back up the hallway to the closet that doubled as a makeshift gun safe. Every Nkosian home was equipped with one. He unlocked the door, and with his beer between his teeth, he searched for the second key – the one that would open up the safety cage's door.

The key made a rough noise as it entered the lock. He turned it slowly, not wanting to keep Nyla awake with the cage's heavy clicking. It swung open with a loud whine. Stefanus winced, but Nyla, tucked into her bed, smiled. The click and the whine made Nyla feel safer. She liked it when Steffi slept armed.

He looked around the storage closet. Amongst the light bulbs were a few weapons: an AK, an M16 and a small black box, high up on a shelf. Stefanus reached up and pulled it down. He opened it; beer bottle still hanging between clenched teeth, and took out a simple pistol. He loaded it and, taking it with him, pulled the cage closed and turned the key. As he took his beer back into his hand, he proudly took in the two state-of-the-art prosthetic legs that Nyla was getting for her self-proclaimed birthday. She had chosen it on a whim.

"The 27 of March please!"

"Funny, you don't seem like a Gemini."

"What's a Gemini?"

"It is a horoscope sign. Gemini are two faced ... they can turn on you. They can turn on themselves."

Nyla didn't know what a horoscope was, but she bore her teeth and clawed her hands anyway. She growled at Stefanus. He had to laugh and let her have her date.

"OK, the 27 of March it is kid."

The War Amps of Canada had donated the legs. Stefanus had sent pictures of Nyla along with an essay of her survival story to every relevant NGO he could think of. War Amps were the first to reply. They had fallen in love with her dimples and her strength. Not only would her new legs walk, but they were capable of running, skipping and playing too. Stefanus had a vision of her doing hurdles in the Paralympics. He screwed his forehead and wondered what country she would represent: the Netherlands or the Republic of Nkosi?

Regardless, he was very proud of himself because his little girl would soon learn how to skip. She would soon be playing with all the other girls at the orphanage in the Princess Marina courtyard. The very thought of her jumping with glee gave him a rush like he had never known. Pure, unadulterated joy flushed through him, cleansing his doubts, cleansing his fears. He would sleep well tonight.

AT NIGHT

In Nyla's bedroom
8 February 2009

Her heart beat … it beat … it beat … waking her from her troubled sleep. The heaviness of wondering about Severin pressed her down into her bed. She pushed herself up and peered out into the moonlit garden, hoping with all of her hope that he was looking at the moon at the same time as her. The moon gave her no hint of it. Nyla sensed that her night would again be filled with sadness. It always paid a visit when she thought about her brother. She hated it for its tyrannical coups. She had no reason to be sad anymore. She was well fed, loved and safe. That is, as safe as a child could be in the Republic of Nkosi.

The floorboards in the hallway creaked. She thought of Stefanus and his gun in bed. Would that gun be enough? She remembered what a "Freedom Fighter" was capable of. Would a gun scare one off? Terrified that the answer was no, and with images reeling in her head of how an intruder could cause further harm to her damaged body, she flung herself around to face her door.

It stood ajar.

She sat quiet and still, taking slow, unmoving breaths as she waited for the imaginary intruder to dare enter. No other noises came, but little Nyla was not willing to take the chance, so she rolled off her bed, deciding to make the terrifying journey down the dark hallway to Steffi's room. She knew she could not stand one more moment alone.

She pulled her blanket from her bed and squeezed it between her legs as she dragged herself down the hall towards Steffi's door. The carpet burned her thighs as she made her way, but the fear of what could be lurking in the kitchen kept her going. Time was surely of the essence, so she hurried along. She believed with all of her fantastical might that the soldier was right on her tail. Exhausted, she made it to the end of the passageway only to be dejected by the fact that Steffi's door was closed, and – sitting on her seat – she was too short to reach the handle.

A sharp sound came from the TV room. Nyla stared over her shoulder into the darkness.

With characteristic tenacity, Nyla pushed into the ground and stood on her stumps. She used the wall and the door to keep herself standing tall. She still had angry-looking scar tissue from her surgery, and her stubs ached. She gritted her teeth and searched for the door handle. The blackness of the night did nothing to help her, but she finally felt the cold metal of the handle and pushed down on the lever. The door swung open and ushered in a night of sleep at last.

She dropped to the floor with a thud and exhaled a small sigh. She put her blanket back between her legs and dragged herself to the base of Stefanus' bed where she set up camp. She lay down and rubbed at her scars, whispering, "Owie," as she did so. Very tired after her intrepid late night adventure, she let Stefanus' gentle snores lull her to sleep, and she forgot all about the imaginary intruder lurking in the kitchen.

THE DOORNBOS

The bar in Baobab & Doornbos Academy
9 February 2009

Just like every Friday, the bar was electric. The women of the night swayed their tails lasciviously. Like cheetahs, they prowled, hoping to be noticed, feigning confidence. All so they could eat the next day. What would take place in the beds of the townships tonight would tomorrow steal the lives of many infected wives.

Stefanus and Mandeep drank their Castles. Their energy had altered. Onlookers could tell they were fidgety and nervous. After three beers spent in intermittent and unimportant conversation, they were ready to speak about the following day.

It was Mandeep who began. "So. The NAP boys are taking you up river?"

"Uh huh."

"They'll be armed to the teeth, will they?"

"I God damned hope so!"

"Yes ... me as well."

"The Peace Keepers assures me that they have been in talks with a man named Anthony Zaza, the commander of that particular contingency."

"Will you be negotiating with him directly?"

Stefanus drummed the table with his fingertips and muttered, "Unfortunately yes."

"Christ, Stefanus!"

"Christ evidently isn't in the picture, Mandeep. I've survived talks with warlords before, but Rwanda was different. I was there at the end, after they had let out a lot of steam. This time, it is just the beginning, and I fear this Zaza is a fuming lunatic! I won't get much sleep tonight."

Mandeep shook his head. The cool night breeze gently teased at his shiny black hair. "Neither will I. I hate to say this out loud Stefanus, but I'm terrified for you."

Stefanus laughed nervously.

Mandeep continued to ask questions. "Where did Leoson say it was?"

"Doornbos. It amazes me how much these kids know. He's from the LLLS ... how would he know where one of the MM camps are?"

"Perhaps he was a scouter? Wait. Doornbos. That deserted private school up the Crocodile River? It's beautiful there ... well, was in its day. I've seen photographs." Mandeep pursed his lips and whistled out his amazement through puffed cheeks. After taking a swig of beer, he added, "The good ol' days," and raised his bottle in an ironic salute.

Stefanus scrunched his brow as he spoke. "In the good old days they taught mathematics, geography, history, French. Now they teach..." he trailed off.

The two sat in silence again. They finished their fourth round and watched the buzzing room. They noticed Deborah at the bar with yet a few more newbies. The other aid workers they saw a few months ago must have left, unable to hack the pressure of the camp.

Mandeep wouldn't let the subject rest and was in any case unable to bear the scary silence, "So, tomorrow it is."

"Yes, it is, old friend."

"And the children you bring back are going straight to the old children's wing at Marina?"

"Yes. Late tomorrow night ... escorted by the Peace Keepers once we get back down the river. They won't come with us to the camp. Something about traumatized officers.

The men stationed here have supposedly engaged with the MM before, and can't get close to them again in fear of a vengeful retaliation from the kids. Supposedly the children of the MM hold a bit of a grudge against the Peace Keepers."

Mandeep looked confused – a common enough state in Nkosi. He shrugged, shook his head and assured Stefanus, "Well, I'll be waiting."

"Thank you Mandeep. Hopefully I'll see you again."

They exchanged wry smiles.

. . . .

The next morning, Stefanus fed his daughter and doubled her on his bike up Jacaranda Drive. He dropped her off with Shalini and waited to get picked up by the NAP boys in their Land Rover. It felt like a lifetime had passed before they finally pulled up.

Together, they rolled silently through the sweaty alleys of Baobab and passed the morning markets. The air smelled of roasting porridge. The sounds of rough voices moved about in the air as people bartered and argued with one another. Outside, the world seemed normal enough. The confines of the car, however, were tight with apprehension.

They made their way in silence past the displacement camp at the edge of town. The putrid smell of shit pulled at their innards and turned their skin grey. All of them, especially Stefanus, began to sweat. After half an hour of anxious driving, they reached the very last of the tents and arrived at the river. Hundreds of swollen-bellied children were washing their gritty bum holes. Diarrhea was an ongoing epidemic in the displacement camp. There were not enough wells to satisfy all the children's thirst, so dehydration paid its toll. The men from the NAP and Stefanus watched as a group of children drew unsanitary water from the river into household buckets. Stefanus' stomach heaved at the thought of having to drink such water. He sighed sadly as he looked at the children. They had no idea, he thought, how many of their systems were being further weakened by AIDS. Any disease could get them, and get them good.

The NAP Land Rover pulled up to the barge that had been arranged by the Peace Keepers. A couple of young men in blue berets said their bonjours and shook the Nkosians Against Poachers' hands. Not much advice was handed to them. Mushy French accents clucked at Stefanus, "Good luck Monsieur. We will be waiting for you here."

"Thanks ... I guess."

Then the motor roared, and the NAP boys headed alone up the Crocodile River. The trip would take a few hours, so Stefanus lay back on one of the benches. He tried in vain to fall asleep. His mind was racing. He kept designing a fantasy of what Doornbos would be, the forgotten school where the MM had been hoarding and educating the children of tomorrow. Ha. Stefanus couldn't fathom the rebels' lack of foresight. Having stolen so many young, who were their doctors going to be? Who were their nurses going to be? Who was going to educate the next generation? Who was going to look after the old?

Stefanus thought of Leoson, and then of the others he would be meeting today. He could feel their rage, their volatile tempers, and their trigger-happy fingers that would surely be twitching by their sides. He wondered what was going to be most terrifying about the experience. The children's seeming innocence? The sensing of their vicious histories and hopeless futures? The fact he couldn't save them all?

Finally, the barge approached an opening on the eastern bank. Many sets of eyes turned to rest heavily upon Stefanus in particular. Being Nkosian, the other NAPs were indistinct. For many of the children, Stefanus was the first white man they had ever seen. Some of them were not even sure if he was human. Others whispered, "Rambo."

Stefanus surveyed the scene of young boys and girls cooling themselves in the muggy water. His eyes passed over the gaze of a young man who stood tall upon a rock. The boy's palm held the neck of his AK's barrel. He had sharp, enthralling features – a slender nose, thick lips and arresting eyes that held Stefanus' attention. The young man stood tall like a meerkat, fixated on the visitors. Stefanus could tell the soldier's mind was still, easy, calm, unlike his own. The boy held the power; he owned this space.

A teenage girl waded through the water. The slender boy's chin turned mindfully to watch her. She emerged, shining, dripping and naked, painted with muddy water. Stefanus was transfixed. If it were possible, she was more beautiful than the young man. Her amber eyes shocked him. He felt ashamed to be aroused in such a moment, but the girl had managed it. Noticing Stefanus' admiration, the meerkat jumped from his lookout rock and guarded her. His eyes challenged Stefanus, who collected himself and spoke from the water,

"I am here to see Anthony Zaza."

The boy said nothing.

Disconcerted by the boy's silence, Stefanus persisted, "Is he here?"

The boy nodded his head. He turned his chin over his shoulder and whispered something to the amber eyed girl. She found her clothes on the rock behind her and began to dress herself. He then led Stefanus and the NAP boys away from the water and towards an overgrown soccer field. Behind it stood a series of architecturally magnificent schoolhouses, classrooms, dormitories and a mess hall.

'What a waste,' Stefanus thought.

He watched the back of the boy who was leading him to Zaza. It moved stealthily under its sweat, taut muscles asserting themselves from beneath the skin. Stefanus followed the lines of the boy's body towards his feet. He noticed short tracks the teenager was leaving in the dust. The kid couldn't have been older than sixteen.

Paris brought him through the playground, where the children stopped their painting to take in the strange visitor and the Nkosians trailing behind him. Paris wondered how uneasy the man must feel with all these eyes on him.

In truth, Stefanus did feel deeply disturbed. His stomach roved as he took in the children's hands, matted with drying multi-coloured paint. He noted the children's newly patterned AK's laid out in the sun for drying. Masterpieces. Pretty guns. The taste of metal grew in Stefanus' mouth as he and the men from NAP moved passed the watch-full eyes of these little killers.

They came to the headmaster's door, and Paris knocked lightly. He placed his ear gently against it. From inside he could hear Zaza on his special phone. "I too am glad we've come to a position of unity. Together we will conquer!"

Paris stepped back from the door and, keeping his eyes on the children in the playground, told Stefanus and the men for NAP, "We wait."

Stefanus stood, his heart beating harder than he imagined possible. He kept telling himself that he had done this before. That Rwanda was no different. That he would be safe. That he would eat a streopwaffle[31] again...

Paris finally broke the silence. "What is your name?"

"My name is Stefanus Abraham. I'm from Baobab."

"OK."

A booming voice came from behind the closed door. "Who the hell is it?"

Paris opened the door and, before walking in, poked Stefanus with his finger. "Only you come."

Stefanus could not move. He pretended his fear was politeness, and tried to look a bit bored as he waited outside until the boy had made the introduction.

He saw the child talking to a man of surprising girth. The commander wore a confident smile and stood leaning

---

[31] A stroep waffle is a Dutch dessert of caramelized sugar.

against a desk. "Ah yes!" Zaza had been waiting for his arrival all day, looking forward to abusing this idealistic and arrogant aid worker that the pussy-UN had sent in lieu of themselves.

"Mr. Abraham! Do come in!"

It took all of Stefanus' courage to move forward. One of the men from the NAP whispered, "You can do it, Stefanus."

A lump rose in his throat, and he feared for the breaking of his tears as he entered the room.

"You have met my boy Paris." Zaza offered an open, proud palm to the meerkat who stood at his side. "This," he said, pointing to his left at a boy loading AK cartridge wheels, "is the newest addition to our family, Babba. He is very good with his little fingers! You would not believe it. Ran away from home he did. Found his rightful place, here, with the MM."

Stefanus nodded. "How do you do, Mr. Zaza? Hello, Paris. Hello, Babba."

The tiny boy looked back mutely.

"Babba, will you get Mr. Abraham a chair?"

The little one got off of his child-sized seat and dragged it toward the white man. He stood only a little bit taller than Stefanus' knee. Perhaps the same age as Nyla, but given the swelling of his belly, he could've been older. Stefanus presumed he had a tummy bug, and malnutrition had probably interrupted his growth.

"Please, Mr. Abraham, sit."

Stefanus took his place beneath the commander. Zaza began with niceties. He spoke about Baobab, and the good old days, and about responsibility. He spoke clearly, booming his voice about the room while Stefanus responded quietly, timidly, mainly because his stomach was too sick to muster the strength to give true answers. He was wavering on nausea throughout the conversation and could not wait until the deal was done and he was home with his daughter.

Stefanus finally found it within him to take command of a conversation that was tortuous and banal. "Mr. Zaza, no disrespect, but we need to make it back in a timely fashion as the Peace Keepers are on alert. They are expecting us back at 11 o'clock. I'm sorry, but I need to request that we hurry the negotiations along." Else they may come looking for me, and neither of us would want that. Stefanus' heart hammered. He could not believe his own curtness.

Zaza stepped back and studied the Dutchman before apologizing, "No! No ... you are right, Mr. Abraham."

Relieved, Stefanus, sighed. He had anticipated being shot for such bluntness.

Anthony walked around his desk and sat down. He rocked back in his chair and crossed his boots upon his table. He smiled condescendingly. The name of this game was Unease.

"What the fuck are you doing here, Mr. Abraham?"

Stefanus, rattled by the harshness of the man's voice, stammered forth, "I-I-I-I have come for an exchange, as was discussed. Money, food and supplies for the wounded."

"No. I know why you are here at Doornbos. But, what are you doing in this godforsaken Republic?"

Stefanus had no answer. He watched the commander rock back and forth comfortably in his seat.

"You can say you care about things, Mr. Abraham. You can read your books and learn our languages. You can come to learn of lives-lost. You can pay your way out of unspeakable guilt by spending time with us here, but you will never know pain ... because you are lucky ... because you are lucky that your heart beats freely and your eyes see beauty."

Paris' hands gripped his AK as he wondered if falling in love with Helena meant that he could still see beauty.

"I ... I am not as lucky, Mr. Abraham. I have seen it all. I have seen the ruination of my country. I have seen the death of my mother and father, and I do not miss them anymore. Because, in our world, I know that mothers and fathers are not real. They are figments of our imaginations. They exist to tease you. They, and their love, are the devil, because when they are gone – and they always go – they leave you lonely. They leave you terrified, and the only way to make it without them, believe me, is to be angry. Because once the fuckers who brought you into this world are gone, one is either a slave to their memory or a master of his calamity."

Paris caught Babba's bewildered eyes and, sensing the child's confusion, softly smiled at him to try to make him feel safe.

"I choose to be a master," Zaza continued. "I choose to own this war. So I am teaching these boys to do the same. Believe me, you would too if you grew up like we did." Anthony waved a pointing finger back and forth between his two boys.

Stefanus sat in Babba's diminutive wooden school chair. He had become the insolent child in the Head Master's office. Meanwhile, Anthony sat high above him at a desk littered with hand drawn maps, knives, handguns and lists of names. Stefanus found himself wondering if they were records of stolen children.

Zaza followed the chastised man's gaze. "These are the names of the boys I am giving to you. You want to take parts of my family? You think you can do better? Go ahead. Have the ones who are too weak, but the girls you cannot have. They care for the boys, and they care for me."

Stefanus bowed his head. "Thank you." He said, suppressing rage. He felt as though he could kill for the very first time in his life, and he thought he might enjoy it.

Stefanus tentatively added, "But the girls. What of the ones with babies, Mr. Zaza?"

Anthony looked amused. "What babies? Pah ... the babies! They do not last. If they do, it is the girl's problem. Little sluts."

"You are suggesting they sleep around willingly, Mr. Zaza?" Stefanus noticed with regret that his tone was bordering on patronizing.

Anthony's voice hardened. "Not at first, Mr. Abraham. Like wild horses they must be tamed, but I assure you they come to like it. They soon trust their riders. The way they let every man fuck them in their assholes. They're as stupid as horses, you see? Pretty little beasts." Zaza leaned farther back in his chair, adding, "And like horseback riding, it is a sport. A gentleman's game. Not all men have it in them to fuck women the way we do. It takes time to learn that it is not only a service for one's own needs, but a service for one's country!"

Stefanus recoiled. The initial fear he felt stepping into the room was now burned away by Zaza's dementia. He contemplated what it must feel like to strangle a man. This man. If it weren't for the village of Little Warriors outside, he would happily do it right now.

"May I talk to them at least, Mr. Zaza? Find out if there is anything that they need, perhaps sanitary pads for their periods? Formula for the babies?"

The man roared, "You think you are God? You think you will fix their lives? They are here for us! Their job is to do right by us and make our lives easier!"

Zaza restrained himself, and attempted to explain further. "My girl Helena is my solace in this mad fight."

Paris' flinched at the mention of her.

"She, believe me, is stronger than any one of those boys out there. She killed her own mother! It was incredibly sexy watching her slice the woman's throat…"

Paris' skin burned while listening to Zaza talk of her. He blinked back his fury as Zaza continued his rant.

"Don't think they're innocent little kiddies. They are Warriors! They are Nkosians! They are fierce, like all Nkosians who have fought for their country before them! That little bitch doesn't sleep. I feel her watching me, that dangerous conniving bitch!"

Paris' tears began to slip down his cheek, an event that did not go unnoticed by Stefanus.

Zaza, lost in his own depravity, raged on. "Sometimes I am afraid she will slit my throat in the middle of the night. When you leave today, which I can't wait for you to do, take a look at those girls as you go. Their eyes are wild. Nobody is innocent here boss.[32] So do what you like. Be God if you want. Bring them lipstick and perfume. Bring their bastards bonnets, but it only makes you a fucking fool!"

Stefanus stood his ground. "Thank you Mr. Zaza."

Anthony, amused, shook his head. "That is the problem with you aid workers. You're all a bunch of pussies. You never demand anything. You take only what we give you. Is it because we scare you? Are you scared of me, Mr. Abraham?"

Stefanus relaxed in his seat. "I'm fucking petrified of you."

Anthony erupted uncontrollably with laughter. "An honest man. A word of advice for when you meet the rest of us, you are a big Dutchman. Wear it a little prouder. We may have guns, but you – your body is one of a real warrior's. It can intimidate. You should use it that way. Though we sadly no longer have old-fashioned warriors in Africa, we still tell the old stories. You resemble those warriors, other than the white skin, of course. Stop being such a pussy. It's pathetic."

Stefanus pitied the man. He realized that Zaza was petrified himself. Petrified of losing control. If he ever lost the means to kill, he was nothing. Nobody.

"Thank you for the advice," Stefanus said. "Now if you'll excuse me, I have some children to take to Baobab. Where do I find them?"

"My boy Paris will take you to the wounded. You can have them all. They're expensive little fucks. They snort too much brown brown. Hope you have some to keep them from going mad."

The exquisite meerkat opened the office door. Light flooded the room.

---

[32] 'Boss' was the superior term used by an African man to address a white man before independence. It is still commonly used on farms. Of course, Zaza is using it ironically here.

"Thank you for your time, Mr. Zaza. Until we meet again."

Anthony smiled creepily. "Yes, boss. Until we meet again. Do not think the kids will go happily. If you think they do not love me, you are mistaken. They love me, you hear? See this little child here?" Zaza pointed under the desk. Stefanus found bug-eyed Babba staring at him. "He may not say a word. Has not since he arrived. We are pretty sure he cannot speak, aren't we Paris? But he polishes my shoes and makes my tea not because I order him to. No, on the contrary, because he loves his Pappi Zaza. Don't you my child?"

Anthony reached under the table and pulled Babba onto his lap, bouncing the boy on his knee. Feigning affection.

Stefanus noticed the flinching of Babba's skin as it pulled away from Anthony's touch.

As he sat there on Anthony's lap, staring at the wild white man, Babba remembered the day Anthony had walked in on one of the other commanders who was holding him down and ripping into his bum with his willy. Anthony had done nothing. He gave orders to Babba above the grunts of the man raping him. Babba hid in the bushes afterwards, trying to push the blood that poured from his bum back into himself, but it hurt too much.

Stefanus taunted Anthony. "This one is a bit young to fight, no? Can he even carry a gun?"

Zaza, scoffing at Stefanus' naivety, retorted, "He will be able to soon enough. Won't you Babba?"

Babba looked from Anthony to Paris, and then to the He-man look a-like.

Stefanus was feeling brave. He had lost patience with the commander. "Do you like guns, Babba?"

Before the boy could shake his head 'no,' Anthony took control. "You can't have this one!" he snarled. "He is perfectly healthy! Now if you'll excuse me, I have things to do while you go and save the world!"

Anthony took Babba on his hip and walked out of his office.

Stefanus turned to Paris whose meerkat face looked on, unchanged. "Where are the injured boys kept?"

Paris did not reply. Instead, he walked towards the doorway, looked back and nodded his head out towards the sun, as if to ask Stefanus to follow him. The men from the NAP patted Stefanus on his back as he stepped out of Zaza's lair. They joined Stefanus as he followed Paris through the dying gardens of Doornbos. Children lay bored in the sun. Some kids smoked cigarettes while others drank fermented cane juice from old Coke bottles. Some cleaned handguns. They surveyed the burly white man as he passed. Stefanus had never felt so out of place, so useless, so meaningless. 'How can people treat children like this?'

Paris finally came to a dormitory with white Dutch gables caked with mud. Broken glass littered the unflowering flower beds. Paris opened the door and led them into a hazy hell. The smell was violent, and the moaning voices of the sick children tangled Stefanus' guts.

"There are so many of them," he said, amazed. "Are they just left here to die?"

Paris turned and looked at Stefanus. Confused by the man's motives for asking, the boy didn't offer an answer. He did not understand where this man was from, or what he was going to do with these Little Warriors.

Stefanus tried another line of questioning. "Are they all wounded?"

"No, some are just sick. In the head or in the tummy."

Surprised and pleased by the boy's sudden responsiveness, Stefanus urged the child to talk. "You mean dysentery. E. Coli?"

Paris looked puzzled, but tried to be of help, "They have very sore tummies. They poo too much. Mr. Abraham ... where are you taking them? Why are you taking them?"

Stefanus learned only then just how little these children knew. "My child, I am taking them to a place that can make them better. I am taking them to a hospital in Baobab called Princess Marina. We already have a boy there. His name is Scarface. He ran away from the LLLS a few months ago. He is well fed and does not have to fight anymore. He is able to be a boy again. A child. Would you like that, Paris?"

It took all of Paris to manage a strained reply. "Princess Marina? In Baobab?"

Stefanus stepped closer to Paris and encouraged him by fastening his large hand around the boy's forearm. Lowering his voice, he whispered, "Son, if Scarface could do it, you can too. Just follow the river to the jungle. From the jungle, make your way to the Dunes, head south along the beaches until you reach the Nothingness. This will be the hardest part – but make a run for it, Paris! Come to Baobab. We will be waiting at the hospital."

Paris' breath hardened. He looked down at the hand wrapped around his arm. Stefanus removed it quickly, scared that he may have offended the boy.

Paris knew that the journey Mr. Abraham spoke of was nearly impossible. He hated Zaza for not letting them all go with this man with pale eyes. He could not manage to speak anymore to Mr. Abraham about escaping. It had been a fantasy for so long, and now that he had been granted such a gift as a map to a place of idyllic safety, fear brewed. What if they failed? What if they were eaten by hyenas? Or worse, what if they died slowly from thirst?

His eyes began to tear, so he spoke quickly. "Sir, these are all your boys. I will get the new soldiers who are in training to help you carry them out to your boat."

Paris sniffed back his fears and left the dormitory. Stefanus and the NAP men stood looking at the sixty or so boys who lay about the dusty room, bandaged like patchwork denim. In the corner, a shivering child adorned with a mucky bandage around his waist lay with his head in the lap of a friend. Something was very wrong with him.

Stefanus moved towards the stronger of the two boys. "Excuse me," he said softly. "May I take a look at your friend?"

Severin looked up at the newcomer he had seen talking to Paris. He had not let anyone near Dorian in a few days. He had stayed with him since the slashing. He had not slept, fearing death for Dorian if he did. But, for some reason, he trusted this new man. Paris had seemed very calm with him, so Severin nodded his head.

Stefanus squatted until he was seated on his haunches and lifted the shuddering boy's bandage. The child had a deep gash running from his side-ribs to his belly button. His breath was short. He was suffering.

"How long has he been like this, young man?"

Seve shrugged his shoulders, but the care in the man's voice invoked tears. Stefanus brushed Severin's cheek, and placed his other palm on the sick boy's forehead. Dodo's fever raged.

"I am going to take him somewhere we can make him better."

"No!" wailed Severin, as he pulled his friend closer into him.

"I know this is scary, my child, but you want him to survive, don't you? He will be waiting for you in Baobab."

Severin felt as if his greatest possession was about to be stolen right in front of his eyes. He squeezed protectively at Dodo's arms and legs. He pulled him close and hugged him tightly. Dorian lay rag-dolled, oblivious to his best friend's fight.

Stefanus pulled him away while Severin clamped on tightly. The Little Warrior fought with all his might to keep Dodo, but he was exhausted from sleep deprivation and malnutrition. Besides, his meager weight could not compete with that of the white behemoths. Finally, Severin gave in and Dorian's smell left his nose. Severin slumped to the concrete, huddled himself into a ball and wept. For he knew, undoubtedly, that he would never see Dodo again.

From the floor, Severin watched the white man's felt schoens[33] walk away from him and across the dorm. He watched the light enter the room as the door swung open. Dust twinkled in the streaming sunlight, and then everything went dark as the door shut behind them.

At the barge, Stefanus was met with more resistance. The girl with the amber eyes came screaming towards him and tried to rip Dorian from his arms.

"Be careful!" he shouted.

She protested, "He is my brother! Where are you taking my brother?"

Helena was like something possessed, and she struggled ferociously to gain possession of Dorian. Stefanus tried to fight her off. She scratched at him like a lioness, the greatest protectorate. Stefanus stumbled back in the water and almost dropped him. The girl persisted. Stefanus was sure that she would kill him. She was filled with unprecedented rage, and her curses filled the air until a gunshot fired. The two of them looked back towards the shore.

Anthony held his handgun up towards the sky. "Helena! Have you no shame? You disgust me. Go to our room! I will deal with you when I am drunk enough to beat you!"

The children watching from the bank stiffened. They knew all too well the sounds of Helena's harrowing yelping that would invade Doornbos tonight.

Stefanus, stunned, turned to the commander. "Please Mr. Zaza, no. Leave the girl out of it."

"She is mine! I will treat her how I see fit Mr. Abraham ... but I hope you see that what you are doing and what I have done are very similar. We rip apart families for our own opinion of a greater good." Anthony's lips curled up cheekily. "Goodbye Mr. Abraham. May the LLLS find you on your way home and steal all your children."

---

[33] Shoes worn by expats in the bush.

Stefanus felt sick, for Anthony was – at least partially – right. He was ripping apart a family, and he had not even thought of this possibility. Nor had he considered that the LLLS might be waiting for him. It was too late now. They had to go back the same way they had come. He still might die today. Infuriatingly, the task was incomplete. "Fuck."

Stefanus turned to the girl with the amber eyes. "I can leave him with you to die, but if you let me take him to the hospital in Baobab, we may be able to save his life ... Let me try, please?"

Helena, conflicted, finally nodded her head, laid a kiss on Dodo's forehead and then rushed from the water, up the bank, past Anthony and to her prison.

The wounded were loaded onto the barge. Many were given shots of morphine, and others that were strong enough to eat were given oranges and Coca Cola.

The children being loaded onto the barge grew nervous. Those strong enough protested, thinking they were being stolen again. Many tried to jump back into the river to swim ashore. Anthony laughed from the bank as Stefanus and the NAP men tried to keep the hysterical children from the edge of the barge. No reasoning could say them. The NAP men had to forcefully pin down the most tenacious of the children, until Doornbos had shrunk into the distance. They settled in nervously for the ride to this so called, Baobab.

It was quiet in Doornbos too. Though Zaza's brutality was no different on this night than any other, the loss of her brother numbed Helena from Zaza's brutal playtime. After he was finished, she stared into the blackness while he snored. Whenever she wanted to feel better, she would think of Paris. Thinking of him now ignited her courage.

For the first time, she left Zaza's bed in the middle of the night. Now that Dorian was gone, she did not care if Zaza punished her for disobedience and beat her until she was breathless. She padded her way to the door and turned the handle slowly. The door creaked as it opened. Helena froze and waited to hear if Zaza's breath changed. The snoring persisted, so she slipped out and sat on the cement in front of the headmaster's office.

Paris was not in the courtyard for once. Instead, around a glowing fire, several of the commanders spat drunken jokes at one another and cackled into the night. One of them noticed the girl and started hissing lasciviously in her direction. Privacy was not hers to have or to hold. Nervously, she stood back up and returned to her master's bed. It felt like the safer option.

. . . .

Paris guarded Seve's door. Leaning against it, he listened to the whimpers of longing from within. Once in a while he'd sneak a look at the child crying in bed, hugging his AK as though it were a body. Dorian's. This was a night of mourning, and even Babba took it very seriously. He puttered about cleaning Severin's room, digging up memories from under blankets and placing them on the school desk in a neat little row – a sling shot, a He-man comic book and a pack of cards that Dodo and Severin used to play with. Severin could go through them when he felt like it.

The night felt lonely. Not many of the children slept. Most of them played cards and smoked cigarettes. They bet bullets, sniffed some powder. Eventually, the night softened from black to grey. Finally, in the early hours of the morning, the camp grew sharply silent, as the kids pretended to rest for another bloody day.

THE DECOY

Down by the Crocodile River
11 February 2009

Determination lined Paris' face as he set out to find her. He fastened his grip around the shovel in his hand as he pushed through the whispering fog.

He came to the thorn tree where they had buried the faceless girl. They had dug out a hole the same day the crocodile took her. They dug deep to keep the hyenas and jackals from sniffing out her corpse. Then they'd covered her with sand. There she stayed, their horrendous secret.

He began to dig. The soil was soft and gave way readily. Fatigued by the pain that still lurked in the shoulder where Joshua had shot him, Paris cast his shovel to the side and went at it with his hands. Finally, he neared her corpse. He brushed away the last of the coverage and found that she was still quite fresh.

Except for her smell.

A brittle staleness overtook him while he rested beside her. He peeled off her shirt and replaced it with one of Helena's, then dragged her gently, limp as a wet rag, from her grave. He refilled the hole while she lay obediently beneath the thorns that twinkled with dew against Nkosi's early morning sun. After he had ensured the earth was back in its rightful place, he waded her into the water and softly washed her torn apart body. He gently swayed her and, making a cup of water with his hand, poured it over the gouge where her face used to be.

Her size and shape resembled Helena's so closely, this body destroyed by the great lizard's hunger. She would serve as the perfect decoy. It would be impossible to tell it wasn't Helena, thank Nkosi. As she floated, Paris touched his palms together and prayed to her ancestors for support. He hoped that this plan of theirs would work, because if they were caught, the four of them would be hung in the courtyard.

Paris pulled his decoy ashore and banked her.

While he had been busy setting the stage for his trickery, the sex slaves were cleaning themselves in the river and filling large troughs with water. Every morning, they got up to perform these chores while their rapists slept. Once they had bathed, they joined him, and her, on the bank. Kneeling, they gathered around the girl. A couple of her friends began to whimper. Others consoled them by wrapping the mourning girls in their arms and cooing softly into their ears.

Then Paris began to speak, his stomach churning with uncertainty. "Alright ... you know what to do ... and you promise you will all keep quiet about the truth. I am asking you as a loyal friend."

The girls nodded, and slowly, one by one, the mourning song flew from their throats. A depressing chorus erupted. They did not sing for the death of the faceless girl, they did not sing for the imaginary death of Helena. Instead, they cried out in search of themselves. For if they could not guide their wandering souls back into their bodies, they would be lonely until it was their turn to lie on the bank of the river, naked, torn apart, faceless.

The girls called out, "Wayayayayayaya!" They called and called and called. Their voices rang out, puncturing the soft, hanging clouds of the morning, and woke up their men, who came running.

Anthony staggered towards the great crowd of child soldiers and commanders who had gathered on the bank. He pushed through them, demanding, "What's going on? Shut up, all of you!"

Some of the commanders tried to warn him. They pushed him back saying, "No Sah! No Sah. Don't look!"

But Anthony did not understand the word no, nor was his arrogance capable of heeding a warning, so he pushed through until he stood over the beached and tattered girl.

He then surveyed the crowd of wrenched hearts. The girls in mourning sported bloodshot eyes. The men clucked their tongues and folded their arms across their chests. Shock fired through Zaza. His hair stood up on end. His stomach churned violently. His brow sweated sorrowfully. His knees buckled and he found himself in the mud at the faceless girl's side. The sex slaves' voices hammered into his ears and reverberated against his brain. His hands, suddenly remorseful and guilt-ridden, reached for her body but he could not bring himself to touch her.

"Helena?" His heart broke loudly within him, sending the taste of acid up into his throat. The world swayed. Anthony grew seasick in its motion. Lost in the abyss of death's wake his senses began to slip away. The world grew blue. The girls' cries softened into a gentle humming and numbed his chest. Loss consumed him.

Paris took the opportunity shock had provided. He placed his hand on Zaza's shoulder. "I will take my boys Zaza. We will kill that fucking crocodile!"

Too consumed by shock to respond, Anthony nodded. The boy's silhouette faded away. He heard Paris call for Babba and Seve, but the commands sounded as though they had come from over the hills, in a place far, far away.

That was the last Zaza saw of those Little Warriors. He did not know what happened to them. Perhaps the boys had been caught by the LLLS during their hunt. He would never admit it to anyone, but he missed them. Of course, he soon found a new Helena. A girl is easy to replace, but Paris was his child and Babba his grandchild. He longed for their smiles, and turned sourer because of their absence.

If only he had known the real story … that they had run away from him … that they had gone looking for Dorian.

For a future. For peace. For a release.

. . . .

As soon as he had gathered his little group, Paris led Severin and Babba around to the other side of the school. They found Helena behind the tennis courts with their packed supplies, and leaving their AK's behind, the Little Family had set out into the Nobody-Knows-How-Vast-Jungle of Nkosi.

MOKOLODI

Rushing through the Nobody-Knows-How-Vast-Jungle of Nkosi
March 2009

The children had been running for three sun-scorching days and three mosquito-biting nights. They were unsure if the MM were looking for them, or if they would be ambushed by the LLLS. They were unarmed, deliberately leaving their unchosen professions behind them. This route was indeed more dangerous, but they had chosen it because if they had taken the river to the city they would have definitely been found and punished by either militia.

Hungry, thirsty and exhausted, they stopped to rest at a pond. A short and sweet waterfall trickled down the rocks of the hill they had been using as a guide through the Jungle. The children lay, eyes closed, as the trees rustled lightly about them. The three eldest fugitives spoke of what it felt like to be free. They went further to determine that even if they were recaptured and punished, at least they would bear the beating – or death knowing that they had felt freedom again. Babba rested coolly by their side.

Paris turned to face his girl. She lay back with her hands behind her head. A soft smile had settled upon her face. He had never seen her smile like that. "You're beautiful," he whispered.

She rolled onto her side and faced him and lifted her lids. Liberated from wretchedness, the embers of her eyes were more beautiful than ever. Her spirit emitted golden fragments of warmth upon him. Paris reached for her. She edged towards him and rested her head on his arm. They slept in bliss' keep, embracing, smelling, loving.

. . . .

Severin's eyes shot open. Above him the silhouette of a sturdy man disrupted his view of the sky. A machete glistened in the early light. The boy fugitive tried to take a breath. His lungs would not inflate. They had been found.

He tried to break away, but the man tackled him back to the ground. He rested all of his weight upon the child, digging his elbow into Severin's diaphragm, immobilizing his breath further. The child wrestled his throat away from the warrior's machete, which softly sliced at his skin.

A gruff voice demanded, "What you doing here, boy?"

Severin caught sight of the other three who were rounded up by a group of traditional warriors. Their arms were tied behind their backs. The warriors stood proudly, adorned with hides around their shoulders and leather wrapped around their waists. They held spears in their fists and looked on with fiercely painted faces.

With pleading eyes, Severin searched Paris for an answer, but his mentor – a child himself – was scared of the ferocious Nkosian warriors and stood frozen, unable to help.

"You some of those Child Soldiers? You come to take our village? We want to see you try!" His painted face reminded Severin of Dodo's father – a man who spoke little, but whose mere presence was enough to excite a child into admiration … or intimidate a foe into wetting himself.

Severin grew lightheaded. He needed a breath. He tried to sound out some words. He opened and closed his mouth in a vain effort to beg for mercy.

It was little Babba who came to his brothers' and sister's rescue. After months of silence, his screams were alarming. "We ran away! We were scared! We don't like big guns! We don't like the MM. We want to be safe!"

Intrigued by the squealing boy, the man on top of Severin lifted his weight. Severin gasped for air and coughed out in anguish. The man approached Babba. "Why should I believe you? Three of you wear the markings of the MM! It is our job to hunt you out and kill you!"

Unwavering, Babba continued, "The MM killed my family! They stole me and put me in a cage! They made me dig in caves so they could get rich!"

He pointed at Severin and continued to howl. "They killed his little sister."

He pointed at Helena. "They raped her every night!"

He pointed at himself. "And they raped me too…"

The boy, exasperated and embarrassed, trailed off.

Severin stared at his little brother, astonished by the news and sickened at the likelihood that it was true. Nausea pulsed within him. Severin did not need to imagine Babba's experience, having seen what the soldiers were capable of during raids. He knew firsthand what Babba had endured. Severin threw up the water he had guzzled earlier. Acid bit at his tongue.

He spoke through his wheezing. "Babba ... my baby Babba ... why didn't you tell me ... we could have kept you safe from the commanders!"

The little brother dropped his big, beautiful eyes to his feet. His toes cocked towards one another. His hands wrung behind his back. Then he shrugged and began to cry. His chest hiccupped as snot dribbled from his nose. He looked up expectantly at the warrior, whose eyes also glistened with tears.

"What has become of our country?" asked the warrior. He picked Babba up and placed him on his hip. He petted the child's head and wiped away his tears. "Come, we will take you to our chief. He will know what to do with you."

The children were taken to a village that lay at the foothill of the other side of the mountain. As they entered it, a wave of nostalgia greeted them. It reminded them of better times.

The villagers watched the children as they were marched directly to the chief's hut. They were placed, on their knees, before the fat man. He wore trinkets around his neck and swatted a calf tail about his face, shooing the flies. Sternly, he looked upon the four children. The man with the machete addressed the chief as villagers began to close in. A trial was taking place, and an interesting one at that. It would be the talk of their community for months.

"Chief, we found these children in the jungle. They are ex-MM child soldiers. They have undoubtedly killed many people with their pathetic machines. They must be punished."

The chief watched the children and grunted in response. Paris, Helena, Severin and Babba stared up at their judge.

"Children!" he boomed. "You have weathered a long journey?"

Paris nodded, his head bowed.

The chief continued. "How do we know you are escapees and not scouts for the MM? If you are scouts, you know we have no other choice but to behead you – as much as it would harm our minds and hurt our hearts. You are Nkosian. You are our future."

Severin spoke swiftly, "Sah, may I have a knife?"

The chief erupted with laughter and the rest of the village joined in. The noise of their amusement unnerved the children. Babba reached up for Helena's hands. She held his small fingers in her palms and against her stomach. Her skin felt hot as fire, but was wet like a muddy pool.

Severin continued, "I know it sounds crazy to ask for a weapon Sah," shouted Severin over the patronizing laughter, "but I wish to prove myself to you!"

The grinning chief directed one of the warriors to give Severin a knife. The warrior did as he was told, but stood nervously nearby, his machete in his hand. Severin took the knife and lifted his branded arm. He brought the knife's tip to the double M and began to cut. The audience gasped and shouted in horror at the boy's self-mutilation. Severin screwed his face as he carved deeper into his own flesh. He cut around the brand and then slowly sliced beneath it.

"Aaaay!" he screamed.

A patch of skin fell to the ground and blood poured from where the marking had been. Severin passed the knife to Helena who did the same, and then onto Paris who too de-branded himself. All the while the audience ooohed and aaahed, and then shouted out to the chief, "Free them!"

The three children knelt, bleeding. The chief, mouth ajar, struggled to process the children's courage.

"And the little one?" he asked.

Babba grinned upwards and shrugged his shoulders. "I don't got one to cut!"

The audience laughed. Babba looked around at people of Mokolodi and smiled, proud of his joke. The chief spoke. "Very well … it is proven then. You are not scouts, but fugitives. We have received one of your kind before. Like we did with him, we will give you food and shelter. But, you cannot stay here for long in case the MM is hunting you."

"Sah, we are on our way to Baobab to rescue my brother," Helena explained as she held her bloodstained arm.

"Very well … but you must rest here now, especially since you have lost so much blood. Our medicine man will clean you up, and then, tonight children, we must celebrate your freedom from the MM. It takes courage to do the right thing."

The children were led through the chattering crowd and to the medicine man. After he patched them, they were taken to the market square where the villagers had built a humongous fire.

"Tonight we have a celebration for you," said the warrior with the machete. "You must now eat and celebrate with us."

. . . .

The little boy Babba shivered with ecstasy as he bathed in the attention. He looked up at the night sky. Flapping his lithe arms above him, he waved cheerfully at his ancestors. They twinkled lovingly down upon him, shedding ancient sorrows in silver tears.

A light drizzle cooled the dancing child as the drums penetrated the night sky. They set the once-mute boy into a giggling wriggle. He scuffed his feet into the sand while he dipped at the knees and pushed and pulled at his hips. He rolled his head from side to side, smiling brightly, as he undulated his shoulders and slid his slippery backbone.

The child danced. Hell-bent on emotional release, the child danced!

The other three revelled in his happiness. They laughed and cheered him on with proud whoops and hollers. The villagers slapped their drums and clapped their hands, encircling him with their compassion and joy. A little girl Babba's age squeezed out from the crowd and stirred the dust up with her feet as she shimmied towards him. She placed one hand on her hip and waved the other at him as she closed in as if to say, "Hey!"

Then the two held hands as they twisted and shook to the mesmerizing rhythm. The audience cheered the dancing children on. The entertainment brought much happiness to everyone, but most of all to Babba. For here were a people who would encircle him with love, who would watch him dance and cheer him on as he moved. Here was a little girl who would be his friend and hold his hand. Here were his three guardians who had brought him to this safe place. Tears of joy welled up and spilled over. He continued to smile and undulate as he cried until he was blind with happy tears.

Then, from the pit of emptiness still deep within, a warm flow of energy surged. Like a balloon, it expanded his lungs and caused his body to shake. To his own wonderment, the warm feeling turned into a magical sound: full-bellied laughter. Babba wiped his tears from his eyes and reached out his other hand for Severin, who had also begun laughing and dancing. Seve flapped his wings towards his precious Babba. He was wearing a hearty grin. Together, the boys danced.

Helena, filled with unmitigated joy, led the young man she loved through the bodies of the celebrating villagers and out of the market square where the big fire was burning. She led him into the residential cluster of huts until she heard the goats bleating. She held his hand tighter as they said their hellos to the young shepherds. Then she squeezed it even more as she passed the night watchmen with their guns and their machetes.

"Good night, gentlemen," she whispered.

The men nodded their heads at the beauty as she and Paris passed. She cast her eyes downward, inexplicably ashamed that they might divine what she was about to do. They looked upon her as if she were still a girl, even though she had lost her girlhood long ago. A twinge of uncertainty squeezed at her, but then the love spoke from within.

'No, this is what you must do.'

And so she raised her chin and continued on. The dry veldt crackled beneath their feet as they advanced. They felt as though they had covered unfathomable distances to reach this safe place, and they knew there would be unfathomable more before they finally arrived in Baobab. Still, this pathway to the hut they had been granted for the night felt the longest of all. Teenage nervousness is a daunting and arduous thing.

As they reached the doorway, Paris pulled Helena back. He placed his hands on her face and pulled her toward him until their lips were touching. The softness of her mouth made him hard. He ran his fingertips down her neck, sending an unknown, yet excitable sensation that quivered over her skin. She opened her mouth and gently placed her tongue on his. Her nipples hardened at his taste. He found them with the palm of his hand and gently pushed into her small breasts. He did not stay there for long. He felt like it was not his place – that they belonged to her, and he should be cautious of lingering on any part of her lest she change her mind.

Helena felt his uncertainty and reassured him. She kissed him harder and wrapped her arms around his shoulders, placing her palms on the nape of his neck. To have her hands warm such a vulnerable part of his body gave him great pleasure. He pulled her closer and opened his mouth wider, allowing their tongues more space to caress.

Helena pulled Paris into the hut. They lay down upon the sand floor and eclipsed the harsh reality of their lives with a glimpse of nirvana. Their minds cleared themselves of misery and opened ever so slightly to a future filled with radical tenderness.

When the drumming outside subsided, they got dressed, snuggled into the safety of the other and waited for their little boys to come home. Exhausted by love, Paris did not wake when the giggling boys entered the hut and settled down on the floor beside them.

The three boys slept soundly, and when the sun climbed up the sky, they winced into its bright glow. For once, were excited for the new day.

Helena, however, barely slept. She lay shivering against Paris, despite Africa's heat. Her dreams the night before, when she did slip into compromised slumber, were lucid, decrepit, and violently fantastical. Her body ached and her spirit suffered. She used all of her might to feign happiness, but she could feel that she indeed was very, very sick.

She sat up and looked out of their hut. Women pounded millet, children chased chickens. The nose of the day battered about in her brain, echoing into the hollow of her thoughts. Paris pulled her to a standing position. She swallowed down her approaching illness. She looked for him through the intruding sunshine. Blinded by the heat of her fever, his voice faded into kingdom come when he spoke to her. She nodded, pretending she understood.

Then, without understanding how she had made it there, she found herself standing before the chief. He was indicating that they should sit down and eat. Obediently, the children sat cross-legged and ate a hearty breakfast of millet porridge and goat's milk. The chief marvelled at their childish mannerisms. They all ate a touch too fast. They all chewed with open mouths and gulped greedily at their milk. It was clear that their mothers had not trained them for a long time. It was clear that they had lost the decorum exclusive to those children who had never been stolen.

The chief decided that they needed to be re-taught not only how to eat properly and respectfully all over again, but also that it would be crucial to reacquaint them with other teachings traditionally passed on to Nkosian children.

With these thoughts in mind, he offered for them to stay a while longer, just as he had done for Scarface. "Young ones, the four of you have lost much time. You deserve to be as safe, and as protected, as all the other ones of your age in this village. Nkosi's youth should be protected; as you are our future ... you do understand that, do you not? That there are some of us who still care. However, you are on the run from the MM, and it is safer for you as well as for my village for you to push on. If the MM come looking for you and uncover that we have been hiding you they will slaughter us all. That being said, you are children and you need protection. We can offer you at least one week of this."

Paris interjected, "Chief, thank you, but we cannot accept. We understand that it is unsafe for everyone if we stay here."

The chief nodded his head, impressed by the oldest one's selflessness.

Helena spoke as well, though it took all of her energy to do so. "Chief, may I?" Some decorum had not yet abandoned her and she knew, as a girl, she had to ask for permission to speak directly to such an authority.

The chief obliged with a nod of his head.

"My brother ... we are looking for Dorian. He is in Baobab, the city at the end of the Nothingness. I must find him; he is all alone and wounded. We thank you for your and your village's kindness. We cannot believe our luck. Honestly, we thought we had lost all of it a long time ago. But blood is thick, and he is my baby brother. He is my home. We desire to move on as soon as possible."

The chief held back his tears. The passion and love that emanated from this young woman's voice broke his heart and agitated his mind. How could grown-ups from these children's own country commit such crimes? How could they ruin such bright futures?

The chief's voice broke, as he turned to the two youngest. "As for you little ones? It is a very dangerous walk across the Nothingness, and you are already frail. Even if your bodies could make it, could your minds? Are they not exhausted? Are they not strained?"

Severin rose, his chin proudly embodying the entitlement of the cats of the delta. "My story is like Helena's, and my heart is in the same place as hers. I must find Dorian. The very thought of him has kept me going this far. I will fill the Nothingness with the tears of my affection for him, and from those tears I will drink. I may feel thirsty, but my body will remain strong, and my mind will be quieted by the longing in my heart."

"Young man, you speak with the wisdom of the ancients! I don't believe I myself have that much courage, nor such a way with words. And what of the little one? He will surely not make it..."

Severin interrupted, "He has travelled farther than any of us. He is our tracker ... out of us all, he is the one we are least worried about."

Babba put his bowl down and climbed into Severin's lap. Once again, unwilling to speak, he pulled himself into the elder boy's body to relay the message that there was no way that he would be ripped from his family again.

The chief clucked his tongue. "I cannot believe that Nkosi has come to this. You are all Little Warriors that is certain. Please stay here for the week to fatten up. My wife will feed you morning, noon and night. We will give you shelter in exchange for chores, just as you experienced in your old villages."

The children nodded, understanding the value of reliving the routine of daily life in a humble village of Nkosi. It was indeed a bigger gift than food and water. It was their culture. That was the nourishment of which they had been deprived for so long.

LULLABIES

Princess Marina Hospital
1 March 2009

Dorian would later share with Mandeep and the professor that the first thing he remembered when he 'came to' was the smell. The hospital air around him was overly clean. Antiseptic drilled his sinuses while her voice pulled him from the light.

He told them that his body had felt extremely heavy and that in his dream, he pictured her moonlike eyes in the far corner of her family's hut. He felt as if it were an early morning from a long time ago.

He remembered thinking that if he opened his eyes, he'd find Severin snoozing beside him and the sun highlighting the room's floating dust. The cuckoo burrow would soon call, and the bells around the kids' necks would clank softly as the goats passed the hut on their way to the watering hole. There Helena and some of the other girls would be washing clothes. Her song continued as he was coaxed into reality. "Tula Tu Tula baba Tula sana Tul'umam 'uzobuya ekuseni." Her voice pulled at the pain in his side.

Dorian decided to let his eyes open. Coming into focus out of the stark light of the hospital room was a little braided head. He watched the girl's lips move around the words of the soothing melody sung to all babies who cannot find sleep during a thick Nkosian night.

He remembered not being able to determine what was a dream and what was reality as he swam through layers of consciousness and finally woke up. He did not care one way or the other though. He had not dreamt sweetly for a very long time. His eyelids fluttered, and though he fought for consciousness, Dorian was sucked back into blackness.

Nyla leaned over and held his hand. "It's ok, Dodo, you can wake up now. You're safe."

He understood, but he couldn't muster the strength. He only had enough to reciprocate the hand-holding.

Mandeep approached, saying softly, "He is on lots of medication, Nyla. He will wake up when he is ready. You were like this too after your operation."

"Can I still stay with him?"

"I don't see why not," said Mandeep as he checked the boy's levels.

"Dr. Mandeep?"

"Yes, my girl?"

"They were always together, but Dodo is here alone..."

Mandeep studied the worried child, "What are you saying Nyla?"

"That my big brother is dead and gone."

Mandeep sat on the bed and pulled the little girl onto his lap to hold her. Her body was hot against him as she wailed. He thought of all the Nkosian children that don't get held when they cry over such a great loss.

"Nyla, Dorian will wake up and will give you news of Severin."

She sniffed back some snot and looked up at the man from India. She wondered at his long lashes. She thought she might be in love. She rested her little head against his chest and sighed her burdens into him.

The heaviness of her breath calmed him too. They had all been on edge since the news of the uniting of the two militias in the Nothingness. The people in the bar the night before had been gossiping. Whispers of Militia for Minerals and the Liberating Land and Life Stealers tickled every conversation in Mandeep and Steffi's watering hole.

The two of them had also questioned whether it could possibly be true. Could they possibly have solved their differences and rallied together? As he sat there holding a little girl he never would have met if he hadn't foolishly thought it appropriate to bring his wife into this place, he thought of how he could not imagine a world where he did not know these kids. He wholly believed that he was put on this earth to have saved their lives and to have helped battle their nightmares.

One of the professors from the university had recently arrived and taught Mandeep what he knew of REM therapy, a non-invasive tactic used on veterans of the Vietnam War who suffered post-traumatic stress disorder.

Leoson had been their first trial. He had watched the professor tap the back of the boy's palms as Leoson's eyes followed the man's finger. Left, right, left, right, left, right. He had then listened to the child's answers to simple questions. The boy's pupils moved in a REM-like state – left, right, left, right – as he spoke. Stories of his killings and his family unfolded. The child had trembled slightly when he spoke, but the process didn't seem harmful.

Mandeep had taken exhaustive notes. Sometimes he struggled to put Leoson's memories down, but going over them with Shalini, week after week, they marvelled at the progress. The boy's understanding of his journey – his piecing it together – was impressive. Memories, good and bad, were being unearthed. More importantly, Leoson sometimes understood that regardless of the murders he had committed, he was innately good.

Mandeep squeezed Nyla tightly against him as he recalled the session where Leoson had looked up from the professor's tapping and said blankly, "This wasn't supposed to happen to me, was it?"

THE BURIAL

Just outside Mokolodi
Early March 2009

Paris had only noticed her fevers a few days before the Little Family was supposed to continue on with their journey to Baobab. She had begun sweating through the nights and moaning into him through the days. It had made him furious, her sickness, because he couldn't conquer it.

The malaria that spread through her blood and found her brain scared little Babba. He cried by her side as she suffered through its nightmares. She faded towards eternal sleep, cold despite the scorching days.

When Severin dragged Babba off of her emaciated body, the little boy hung onto his new Mammi. When his hands were finally ripped from her neck, he reached desperately for her, as all babies reach for their dying mothers.

Paris watched his little brothers go, shaking hands and bowing heads to those who had cared for them during their stay in Mokolodi. Soon, the trees swallowed them, and then they were gone. Severin carried the crying child along with their supplies into the Jungle, searching for the other side ... the Nothingness. Beyond nothing lay Severin's everything: Dorian.

Severin prayed that Helena would be well enough to follow shortly, but he could no longer wait. He left the sick girl in Paris' keeping while he and Babba pressed on.

He had to reach Baobab. He had to find Dodo. They had already wasted one week in the village. Judging by how Dorian had been when they parted, time would surely take him soon, if it had not already. So, Severin bore the weight of fattened little Babba and thrashed at the vines of the Nobody-Knows-How-Vast-Jungle of Nkosi.

. . . .

With each of her struggling breaths, anxiety ripped at Paris' innards. Oh, if only he could breathe his health into her. Oh, if only love were enough to save her.

Days later, after many helpless nights, Paris felt her spirit leave her body. The amber of her eyes diminished. She sighed one last time and expired. She let go of all that she was, all that had happened and all that ever could be. She left Paris all alone.

The irony of her death infuriated him. She survived the heartbreak of killing her own mother. She endured the rattling of rape. She weathered a great trek with no food or water. How could a tiny insect, in a safe place, have then taken her? Paris raged. How was he going to tell Dorian? This was assuming he ever managed to make the journey across the desert alone. Surely, without Severin's help, he would die.

Then again, he no longer cared to live.

Burying his death wish, he summoned up the strength to live long enough to find Dodo because if he didn't find her baby brother, the escape would have been an utter waste, and Helena needn't have died from the bite of a mosquito.

191

THE BEACHES

Burning over the Nothingness
March 2009

The boys walked, their skin leathered from the long hours between sunrises and sunsets. They ended their injurious days with famished sleeps. They lay huddled as one, as the stars bled silver above them.

Black specks in the vibrating glare of the afternoon light, their bodies hunched as they pushed and pulled their raw soles through the sucking sand of the desert. Their arms hung, unbearably weighted, as they pursued the end of the never-ending. Tricked by mirages of water holes and huts, they dragged themselves from one false solace to another in search of the safe haven: Baobab. For there was where their last brother was ... there was where their love was.

Passing hordes of scattered skeletons, Babba imagined parts of himself in the belly of the vultures circling overhead. He shuddered at the thought, said 'No!' and kept moving. Young nomads seeking liberation, they travelled as they had both done many times before. Finding their way ... proving their incredible resilience and ingenuity.

Then, after days with little water and barely any food, save for a stolen ostrich egg, Severin and Babba approached high dunes of sand. It was there where they first heard the roar. The whirling sounded like a wet wind, a rolling river, or a toiling machine. Their desperate yearning forced them upward, fatigued though they were. Backs arched forward, wavering close to defeat, the boys climbed the dune. Reaching its summit, they saw it, heard it, and smelled it: salty and terrifying, the ocean heaved, stretching out to the horizon where it met the sky. Two beautiful blues introduced themselves at the end of their world. Knowing that they were experiencing a wonder, the boys' hearts surged. Seve lovingly took hold of Babba. He was coated in sand. He knew they had accomplished something by making this journey to this mass of washing water that stretched out before them.

Then he began to laugh. The moment was exhilarating, and the boys smiled at one another before hurling themselves headlong down the dune, crashing onto the beach and rolling across the scorching sand. They threw themselves into the tender, lapping lips of the tide. Severin and Babba touched the sea for the very first time.

The boys played and played and played, forgetting the trials of their journey and letting the water wash them of their fearful folly. They drank in the salt not knowing that the sea that blew up their bellies would cause runny tummies.

They splashed and wrestled one another in their newfound happy place and then ran up onto the beach and collapsed on the sand where the sun dried them. The wetted sand swelled around their skin, cradling them, supporting them. Losing themselves in the heat, and lulled by the rolling of their new friends, the waves, these children slept a magnificent sleep.

Nearby, a tired old Nkosian fished upon a rock. Lanky and frail, he had been watching them all the while. He marvelled at the innocence of their joyful inquisitiveness. Once they were asleep, he walked back to his hut, sheltered from the Nothingness' winds at the foot of the dune. There, he gutted his catch as he did every evening, alone, in his hideaway home. The Rra[34] pulled pieces of flesh from the limp skeletons. He slid chunks of meat down a long stick and rested it against the wall of his hut. He built a fire and began to cook. He left the fish to hang above the emanating heat and made his way slowly over to the basking children.

'They must be lost,' he thought, as he had not seen anyone on the beach for a very long time.

The sleeping children sensed his shadow stealing across them. They blinked upwards into the old man's toothless grin.

'Not again,' thought Severin.

Nervous, Babba sang out, "We come in peace!"

The old Rra chuckled, "Of course you do ... you are children!" His voice was joyful. Magnanimous. Warm. He shook his head and waved a giving hand. "Come boys, it is supper time."

Blurry-eyed, Severin and Babba rolled from the sand. They followed the withered man with the trust of innocent children. The smell of cooking fish ignited their appetites as they approached his hut. At the Rra's indication, the boys took a seat and made themselves comfortable. Severin pulled Babba down beside him and patted his lap so that Babba would know he could rest his head.

Babba lay down and looked out over the ocean. He spoke. "I like it here, Rra."

"Yes, it's calming, isn't it?"

"What is it?" said the wondering child, pointing towards the vast expanse of water.

"That, young boy is what we call the sea. It lies between us and everything else."

Enthused, Babba squealed, "I love it!" Then, interested in their new friend, probed, "Why do you live here, Rra?"

"I chose to come here after I fought against the White Man."

---

[34] Sir/grandfather'

"What's a White Man, Rra?"

"He is much like you and me. He bleeds the same. He loves the same. But what he knows is different; therefore, what he feels is different too."

Severin stroked his younger brother's head. "You have seen one Babba. The man who took Dodo was a White Man."

Babba giggled, "I liked that wild man! Why would you fight the White Men if they are nice like that, Rra?"

"My child, we were all very confused. We did not know what we know now."

Severin looked up at the Rra's old face. He read its lines and enjoyed its eyes. Eyes the colour of sap. He studied the Rra's creaking hands as they turned the spit over the fire. He understood that the old man had used those hands to kill.

Severin wanted to know more, "Rra, what do you know now?" "Inside all of us are two warriors. They fight one another all the time. Do you ever feel them?"

Severin nodded. He knew exactly what the Rra meant. There was a 'Yes' Severin and a 'No' Severin. There was a Severin who loved himself and a Severin who loathed himself.

"What happens, my child, when we let our negative inside warrior win and someone else lets their negative inside warrior win as well? The two of them forget that they both come from the same seed. When they do not recognize one another, they become irrationally afraid and lash out. They fight, and the most negative self wins."

"I see," Seve murmured, as he looked down at his brother. Then he added, "Babba has never let his negative warrior win. He has never lashed out."

"It looks like neither have you, young man. You are here, are you not? Looking after your brother? The good you is winning."

Severin looked down at Babba's little face. Marveling over the boy's innocence Severin thought on how his bad self had won so often before.' His mind reeled with days lost to cocaine and spent stealing something he could never give back: life. His skin burned as memories flared. His nose stung and his breath stopped short.

Babba felt the transformation in his protector. He sat up and took hold of his big brother's hand, massaging away the tension. Together, they took deep breaths to tackle Severin's rising trauma.

Not noticing the boys' attempt to calm himself, the Rra wandered into a moment from long ago. His eyes drifted over the washing tide, and he spoke as if he was in a dream. "It was a terrible war. Those poor young white boys had no hope against us warriors. They couldn't have been older than seventeen wet seasons."

"Seve is a warrior!" Babba cried out. "He used to fight in a war, and he's only twelve wet seasons."

"Ssssh Babba!" Severin pushed the little one from his lap and flashed resentful eyes up at the Rra. He felt certain that he would be scolded for having been a killer. He awaited the old man's disappointment. Babba's pulled himself into the corner, feeling the sting of remorse for having inadvertently betrayed his kin.

The Rra lowered himself into a squat and poked at his cooking. After a while he returned Severin's gaze and peered into the face of the Little Warrior. "You have killed young man?"

Severin's eyes burned with his rising tears. He could not answer the Rra. He simply couldn't. But he didn't need to; the old man understood. "I feel for you boy. It is a terrible thing to do. We may be animals, but it is not innate in us to hunt in cold blood. Perhaps it is because once our prey is dead, they serve no purpose. In the world of lions and impalas, it is natural. The prey becomes the feed. Don't be afraid, child. You are safe from having to kill here." The old man chuckled, revealing his few remaining teeth. "Except fish. We need fish."

Severin nodded his thanks and the bulge of emotions lodged in his throat slid back down, filling the cracks of his broken heart.

"What war did those bloody so-called Freedom Fighters have you fighting, Little Warrior?"

"My name is Severin, Rra ... and they had me fighting against the LLLS and the Evil President of Nkosi."

"Ah, your army did not like Mfundisi?"

Severin shrugged his shoulders to his ears. He honestly had no clue what they had been fighting for, and the old man could tell that the boy would rather not talk about it.

"Well. All of that is over for you now. You are safe on the beach. Let it heal your past as it has healed mine. We must wait for the lions ... the ancestors have spoken that they will come and save us from ourselves."

Daunted, Babba asked the Rra, "How can the lions save us?"

"My child, when they finally return, they will come in great hordes, in families of hundreds. They will tremble over the hills and swarm the valleys. They will bolt through the jungles and bring courage back into the Republic. They will protect the villages from rebels and the real warriors of Nkosi will be able to rise up and defend our country from itself. Yes ... we will all be saved when the lions come."

Babba wrapped his arms around his knees and studied the Rra. "Excuse me, but how do you know this?"

"It is our oldest tale, child. It is the lesson you learn when you pass through initiation and become a man."

The boys stared back blankly. The Rra, slightly alarmed that the boys evidently had no knowledge of this rite of passage, looked from one boy to the other.

Severin's throat cracked; his voice was aging along with the rest of his body. "Initiation, Rra?"

"Yes. It is a ceremony for all Nkosi boys. It is a tradition that has been passed down for centuries. It is where the shepherds are shown the teachings of the ancestors, and they become warriors."

Severin wrung his hands. Tears again welled up in his eyes. He dropped his head back so that they could be swallowed into his head. He did not want the Rra to see him cry. His voice cracked again as he asked, "What if you are not a shepherd, Rra? Can you become a real Nkosian warrior then? Can you learn the teachings? Can you help save Nkosi?"

The Rra noticed the boy's snot dribbling from his nose, and took in the child's quivering lips – a child on the verge of manhood. "Boy ... you fool. You are the greatest shepherd this land has known. You have guided this young boy to the beaches of Nkosi! You are already a real Nkosian warrior!"

Severn's face opened up with a wide grin. He let the tears pour as he laughed out his anxiety. The three of them laughed together and then sat serenely silent. They stayed that way for the rest of the evening and into the following days. Quiet.

Each night before Severin fell asleep, he planned to leave to find Dorian the next morning, but every day he would wake with a nagging headache and a bout of diarrhea. The Rra took care of him, feeding him well and tucking him into rest under animal hides. Severin dreamed softly and let the nights stretch on, waking late in the morning to breakfasts of fried bananas and coconut milk. The old Rra nursed them for many days until Severin felt strong enough to go looking for Dorian – the other brother the Rra had come to learn so much about.

The old man understood the child's need to reach his friend and admired Severin's devotion. He packed him some supplies for the journey to Baobab. He hugged the boy as if it were his own grandson who was departing. Seve spent his last morning playing with the seaweed and watching the sea.

In the moments before he walked away, Babba stood by his side, holding his hand tightly. His older brother spoke in the deep tones of a man as he reassured his brother-in-arms. "Once I find everyone, we will come back for you Babba. I promise. Stay with the Rra and get big and strong, you hear?" Babba wrapped his arms around his brother's waist.

"I love you Babba."

"Don't forget me here. Please don't forget me."

Severin was uncertain of whether he could make it to the big city with the stretch of desert that still lay before him, but his heart was wild with longing, so he had to try. He kissed Babba's head and bowed in gratitude to the Rra. He then left the two Nkosians on the blissful beach. His legs burned as he pushed his way up the dunes back to the Nothingness. At the summit, he turned back to wave goodbye one last time to his favourite little boy who stood watching, loyal as a kid goat.

Severin turned away from Babba and looked out over the Nothingness. Loneliness mocked him. He shook away his nervousness and gripped the sand with his toes. Finding courage in the earth of Nkosi, he looked out at the journey that lay before him. Succumbing to the inevitability of his first few steps, he let his legs go and felt weightless as he ran down the dune. The heat bore down on him, nagging at his back, but the choice was no longer his. He had to find Dorian. It was his mission because love is like that. It commands devotion in one. It slays the feeble coward in one.

THE LITTLE LION CUBS

Princess Marina Hospital
12 March 2009

Mandeep's office was sticky from the heat. The three men sweat through their shirts as they sat with Leoson, who was fidgeting in front of them. Swinging his legs off an office chair, he sat in simple shorts and a tattered t-shirt.

The professor from the university who had been leading Leoson's counselling sessions sat next to Mandeep and Stefanus. Leoson had come to know the professor well and felt safe with him because the man had grown up in the same area of Nkosi as himself. The professor asked him one more time, "Are you sure you feel comfortable?"

"Yes Sah."

Stefanus stood up and tampered with the fan until it twisted to and fro on 'high.' Every time the air passed by Leoson, he felt the nastiness of his nerves fall away.

The professor then began, "Ok, Leoson, we would like you to tell us some things today before we can begin the therapy. How do you feel?"

Leoson's heart pressed against his ribs. He was nervous, but the truth was he trusted these men and he did feel ready to share his memories. He nodded his head slowly while he massaged his thumb into his palm.

The professor offered, "Why don't you take a few big belly breaths to calm down, like we've been practicing, and then you can start wherever you like? We can talk about your Mammi more if you wish, or we can pick up from where we left off a couple of days ago. Do you remember?"

Leoson's lonely eyes confronted the men as he thought about the many times he had sat in that chair, swinging his legs and going over his memories. "I keep asking myself when I will forget, Sah."

The grown-ups gulped back their feelings of helplessness. Remembering was an emotional journey for everyone, and they understood Leoson entirely.

"Can I talk about killing?" Leoson queried.

Mandeep started to take minutes. The room was so quiet that his pen scratching against his notepad echoed over their breathing.

The professor urged the boy on. "Yes, young man. Of course you may. This process is for you, and if you are feeling strong enough today to begin tackling this trauma, you are more than welcome to."

Leoson scanned the room. He didn't like thinking about what he had done. When he did, his body felt wishy-washy, like hot water. He hated feeling like that, but the grown-ups said that if they did REM therapy on the memories, then that scary sensation would become less frequent or even stop entirely. Since Leoson was a clever little boy, he decided to go with the odds. "Yes. I want it all gone."

"Well young man," replied the professor. "The past won't go away, but we can help you forgive yourself and remind you that you are worthy of happiness. How about that?"

Leoson nodded. He grew hot again, but from embarrassment this time. The professor had triggered a soft spot. Worthiness was his greatest weakness. He didn't feel like he deserved much. He felt guilty for being safe now and in a community of friends and grown-ups who loved him. Even though he had been at Princess Marina for a few months now, Leoson still struggled when he played soccer because he felt like it was a sport that real kids got to play, not bad ones who had done bad things.

"The thing is ..." croaked his tight voice. Leoson watched his own palm in his lap as he revealed his secret. "The thing is ... I didn't know at the time it was bad."

The boy looked up, wanting to read the men's reactions. Their faces were soft and still so he continued; "I didn't know what it meant to put a bullet in someone or to cut their face. I thought that they just fell over and went to sleep. I didn't fully understand that when someone was dead by my hand they wouldn't wake up. I didn't know I was stealing them from someone else. I thought I'm too small to be a real warrior. Nothing I do could actually hurt someone for real. For good."

At this point, Leoson stopped. He held his breath and noticed how his shivered with cold despite the humidity in Dr. Jain's office. He began to think about the many moments he had stolen from people – just as someone had stolen the moments he and his mother could have shared.

"It's ok, Leoson. You know you can say anything here and you will not get in trouble."

"Yes Sah." Leoson looked through the window and saw the girls skipping. He listened to their rope slapping the ground and their sing-song rhyme that drifted over the courtyard to where he was sitting. "One two three four ... Lamore, lamore, lamore!" He noticed how happy the girls were here. Their faces shone brightly against the sun. They were not sad like the girls at the LLLS camp who dragged themselves from place to place.

"Leo?" prompted Steffi.

The boy, still watching the girls play, carried on. "You see ... I just didn't know that when someone was dead, they were dead forever. I had a best friend in the camp with me. He was from my village, and thank God we weren't separated. We trained together with the LLLS, and we held each other's hands when it was too scary. He is the reason I felt I could survive. Then one day he was sent on a reconnaissance trip to find the MM…" He saw the men watching him from the corner of his eye. "… Joshua didn't come back."

Leoson shifted in his seat. He tucked his hands under his thighs and stared down at his feet. Some tears slipped as a memory filled him with a sudden heat. He felt Joshua hugging hard into him, as he had done when they were hiding in a hut together the day the LLLS came for his village. "When he didn't come back, I learned what death was. The daga, the cocaine … nothing could stop me from understanding, and so I ran away because I could not imagine acting like Nkosi anymore. I am not God. I am a little boy. When Joshua didn't come back, I realized that I, too, was stealing people's best friends, Mammies, brothers and sisters. Only then did I understand what it meant to kill. When you kill someone, you don't just kill them. You kill anyone who loves them too. I'm still waiting for my best friend to come and find me … but I know he won't. He is up in the sky now … with the real Nkosi."

Laughter rushed into the office from the courtyard. The sound of happy girls shifted everyone's attention for a moment. Turning their focus back to the ravaged boy, they exhaled, flushing out some of their sadness.

Leoson looked up at the men. "I'm tired … do we have to finish right now?"

Dr. Mandeep shook his head and put his pad and pen down beside him. "Why don't you go play some soccer, Leo?"

"Thank you, Sah," he said, tucking his pain in the back pocket of his mind. Then he grinned and rushed for the door. The sound of his veldt schoens slapping down the hallway echoed back to the ears of the men who sat somberly.

It was Steffi who spoke first. "Do you sometimes feel like they are wise old men trapped in the bodies of children?"

Mandeep, staring at the boy's vacant seat replied, "All children are born knowing. It is the adults who steal their wisdom slowly but surely."

. . . .

Leoson ran through the orphanage past the shrill cries of sick wailing babies. He broke out into the courtyard where Shalini was shushing a naughty toddler. He swept around her to make his way to Dorian. His sickly friend was sitting under the thorn tree by the soccer pitch, watching the older boys play. He was wrapped in a big blanket. Leoson wondered how he could stand such a covering in that heat. He sat down cross-legged and reached for a fallen branch. He used it to draw in the sand while they watched the soccer. A thorn punctured his skin as he worked. "Owy!" Dodo slowly placed his cool palm over Leoson's. He applied some pressure to the small wound. Leo's eyes began to well. "Tula child, Tula," muscled Dorian's strained voice.

THE FINDING

On a hill overlooking the city of Baobab
17 March 2009

Paris put one foot in front of another, meditating on the child Dodo had killed for his takkies, Joshua, the LLLS intruder. He remembered Dodo's words. "He shot you! Take them. Shoes for a bullet."

The wanderer looked down at his ragged shoes, taken from the feet of a dead boy. He watched them for days as he travelled through the Nothingness, feeling little emotion over them as he traversed the great expanse.

After countless back-breaking days and tear-soaked nights, Paris lifted his eyes from his tattered shoes to see Baobab, finally, sprawled beneath him. The boy's heart stood still. He basked in the light of his spirit's joy. He felt elation rise up from the innermost part of himself, filling the void that loneliness and despair had created, warming him until his eyes were hot with exasperated tears. Before him sprawled the biggest village he had ever seen. It sprawled as far as he could see. Overwhelmed, he could not move. So he stood, breath suspended. He watched smoke rise from chimneys and bodies move between the green tents of a vast camp that stretched from the edge of the city all the way to the bottom of the hill on which he now stood.

Paris let his eyes run back out over Baobab. He looked over the sandy-coloured buildings. He could not believe what he saw. What a metropolis. How on earth would he find Dodo in such a place?

Interrupting his astonishment, a small voice behind him broke the silence. "Paris?"

He turned to find an exhausted Severin stumbling, blurry eyed, towards him. "Jesus, Seve ... how did I beat you here? Where is Babba?"

Severin hobbled towards his older brother. "He stayed with the old man."

"What old man?"

"The man..." his voice drifted off as he took in the solitude of the bigger boy standing in front of him. "...Paris ... where ... where is Helena?"

Before Paris could answer, Severin's fatigued body gave way from under him, and he fell forward into Paris' arms.

"Seve? Seve! Wake up!" Paris, despite his own exhaustion, picked up Severin and hurriedly tripped his way down the hill towards the camp. Dust flew up behind him. It soared high into the air and then showered back down to the earth as Paris bolted on, desperate to find aid for his heavy brother. Suddenly, he found himself thronged by people. They took no notice of him. He was small and meaningless in desensitized crowds like these. Paris rushed through the camp's alleys, begging adults for help, all of who shooed him away with a wave of a hand. In spite of his exhaustion Paris persisted, hunting for someone who would react to the child dangling in his arms. Yet, misery was commonplace in the camp, and no one gave a damn about the boy's suffering.

Finally, he came across a tent with white people standing outside. Seeing them triggered the memory of the wild white man who came to Doornbos. He carried Severin over to the only Nkosian woman amongst them. "Mma![35] Mma!" Deborah, stunned by the sight of Paris' desperation, took Seve from his arms. "Mma! We are looking for a Mr. Abraham and Princess Marina Hospital!"

---

[35] Madam in Setswana.

"Jesus! How long has he been without water?"

"I am not sure. Days possibly."

"Christ!" Noticing Severin's scar on his upper arm, Deborah immediately understood they had escaped from the MM the way Leoson had escaped from the LLLS. "Did you make it through the Nothingness?"

Paris started to stagger. "I - I- We..." And then he collapsed at Deborah's feet.

. . . .

The boys woke up in the back of Deborah's Land Rover with drips in their arms. Their heads bounced against the seat as she drove over potholes and down windy roads of a shantytown. The ambient sounds of the settlement seeped into their ears and finally dragged them into full wakefulness.

Paris rolled his head to find Seve at his side. He took his hand. Through cracked lips came the scratchy words, "You made it."

Severin rolled his head towards Paris, mumbling, "Where is Helena?" Paris pursed his lips and turned his head. Severin took his hand and squeezed it remorsefully.

As they held hands and looked out the window, they took in the chaotic streets of Baobab.

"Mma?" came Paris' crackled query.

Deborah looked at the boys through her rearview mirror, "Yes young man?"

"What is that big white building over there? I have never seen walls so tall."

"It is where the president used to live." As they passed Mfundisi's old home, Paris recalled all the lectures he had heard protesting the president's regime. In the back of his ears, he heard Zaza inciting hatred for the man over meals at Doornbos.

"Mma?"

"Yes?"

"What exactly is a president?"

Deborah had spent half an hour answering his question as she drove them to Princess Marina. She had explained how the war they had been fighting began and for whom they had been fighting. She had said many times that it was not their fault. Severin was distracted from her lecture by the magnitude of the buildings. Paris, intent on Deborah's lesson, could not believe how a president could run away from his duties. If he was the biggest, best chief, then he should stay at all costs so that the children of Nkosi could be safe.

"He is a very bad president," he said.

Deborah tried to explain, "He is a leader in very difficult times, young man."

Paris sat pouting in the backseat until they turned onto Jacaranda Drive. Its architecture, tall trees and flowers shifted his interest.

"Wow!" Paris exclaimed as he took in the buildings. "Seve! It looks like Doornbos!"

Severin looked out of his window at the soft scenery of the drive.

Deborah noticed his raised eyebrows. "We are nearly there."

Paris smiled at Severin, who wasn't nearly as excited as he was. He whispered, "What's wrong with you? We are here!"

"What if he's not?" Severin said woefully. "Then I came all the way to this strange place for nothing?"

Paris squeezed Severin's hand reassuringly. "He will be here."

The Land Rover pulled through a set of gates and made its way into a courtyard. There was a bicycle at the front steps of a huge set of doors. They reminded Severin of the doors of the chapel they had ruined in the clearing of the Nobody-Knows-How-Vast-Jungle of Nkosi. He thought wryly to himself, 'Well, I suppose I do know how vast the jungles of Nkosi are...'

Deborah parked and reached back between the front seats to unplug the boys' arms from their intravenous drips, which hung crudely from the window frames. "We'll get you other ones in there. I have to take these ones back to the camp." She gave the boys each a bottle of water and an orange and ordered, "Come with me."

The boys followed the nice lady up the steps of the hospital as they drank. She led them through the big doors. Its insides were sterile, stark and clad with metal. Women all in white and with little hats on their heads moved about busily.

Deborah stopped one of them and asked, "Excuse me do you know where Stefanus is?"

The woman pointed through a window that looked out onto the courtyard. There, in the orphanage's playground was the white man.

"Thank you." Sophie nodded politely and, looking at Severin, was startled. A familiarity in his face stirred her heart.

Severin watched the courtyard where girls were skipping and boys were playing. He took Paris' hand, nervous that Dodo would not be there. Deborah looked back at the boys, saying, "Come on then," and continued down the hall. They followed her to another set of doors.

Upon exiting the building and turning towards the courtyard, they could more clearly hear the children's voices punctuating the air. Paris and Seve found the white man once again, and relief covered them as they saw a sickly looking Dodo at his feet. He was wrapped in a blanket and he was smiling at the other children playing. He was not only alive, but in good spirits.

Severin then noticed that Dodo was giggling at another child. He followed his friend's gaze. Bouncing around on a pair of mechanical legs was a little girl. At first, Severin didn't recognize this girl given her upright posture and perfect confidence. Nyla was equally unaware of Severin standing such a short distance away as she played on her prosthetic birthday presents. As she wobbled from one new leg to another, her face broke into a wide grin and then she took in air and laughed.

Upon hearing her laugh, Severin's heart exploded. He crushed Paris' knuckles with an excited squeeze before letting loose and running for her! Screaming all the way across the courtyard, he alarmed the orphans.

Unable to believe in his existence, Nyla could only whisper under her struggling breath, "Lamore … lamore." Finally, after torturous months spent apart, months where he had thought her dead, months where she had thought of him with deep dread, the two held each other again. Each was alive and – she at least – was very, very well!
He felt her whispering the magnificent word into his neck, so he cried out in reply, tears raging down his cheeks, "Lamore! Nyla! Nyla! Lamore!"

THE YOKING

The courtyard at Princess Marina Hospital

Dorian struggled to stand. He limped towards the reunited brother and sister, who were collapsed on the ground in an embrace. Despite his confusion, he cried with happiness. 'Happiness,' he thought. 'Happiness is once again in our lives.' He let his blanket slip from his shoulders and fall to the dust. He stopped as it did so and felt his rebirth as the sun warmed his soul. He closed his eyes for a moment to compose his emotions.

When he opened them, he looked into the eyes of his confidante. Those eyes he knew so well. Those eyes to which he had entrusted his secrets and his safety for as long as he could remember.

Limping closer, he spread his arms wide and high like a kite that soars in the Nkosian sky. He had not unwrapped his arms from his own sick body for a long time. In releasing them now, his heart finally remembered its full capacity. He tangled himself around Severin and Nyla and whispered the sweet sorrowful song of Nkosi. "Lamore."

There they stayed. The two boys could feel little Nyla's shuddering happiness from within the hot cuddle of love. Her excitement tickled at their bodies and together the three of them began to giggle little childhood giggles. Paris looked over the children, wishing their eldest sister was holding them all.

Stefanus, overwhelmed, started to cry. He wheezed a little and crossed his arms over his chest, afraid that his heart might explode. He was so moved with gratitude for Nyla's brother who had made the courageous journey back to her. If only he had known that the boy in the classroom at Doornbos, the boy that begged to keep Dorian with him, was her elder brother. Through teary eyes he looked over to Deborah, who was also crying. Even though she was well acquainted with the raw emotions of Baobab, she had never seen or been a part of anything quite like this. Stefanus looked at her with profound admiration and mouthed the words, "Thank you." Then he joined in on the laughter as well. His baritone boomed about the courtyard and soon, because of its greatness, forced everyone into a fit of hysterical giddiness.

The children all sat down in a huddle. Instead of speaking, they reached over with their little hands, caressing faces and wiping away tears. They gripped at one another's palms and leaned across the circle to give one another eager hugs. The world has never known a reunion of such gentleness, of such tenderness, of such forgiveness.

Dorian watched as Stefanus commended Paris with a warm hug, "I cannot believe you made it here, my boy!"

In all the fury of beautiful emotion, Dorian had overlooked the absence of one important character in the saga of his life. Now, looking behind and to either side of Paris, he came to the realization that Helena was not with them. His throat became dry, but he mustered a quiet question. "Paris ... Paris, where is my sister?"

Paris had been bracing himself for this inevitable conversation. He had spent his days walking through the Nothingness trying to configure the best possible way to utter his heartbreaking news to Dorian. He released himself from Stefanus' warmth and came down to his knees. He took Dorian's face in his dirty palms. He brought the child's forehead to his lips. He silently blessed Dorian's strength and spirit. He let his lips leave Dorian's skin and looked at him with brotherly love. He placed his hand on Dodo's heart, "She is in here, Dodo. She is in here."

Severin stole Dorian's hands and gripped them firmly as Nyla wrapped herself around him. Unable to summon up any more emotion, Dorian looked blankly back at Paris, who was now overcome by weeping.

A crowd of rehabilitating child soldiers had clustered to observe the reunion. Among them was young Leoson, whose mind was churning once again with a recollection of something his Pappi had said to him when he was a little boy. He often repeated it to himself as a reminder of his father. It had sustained him when nothing else could. He had wanted to share the words with his new family for quite some time, and now was the perfect moment. He raised a voice of self-assurance and reassurance. It was strong and clear. He spoken just as a real Nkosian warrior would. He spoke to console Dorian. He spoke to console them all. His words were intended for every one of the children lucky enough to find themselves in the care of Princess Marina. His voice rang out around the courtyard. "When we discover, as a family, that we are all in it together, the yoking becomes the most generous of soils, the most thrashing of seas, the brightest of lights and the most courageous of lion hearts … Lamore, Dodo … Lamore."

THE BUCKIE

Baobab
August 2009

Starting with Paris, because he was the eldest, they had all taken turns. Severin was next because he was confident he could get the hang of it. Leoson was third because, well, why not? Finally, though he had to be coaxed by the rest of them, Dorian took a turn behind the buckie's wheel. The boys had enticed him to try by saying how encouraging the feeling was of gaining ground without using one's feet.

Stefanus sat in the passenger seat issuing instructions while the rest of them teased the learner. The group spent the day moving through the alleys of Baobab until they had mastered the clutch and gears.

When it was Dorian's turn to drive in earnest, he did so steadily with hands at ten and two through the tight and bustling alleys of the old quarter. With the boys laughing in the back of the truck, they left the town on the dirt road that would take them west towards the sea. Dorian bounced on his bum and stretched his chin up over the steering wheel to navigate. The brittle scenery stretched out before them all the way to Nkosi's army base. Apprehensively, Dorian pushed in the clutch and lowered the gears down to first. The boys in the back also felt unnerved by the sighting of the artillery and dropped to their bums.

Sensing Dorian's anxiety, Stefanus assured, "It's ok. That army is here to protect you."

Dorian dropped the car to neutral. The car jolted until it finally stopped. "Whoa Dodo!" came calls from the back of the buckie as the boys battled to stay afoot in the cab.

Dorian put the car into park and shut off the ignition. He looked up at Stefanus. "They're here to protect me?"

"Yes." Pointing at the barracks that lay ahead, Stefanus added, "That is the army of Nkosi."

Dorian, suddenly furious, flung open the door and rushed from the truck. He pushed into the dirt the same way he had done that day when had wanted to hack the MM soldier to bits for hurting Nyla. His thighs burned, his arms pumped. The rest of the boys hopped out of the buckie and chased him as he screamed at the barracks in the distance, "Protect me? You were supposed to protect me!"

Still weak from his war wound, he finally wound down. His heaving chest rose and fell and his hand clutched his side, as he stood planted in the dirt. Under his wheezing breath little Dorian told the army of Nkosi just what he thought of them as the other boys rushed in. "You worthless pieces of shit. You were supposed to protect us. You were supposed to save us. Cowards!"

Groups of officers lounging around in the barracks noticed the group of children in the distance. But they soon lost interest in the distant scene and returned to their cigarettes and card games.

Paris wrapped himself around Dorian who, exhausted from his tantrum, fell to his bum. He sputtered one final slur, "Those fucking assholes."

"I don't understand," said Severin. "Why are you so upset, Dodo?"

Dorian pointed towards the barracks. "That's the army of Nkosi. Stefanus says they're here to protect us, but where the hell were they? Where the hell were they when we needed saving?" Dorian's sputtered up tears of fury. The slash in his side ached. He inspected his now bruised scar. His tantrum had done some damage.

Severin looked to the barracks. He took in its many Land Rovers, its tents, its soldiers. He turned to Stefanus asking, "Do they know there are children stolen every day in the interior, Stefanus?"

Stefanus nodded. "They do, but Severin, they don't know how to engage the MM or the LLLS. How can a man fight a child?"

Leoson chimed in, "That's true ... But why are they here and not protecting the villages from future raids?"

Paris surveyed the camp as Stefanus answered. "I wish I knew, Leoson."

"Come boys, let's go home." Stefanus led them back to the truck and helped them pile into the buckie. Dorian and Leoson took the passenger seats in the cab and buckled themselves in next to Stefanus. Watching the barracks as Stefanus made a large arch back towards Baobab's old quarter, Leoson said under his breath, "One day I'm going to run that army, and I'm going to run it properly."

"You want to be a soldier again," asked Stefanus, "after everything?"

Idealistic Leoson answered, "I don't want to be a soldier. I want to be a thinker. I want to protect the people of Nkosi. I am going to think so hard that I am going to come up with a way to save them."

"I'm going to think with you," said Dorian and grabbed his friend's hand.

The boys were driven back to the orphanage on Jacaranda Drive where they found Nyla skipping rope with the other girls on her new appendages. She did not pay them any attention, still infatuated with her new found agility.

That night as they lay in their bunk beds, the boys talked again about the army of Nkosi's shortcomings. Before they drifted off, they all made a solemn vow that they would think together. They would think so hard that they would

find a way to protect their people ... because the army of
Nkosi was failing.

The job was up to them. Together, they agreed to find a way
to put their education on war to good use. Together, when
they were big and strong, they would save Nkosi. Little did
they know that Anthony Zaza had made a promise just like
this with his best friends, also survivors of conflict, many,
many moons ago.

GOODNIGHT MOON

The bar in Baobab
16 September 2009

"There was another proceeding today in the camp."

Stefanus could sense from the way Deborah spoke that she was uncomfortable - deflated even.

"Another hungry boy gone wild?" He tried to sound light.

Her face stiffened and she lowered her eyes to her beer. "No ... a rape."

Stefanus played with his coaster. He tore at it as he replied, "But Debs, that's nothing new."

Her heart hardened. "Maybe so, but today I couldn't take it. There this young girl sat in the proceeding, but to the people she was just there for show. Her father was holding her hand and trying to appear brave, but anyone could tell he had been broken by the undertaking as well. Bruises were still purpling from the violation as the proceeding took place. She was still bleeding as she sat in the sand at the trial, Stefanus! She should have been at Marina! They should have brought her to me, but there are some matters that these people will not come to me for. Matters that I am not allowed to get involved in because I'm a woman, or because I was brought up in the city. Matters they do not care to involve me in even though I could have helped her."

Deborah tried to regain some composure. She lowered her

voice. "I could have helped that poor girl. She was in so much pain, physically and emotionally. She was so shaken she barely knew she was in public."

Stefanus didn't say anything in response.

"Do you hear me, Stefanus? Do you hear what I am saying?"

"I do ... but I'm not quite sure why this rape is different from all the rest."

"It's that this girl wasn't just taken against her will. She wasn't just pinned down. What happened to her last night was so vicious that it scared her soul from her body. It's gone! At least, it wasn't there today when she was bleeding in the God damned sand!"

Deborah picked up her cold beer. It stung her palm. She chugged hard. Stefanus put his hand on her shoulder to try and calm her. This optimistic Nkosian had obviously reached the end of her tether.

Pouring the beer down her gorge, her rant continued. "Have you ever had rough sex, Stefanus?"

"Yes, I suppose I have." Tentative about where this conversation was headed.

"Well, let's just say that even if it is enjoyable for us women, there is a price to pay. The next day our labia swell. Our body knows that, physically speaking, things aren't how they should be. I can't imagine what happened to this girl. I've never seen a person suffering like that."

"Jesus, Deborah."

"Oh, believe me, Jesus was not there, Stefanus."

"I've been thinking that a lot lately too. So, what happened at the proceeding?"

With her voice fighting now against her rage and tears, Deborah responded, "It was her words against his. He claimed the poor girl had seduced him, making it her fault. God, you should have seen her father. He was just so helpless ... so broken. What could he do? Screaming and shouting wouldn't have helped. So he slumped next to her, his hand around her shoulders ... his precious possession now worthless. He can never get anything for her now ... no dowry. She is shamed. I could tell he wanted to hate her for not fighting harder for her innocence, for not screaming louder, for not being able to break free."

"So the rapist? He got off?"

"Can you believe it?"

Stefanus' Adam's apple shot upwards as he heaved. "Disgusting. And the girl?"

"I don't know ... I tried to take her to Dr. Jain, but her father wouldn't let me. She had a fever ... I'm worried for her."

"I'm worried for all of them," said Stefanus. "The boys and girls from Doornbos have been here for a few months now, and some of them can't let go of their trauma."

Deborah let images of some of the children flicker across her mind. "But Leoson is responding well, is he not?"

"Yes, he was, but last week they triggered something during a session. He went completely stone cold. He was awake, but comatose. It was very scary. He couldn't respond. He couldn't move. Not even Nyla and her lullabies could break the spell. We put him in a quiet room all by himself, but he did not move for about twenty hours. He just stared into space. This rehab may be the scariest part of all of it. I don't know what's better – to work on these kids' minds, or to let them hide from their pasts so they can just get on with it, you know?"

"What did Leoson say when he finally woke up?"

"Nothing ... we gently pried, but it seemed to us that he thought he had just woken up from a nap. He had forgotten everything. Even the trigger of his brief paralysis."

"Poor boy."

Stefanus lifted his beer high in the air so that the sauntering barmaid could fetch him another.

"You've had too many beers to drive home, Stefanus."

"I'm on my bike."

Amused, she smiled and said, "Well, don't fall into a bush!"

They shared a laugh as she stood, and though she felt guilty, she said it aloud for the first time. "I think I need a break. I think I'm going to go home right now and e-mail HQ for leave."

"I was thinking the same thing. I want Nyla and Severin to see Amsterdam. I think it is a good time to integrate those two into a Dutch school system. Do you think they're young enough to learn the language easily?"

"Definitely! Nyla and Seve? They're equipped. No need to worry about those two."

"Yes, but I'm not sure Severin will leave Dorian."

Deborah leaned against the chair and wondered to herself if she should also take one of the orphans home. If she did, Dorian would be a good fit. He was quiet, discerning, courageous and strong-willed. He also needed a mother very badly, especially having lost his the way he did.

Yet, all these Little Warriors had a sad story. Dorian's was no worse than any other's. Perhaps she should come to grips with the notion that it was no longer worth her energy. Maybe she should ask Stefanus to take her with him to Amsterdam.

She leaned down and kissed him on the cheek. As he was a bit drunk, he turned his face a little too far and the corner of their lips met. Though she was surprised, Deborah let the peck linger and gave his face another quick kiss before pulling away. He looked up at her, knowing full well that she was just like him: incapable of a relationship. They had both been out of practice for a long time.

She smiled sympathetically and changed the subject. "What was the trigger anyway?"

"What trigger?"

"What was Leoson's mind hiding from? Why did his body shut down? What was the last question Mandeep asked?"

"We have been trying to get him to talk about his first kill. Every time the subject is broached he expresses he cannot talk about it 'just yet.' So we let him leave the room to play. This past session we pushed him, too hard as it turns out. We urged him to open up about it."

"Did you get anything out of him? Wait – do I want to know?"

Stefanus studied his hands. "No, you don't."

She watched him for a few moments, half hoping he would tell her anyway. When he didn't, she made a move to leave.

Suddenly desperate to say it out loud, Stefanus started speaking. "He had three younger brothers who, when the LLLS came and stole him, they tied up in front of him. He was given a knife, told to carve patterns into their faces. 'Scarface.' Remember that was his name? When he begged to stop, they cut off his father's hands."

"Jesus, so they're all dead? His whole family?"

"Yes, executed. But what he was most upset about was that he wished he had listened to his parents. They were begging him to stop, begging him to give up and let them all die together. He kept saying that he wanted to stop, he kept telling his hand to stop, but something inside of him – a will to live, I suppose – kept him going..."

"So, on one side the LLLS was telling him what to do and on the other, his poor parents? And he was caught in the middle?"

"Yes, and he wishes he had chosen differently."

"Jesus."

Deborah stood quietly, taking the trauma in. She then said good night, leaving Stefanus to mourn Leoson's history. She shared niceties with the staff before exiting into the quiet of the sparkling night.

Crickets spoke to one another in the bushes, and she enjoyed their stories. Stories that must be nicer than her own. Feeling the booze settle in her bones, she stood wavering beneath the shining sky. "Goodnight moon. Goodnight."

Inside, Stefanus had one more beer and then drunkenly made up his mind. He would take his children home. He had to. He simply had to. He would spend the day tomorrow planning the move instead of going out on patrol with the NAP boys. Once one makes this kind of decision, one has to jump on it before it gets too scary.

Looking over the sickness that moved about in the bar his gut shifted again, and his decision solidified in his chest, "Yes ... home we go."

. . . .

The NAP went out early the next day without Stefanus. They had all woken to the silence of the black morning. Each member of the group had shivered as he left his warm bed, and each had sipped at his sweet, milky tea as his wife loved him from her kitchen sink. Wet kisses had sent them off into the fog of the morning. Their veldt schoens had crunched over the dirt as they each made their way to their buckie. They had met at the reservoir on the outskirts of town. From there, they said their good mornings. With broad smiles, they patted one another on their backs and rubbed one another's heads affectionately.

BUT ... where have all the lions gone?

The day became hot quickly. Knee high socks were rolled down and jerseys were wrapped around waists as the NAP tracked their way through the jungle. Signs of previous travellers were easy to spot. Many feet had freshly pressed the grass at their feet. Vines had been hacked by machetes. The trail was hot and the NAP, for the first time, felt as if they were onto something. They held onto their guns attached to their belts as they stalked, quietly listening for something ... for anything ... until the sibilant sounds of whispers came from the bushes surrounding them.

Hundreds of soft voices murmured them into a frozen tableau. Rising from the lilies stood an army of Little Warriors.

The crowd of children stood, glaring. Confident of their power, they closed in menacingly. Immobilized, the men from the NAP stood.

One croaked, "We are just looking for the Lions."

A child, smiling wryly, said, "Look at us ... united, we are the MM and LLLS. You fool. We are the lions."

Hundreds of wildcats prowled amongst and between the Nkosians Against Poachers.

The same man tried again. "Where are you heading?"

The child let out a maniacal laugh. "Old man, we are headed for the upside down town."

A look of horror crossed his face. "Baobab?" the man asked, thinking of his wife cleaning the dishes in his sunny kitchen. He pictured their baby gurgling on her hip, snot dripping down its nose. His heart spasmed. "No ... you can't."

All the children were laughing now, a cruel orchestra of dissonant sound.

The Little Warrior softened his face sarcastically, stepped closer to the man, pulled a handgun out of his pants and said, "Yes ... I think we can."

. . . .

Their worried wives gathered the following morning. No husbands had returned from the jungle. The women sat in silence on the back stoop of one of their homes. Their babies crawled about in the sun. Flies bothered the toddlers' eyes and buzzed above their Mammies' untouched milky teas.

Throats swallowed hard.

Mouths salivated steadily.

Hands wrung.

But lips? Lips did not move. They dared not sound the unhappy knowing that their husbands would never come home.

THE END

The Jain residence & the orphanage at Princess Marina
Hospital
17 September 2009

She didn't mince words in her proposition. "I want to go home, Mandeep."

Her face was weathered, her beauty drained. Shalini's eyes fell to her lap where her hands wrung anxiously.

Mandeep, astonished by her confession, sat gaping in his seat. He watched a tear fall from her chin into her palms. Placing his fork down and pushing his dinner away, he reached for her hands, pulled them from her lap and held them on the table in his. Love flowed through their touch. She sighed and leaned into him, silently asking him to help her with her fears. He took her weight gladly. Despite all her capability, self-possession and strength, she still needed him. He thanked God for that.

"Look at me, my love."

She lifted her lashes. Wet eyes watched him. She waited, hoping that they could return to the idyll of their youth. Yes, here in Nkosi they could wander among the sweet-smelling lilies and bougainvillea and could go on game watches with Nyla and Steffi. The little girl would tell them all the charming secrets of the animals, like how the zebra got her stripes and how the monkeys learned to swing. Still, Shalini missed her motherland. She was ready to return to the smell of turmeric and chai, cardamom and curry.

Although she loved looking over her garden here in Nkosi and watching the guinea fowls herd themselves from one flower bed to another as she sipped on hot tea and delighted in her morning rusk, she could not wait for Bangalore, with its tuk tuks and her mother's swaying head ... "Eat, Shali, eeeeeat!" She smiled and laughed at the thought of her mother force-feeding her on her visits. "How is our clever Mandeep? We are so proud of him, you know." "I know, Mamma. However, you are not as proud as I."

Upon these thoughts, Shalini had not expressed her pride for Mandeep in a long time, and so confessed, "Mandeep I am so sorry. I have been a very bad wife!"

"Nonsense, Shalini! Whatever are you talking about?"

"I have forgotten to remind you that I am proud of you for doing what you do day in and day out. I have forgotten to mention that when you hold my hand I am thankful that God gave you to me. I have forgotten to show you I appreciate that you chose me."

Mandeep drew in a long breath and then spoke candidly. "Shalini, you are the most beautiful woman in Nkosi; do you know that?"

Her eyes lowered shyly back into her lap.

"I mean it," he continued passionately. "The sight of you still amazes me. You continue to surprise me. When I married you, I did so because you were beautiful and kind to me. You listened. Oh how I loved that you listened to me. You also believed in me - that I could come here and save some lives. But I have done that now, and I am ready to make my journey back to our home also. I have indulged in idealism more than enough now. I must do my duty as a man and keep my woman safe. You are not safe here, and I love you too much to lose you, for I love you now not because you believe in me, but because you believe in yourself. You are so empowered now. You have learned so much, and given so much. You have changed the way this community works in Baobab. You have done your duty as well. You are right. It is time for us to go back to India."

Shalini's grey eyes glistened as they came up to meet the eyes of the man who had vowed to cherish her, and who did revere her. Still. Forever.

She pushed her plate aside and leaned over the table to kiss him. Their lips met with all the enthusiasm of young lovers. As one, they moved towards the floor, where they continued to celebrate their return home by making love and sharing laughter well into the night.

When their maid came into the dining room in the morning, she first saw the baby bushbuck that was skipping across the grass. Then, she found her bosses naked on the floor of the veranda, wrapped up in one another, cradled devotedly into each other. Giggling, she ran back into the kitchen where she waited for the gardener to arrive. Upon his appearance, she handed him his sweet tea and rusk, sat him on the back stoop in the sun, and gossiped all about it.

. . . .

That afternoon the world did not seem to hold so much promise. Mandeep came to see Shalini at the hospital at lunchtime. Pale, he walked up to her, sickened by his recent acquisition of new knowledge.

Shalini was bouncing a little girl on her lap, buzzing a spoon to the little one's mouth – "The airplane goes brrrrrrrrrrrrm. Yum, yum, yummies!" Laughing, the child opened her little beak and welcomed the nourishment of mashed-up bananas.

For some reason the happiness of the scene made Mandeep feel hopeless. He sat down opposite her and slid a piece of paper across the table. Shalini picked up the results and studied them. A lump grew in her throat. She looked over to where a group of children were sitting. They looked no different than any other children. Young, cheerful, innocent. Nyla and Dorian were satiating healthy appetites. Severin was telling a wild story. His arms swung in the air, animating his words. Shalini could tell it was a good story as Paris, Dodo and even Leoson were captivated. Like a pride of lions, they were fiercely loyal and gently affectionate.

Shalini looked back across the table where her husband sat staring, "I just cannot believe that Paris is sick."

The good wife scooped up some more yams and buzzed them through the little one's lips. She made nyummy nyummy sounds as she ate.

"I will tell him after lunch, my love."

Mandeep reached across the table and stroked her face. "Thank you, Shalini. I really appreciate it."

The tired doctor rose from the table and gazed down upon his wife. "Hey," he said. Shalini looked up at him and smiled softly as he continued with, "I love you."

Shalini's smile broadened. "I love you too."

She watched her husband walk towards the mess hall doors. As he drew closer to them, his silhouette grew darker, and then he was swallowed by the light.

. . . .

Paris leaned against the doorframe of Shalini's office and looked out over the soccer field. Pre-pubescent veterans were barely visible through the fog of dust. Bodies swam through it, coming up for air with happy, sweaty faces. He wished he could relearn how to smile freely and largely like that. When he smiled, it was all for show. It was make-believe. Happiness for him was something he constructed from what was left of his imagination. He shape-shifted his skin into something that resembled mirth. It was an exhausting exercise that left him looking uneasy instead of truly happy.

The truth was, Paris had been tired for a long time. The doctors at Princess Marina insisted that depression was the cause for his fatigue. Losing Helena had compromised his ability to even attempt to seek out humour. At the mere thought of pleasantries, his gut would pour into that bottomless dark cave within him. War had sinisterly stolen any real happiness and nothing was left inside of him save for a deep bit of darkness.

He stood watching the glimmers of glee rise and subside from the young players' faces. Seeing a flash of his lost love in her brother's face, he breathily whispered her name. "Helena."

No wonder they had thought the cause of his chronic exhaustion was depression, for he periodically moaned the name of the dead and continuously wallowed over her absence.

He had grown taller over the past six months in Baobab. His feet were longer now too. His big toe protruded from his takkies, yet he wore them proudly – those decrepit shoes that had brought him out of one hell and into another: loss. He had calmed down as well in the past half-year, but he would sometimes be triggered by one of Dorian's mannerisms that shared a likeness with hers. It would send the mourning lover into toxic states of static insanity.

They were all disjointed, these ex-soldiers, but no one's derangement could quite compare to Paris' lunacy. During his fits of madness, the other children would lower their eyes and shake their heads. They all knew they were sad, but were thankful that they were not as debilitated as him.

This is how Paris became the children's measure for their own mental health. Each child would begin his or her day deliberating, "How am I feeling today? Am I going to make it today? Will I smile today? Will I laugh today? ... Or will I cry into the folds of my bedding until I am hysterical with grief? Will I pull a Paris?" They used his name as if his very living and breathing was the embodiment of unbearable melancholy.

Sweat slipped from the living dead man's brow, over his nose and was caught in the crevice of his upper lip before overflowing and meeting the sour taste of fear that swam in his mouth. The world became murky as his tears welled. His heart – the heavy place where he kept her – shrivelled within him.

Shalini let him take his time processing the news she had just given him. She did not want to interrupt his agonizing ruminations. She took off her cap to show respect and placed it on the table next to her glasses. She removed her watch, as it felt heavy. She could no longer bear the weight of it so she placed it on the metal table.

The sound of the two metals meeting clamoured in Paris' mind. A gunshot rang out in his head. He squeezed his eyes shut, hoping that once he opened them the world would change, but it didn't. Shalini moved slowly towards the young man. She lifted both hands, palms upward, revealing an open desire to softly approach his pain and try to mend it.

Because she was nervous, she hesitated before placing them on his rigid shoulders. Relief bathed him as she did so, and he welcomed her warmth. Simply knowing that someone would still touch him calmed one of the worries that taunted him.

He turned and looked down at her. Indecipherable sounds crept from his throat until he could find the words. "So I will die anyway, even though I survived the journey across the Nothingness?"

Shalini's heart twisted within her. It knotted itself protectively. Just looking at the sorrows this young man bore was enough to reignite her occasional loathing of Nkosi, but she knew this was not the time for a rant. She stayed strong for him, refusing to break.

Shalini studied his eyes. They stung with sadness. She tried to reassure him, "We will all die anyway, my child."

"Yes, but not like this," he cried.

Shalini took a deep breath, attempting to summon hope, and added, "It has been caught early…"

The boy interrupted her. His mind was racing, trying to solve the great puzzle that was his scrambled life. He sputtered, "Does that mean that Anthony Zaza will die too? That's who gave it to her. I know. I was there. He would not let anyone else have her."

Shalini tried to keep up. "Yes, if he does not die from his stupid games in the Nothingness, he will also die from this. You will live longer, and live better, because we have the right pills for you here." She pulled him into her to console him.

Upon feeling the embrace of a woman – the first since Helena – he sunk into a sweet memory. He figured while buried in this woman's soft and gentle chest that death was not so horrible. In death he could be taken by the wind to Mokolodi where she was buried. He could seep through the sand of her grave and he could wrap what was left of himself around her forever.

He let Shalini hold him for a long while. He had forgotten what it was like to feel the empathy of a mother or the sympathy of a lover, so he let her try to console him. After a long time, he released himself and turned back to watch the children play. She returned to the table and picked up her things, sunk into her chair and studied the boy.

He watched his brothers laughing and summoned the courage to speak his thoughts to Shalini. "Thank you, but give the pills to one of them. I know they do not grow on trees. I am ready to go."

A great pain gripped Shalini, "I hope you change your mind."

Both deep in contemplation, they stood there well into the early evening. They stood until the children grew tired and dropped to the sand. They stood listening to them rolling jokes to and fro, to and fro, with a soccer ball. They stood there until the sun started to slip down the sky and dripped gold upon the horizon. They stood until the first crickets began to chatter, incessant sounds that reminded Paris of those nights spent lying with his gun upon his chest

– nights when he would stare up into the stars, dreaming of what once was and what could have been, if his life had not been stolen.

The two of them had been quiet for a very long time. Shalini had been so caught up in studying the young man that she had been unable to leave to meet Mandeep to discuss their departure.

The energy of the world shifted as they stood in their private contemplations. Something strange was happening. The air grew warm. It suddenly hung heavily upon their skin. Paris' heart sunk into a weird rhythm. He turned to the woman who had been dreaming into his back. "Shalini, something doesn't feel right."

At first she wanted to console him again. She wanted to remind him that it was not his fault for contracting HIV, but in his furrowed brow she saw he was no longer talking about that. His eyes were wide with premonition. "What do you mean?"

The boys' eyes continued to burn. "Don't you feel that?"

She shook her head slowly.

A nervous rush of knowing passed over Paris' skin.

Softly, softly, softly, a choir of young voices rose in the distance. Paris stepped out on the stoop of Shalini's office and then he sniffed into the dusk. His eyes screwed tight as he jutted his chin towards the hills. He peered into the Nothingness.

She stood up and came to the doorway with a heart full of denial. Moment by moment, its beat changed with the rising sense of danger. The boys on the pitch heard it too. Heads swivelled over shoulders as other boys stood up and placed their hands on their brows, searching like sailors do for the stillness of land. Everyone looked and everyone listened, frozen like the prey on the Serengeti.

And then, the malicious pounding of the drums could faintly be heard.

"There!" Paris saw them at the edge of the horizon. He pointed towards the silhouettes tenaciously pushing through the last of the amber honey of the dying sun. Innumerable Little Warriors spoiled the sunset, timing their arrival in Baobab to coincide with the shadow of the night. They arrived as traditional warriors would ... Trembling the earth with their drums. Sending a warning that they were going to bleed out the town.

They had come, finally, as people had anticipated for years. The madness of the middle of nowhere had come to break the thorax of the body of Nkosi.

Paris turned to Shalini. She had never seen anything like it, and was unsure of how she felt for those children coming towards them. Children who needed saving. Children who, in moments, would be killing. Her courage trickled from her. It hid in the cement at her feet. She felt hollow, light enough to be swept up with the wind. As she'd move in its draughts, the flames of her fear would help paint the setting sky.

Paris looked at her sternly, and commanded her to move. "Run, Shalini."

Tears streamed down her face. She did not know when she had begun to cry. Her voice was trembling. She spoke meekly. "To where? Look at the horizon, Paris. There are thousands of them. Where did they find so many?"

Paris could not answer the question himself, but urged her still. "Go!"

As she ran, she thought of her husband. She had to find him. She could not die without him. She thought of the children and wondered how she would possibly be able to save them all. She ran over to the mess hall and pounded on its windows. The choir grew louder in the distance as she looked in at the children who had all put their forks down to watch this woman turned wild with suffering. The ex-child soldiers sensed that her body crackled with a fire of fear. It smelled the same as those women whom they themselves had terrorized. A painful memory sprang up within each and every one of them, and as surely as fires spread, they felt her heat until they too were burning.

Their ears grew sharp as they listened to the sounds of war cries gaining volume from the foothills on the horizon.

It was Leoson who sounded the alarm. "Run! Everyone! Run!"

They were baby bushbucks, impalas and kudus, and much like the prey of the delta, those boys and girls, unwilling to give into the impending massacre, sprung from their seats and scrambled for an exit. Fiery movement sent the mess hall up in flames.

Shalini was collected in the exodus. She felt one of the littlest girls trip by her side. She picked up the child and swung her up onto her hip and ran for the hospital with the rest of the children. What they would do when she got there she didn't know. She thought of Mandeep and her heart broke within her.

A few children, immobilized by fear, could not make the escape. They sat whimpering in their seats. Paris calmly walked over to them. Leoson too stayed to protect the children. Two boys who had turned into brothers in the sickening panic of war, sat side by side and waited with the little ones ... for their kingdom finally coming ... for their killing.

HELPLESS

In the dining room at Victoria Falls Hotel, Zimbabwe
18 September 2009

But I feel it – no, I hear it:
a long whistle or a moan.
Like a falling pebble,
a plummeting rock,
a dropping bomb.
I look up to catch a glimpse,
and recognize the inner demon.
He explodes above me,
and fear shatters merrily.
And I, the sky-gazer, the day-dreamer, sigh with weighted affection
for my deep and dark affliction.

Mfundisi tucked his fountain pen into his suit pocket. He closed his Moleskine diary and buttered his scones as he awaited the arrival of his Saturday luxury – traditional golden syrup. As he waited, he listened to the sounds of the children of the American expats from the bank. They were playing in the pool again. Obnoxiously.

A young waiter came over and stated gravely, "Unfortunately Sah, there is no more golden syrup ... in fact there is none left in all of Victoria Falls ... we went looking."

Mfundisi sighed, knowing that there was probably none left in Zimbabwe at all. He drummed the table with his fingers but smiled up at the boy, for it was not his fault. "It does not matter. Jam will do."

"How about marmalade, Sah?"

"What – no jam either? I hate marmalade, but I shall have to force it down, shan't I?"

The boy gave a gracious nod.

"And my mail, boy? Has anything come yet?"

"No letters sah. There is no answer."

Even though it was purely a linguistic shortcoming, how the boy had put it stung Mfundisi. The boy meant to say, "You have not received any replies," but his English was imperfect. Sadly, the young Zimbabwean had been, in his literalism, unintentionally astute. There was indeed no solution to Nkosi's predicament. Mfundisi watched the servant leave to get the marmalade and sighed – something he had become very good at – as he spoke to a vacant dining room. "I suppose you are right, my boy. There is no answer. No solution at all."

He looked around his lonely surroundings. Empty chairs. Tidy tables. Nobody came to the hotel that much. Was it because there were no tourists, or was it because there was no food to feed them? He stared at his scones and contemplated the chicken and egg scenario, as if understanding the miserable history of Zimbabwe would help him fathom why there was no jam at the Victoria Falls Hotel. He sighed again. The paucity of jam would persist until one of the young hotel employees demonstrated some criminal ingenuity and hurled himself over the border and into South Africa where he could load his buckie with confectionary goods and sell them in Zimbabwe on the black market. What a sad state of affairs, thought Mfundisi, 'when finding the jam for my scones could make a hungry boy a criminal.'

From across the room, a man dressed in blue fatigues moved towards him. The officer was greying around the temples. He watched the president with tired eyes. Mfundisi studied them as the officer closed in. He had always been intrigued by the different shapes of White Men's eyes. Some were round, others sharply slanted. He very much enjoyed the almond-shaped ones. For him, they emanated a certain calm.

As the Peace Officer approached, Mfundisi noted that this white man had beautiful, golden-brown eyes that drooped like the wings of a swallow.

What most interested Mfundisi about a White Man's eyes is how they perceived the world. They viewed it in such a different manner than a Black Man's did. In the past, some of the ways the White Man's eyes viewed things had been so dehumanizing in both personal and political matters that Mfundisi sometimes struggled to see much likeness between the two races at all. This was a fact that had made diplomacy quite difficult over the decades. 'The eyes,' he thought to himself. 'It is the eyes ... the seeing ... that matters in politics, in war, in life.'

The man saluted the president-in-hiding and stood at ease after dropping his hand from his beret. His eyes were heavy with fatigue. Mfundisi was drawn to them because, for once, he saw a similarity between his own eyes and this officer's: they were both tired of seeing ... seeing anything at all.

And then he spoke and unveiled his accent. French. Mfundisi was grateful for the revelation because even though Mfundisi resented both the French and the Belgians, a Frenchman was tolerable. A Frenchman in Africa was able to shed some of his arrogance. Some of that cultural self-entitlement melted in Africa's merciless sun. Africa humbled the French, whereas the Belgians would not be abashed. Mfundisi did not want to waste time thinking to himself about Belgians, so he cleared his mind and acknowledged the man with a nod of his head.

"Sir, good morning. Forgive the interruption, but we have some pressing news."

"I already know. Do you think I don't know what is going on in my own country?"

"You mean, you know the MM and the LLLS have joined forces as the Militia for Nkosi? You know that they have stormed Baobab, that they are killing all the men? When did you find out? We could have saved thousands." The man's voice was strained and his tired eyes were pleading. He could not understand Mfundisi's apathy in the face of such incredible loss.

But this was not the first time Mfundisi had witnessed such loss. In this reckoning moment he kept reminding himself that it was the normalcy of life, the circle, the rising and the falling. Of course it wounded him deeply, but for a man who had already weathered many life-stealing storms, this was, theoretically speaking, just more wind and hail. "We could not have saved thousands. Nobody in the West gives enough of a damn to have done anything. This was the only way. I had to keep mum so you would jump. What anyone is going to do, however, is beyond me. How can anyone fix this mess? Do you recolonize? Until you figure it out, my army is there..." and he trailed off, trampled by the futility of it all.

The officer's eyes suddenly jumped to life growing wide with wild intentions. "Sir! That is just it! Your army has been superseded. They did not hold. They could not fight them. They could not fight the children." The man shifted from one foot to another while he spoke. He continued, "I understand. Facing a raging boy breaks you. Everything you ever knew about yourself and humanity implodes. They just could not hold, sir. Baobab is uprooted."

Mfundisi recoiled in his seat. The marmalade was set beside him. His eyes followed the confection as the waiter lowered it towards the table. His white gloves were dusty and smudged with African dirt. Mfundisi judged the absurdity of it: White gloves in Africa ... of course they would get dirty!

The officer interrupted his thoughts with, "Sir? Sir? Are you listening?"

The exiled president's eyes flamed, burning through the officer. He snarled, "Of course you fool! Do you have anything important to tell me at all? Or are you just the bearer of pathetic news?"

The man took off his cap and pulled a chair out from the table next to Mfundisi's. He swung it around so that it faced the president, sat down and folded his hands into one another. "We have had a distress call from our boys guarding a hospital off Jacaranda Drive on the outskirts of Baobab."

The president interjected, "Princess Marina. I know the one. It is where I lost my Ingrid. She was a Belgian, like you."

"My condolences, sir ... but I am French."

Mfundisi blinked hard. He could no longer keep his thoughts together. They scrambled through his mind, looking for an exit.

The man felt impatient, because to him it seemed as though Mfundisi did not care about nor even sense the urgency of the matter. He continued, "Anyway, well, you see, they have barricaded themselves in. We have spoken with a Mr. Abraham ... Stefanus Abraham, who reports that the militia has rampaged through Baobab, killing every boy they could find. The city is upside down, sir."

Mfundisi spat, "It has always been upside down."

Again the officer was unnerved by the president's composure. "Sir, you are rather calm. We hate to throw this term around, but we fear gender cleansing is taking place in your capital city. Baobab is burning. Its men are dying."

"A genocide, you mean." The word spewed like lava from Mfundisi's mouth. Genocide. The word suited him, as though he had been born to say it.

"Yes sir." The officer composed himself and reaffirmed sadly, "A genocide."

Defensively, Mfundisi began, "Well it was only a matter of time, was it not? I did try to explain the imminence of this to the West. I begged for help, but no one paid attention to this old Communist. By punishing me, you have punished all of them. What immaturity. What cruelty." The president stopped to think about this for a while, and then continued on a different strain, "Then again, it was also a result of my own folly. I should have had greater foresight and courage. I was too afraid to uproot my country with such a shift from the Red to the West. I should have done so when things began to fall apart. I was frightened, you understand? I thought that such a change would bring about civil war. As it turns out, not changing brought it about instead."

The officer squeezed his beret between his palms, "Sir, I am sorry."

"Don't be. You are as powerless as me. You're just a man in a pretty blue cap. Now, if you'll excuse me I have something to do. Thank you for your visit."

The man rose with the president. "But sir ... we need you to liaise with the UN, sir!"

Mfundisi opened his Moleskine and fumbled for his old-fashioned fountain pen in the inner pocket of his suit jacket. He neatly inscribed his wishes. He folded the torn out piece of paper and dropped it on the table next to his untouched scones. The old man straightened his tie, adjusted his cuffs and cordially excused himself, saying, "Once again, thank you so much for coming, but there is something that has to be done."

"Something more important than this?" stammered the officer.

"Yes, I'm afraid it is the only answer." Mfundisi left the man to tear at his little blue beret.

The president walked across the manicured garden, taking in its sweet smells. He ignored the Americans in the pool, gazing instead at the remarkable vista. He watched the vigorous cascade of never-ending water topple over Victoria Falls. Upon one of its stony edges was a photographer taking pictures of the famous bridge where Ian Smith had signed over Zimbabwe's independence so many years ago. Mfundisi focused on the man taking pictures on the hanging nail of the cliff's edge high above the Zambezi, and then walked across the garden back towards the hotel. As he did so the exiled statesman reminisced about the old days in Rhodesia. That country was by no means perfect, but it had been delightful in its day. He made his way to the hotel's grand foyer with its colonial furnishings and finishings. He paced through it, acknowledging no one. He recalled an ancient memory from his days in training in Angola: the boys talking about blowing up these old hotels. He was glad independence was granted to all of them before it got to that point because, though a White Man could not build a happy country here in Africa, he sure had built some fine hotels.

Exiting the coolth of the masterpiece, he collided with the day's insufferable warmth. An aged bell-boy wearing a ripe grin wished him a good day. The grandpa was adorned with tacky badges from his top hat to the hems of his uniform's trousers. The emblems preached idealistic phrases such as, "Don't worry be happy," "We are the World," and "Viva Las Vegas." Mfundisi asked the old idiot for a car that would take him to the other side of the falls. He growled under his breath, irritated by the old man's idealistic badges.

Mfundisi was driven through the dead town to the other side of the falls. The taxi was stifling, and local beats blared from the tape deck. The president rolled down his window, took in the smell of melting tar and studied the plastic bags that littered Victoria Fall's unkempt streets. He sympathized with the young men who sat sickly on milk crates along the side of the road, selling soap stone curios to what few tourists there were.

The driver turned onto an unpaved road. The dust picked up, and the president felt a filmy layer of African dirt settle upon his skin. Mfundisi did not move to clean himself.

The taxi pulled in under a large acacia tree, and the driver turned off the tired and gasping engine. "You want me to wait here, Sah?"

"No thank you, driver." Mfundisi handed the driver an American twenty. Leaving the man with a dropped jaw, Mfundisi stepped out of the car into the stickiness of the day.

He walked towards the delta, where he found a team of Morwang paddlers lying around and chatting to one another in the sun. He again flashed some American money, to great effect. They chirped and waved their arms at one another, each insisting that he was the safest paddler. Mfundisi was not concerned with safety, so he chose the sickest looking of the lot and handed him the bread-buying dollar bill.

He was paddled out down the Chobe Delta in a Morwang – a hollowed out trunk of a tree. The finest pedigree of African engineering: It was rickety, and it creaked as it slid atop of the Delta. A playful hippo or a naughty crocodile could easily have tipped it. It happened all the time.

The day was hot, and Mfundisi had to remove his suit jacket. He discarded it overboard. He undid his cuffs and rolled up his sleeves. He sweated through the cotton. Suits were not designed with the African heat in mind, and neither was the African man's dusty-smelling sweat taken into consideration. It's the kind that stains the air with its pungency. That is why the hard labourers roll down their one-piece uniforms and knot the arms around their waists, for they sweat a lot when they build, mine, dig or farm. The boat banked upstream from the falls. Mfundisi shouted his thanks to the man that brought him there, but his words were inaudible against the crash of the magnificent water.

By the time he reached the ledge to the right of the falls, where he had seen the photographer an hour before, his once shiny shoes were muddy and his socks were wet. He removed his footwear and peeled off his socks, revealing shrivelled skin. Watching his footing, the old man carefully climbed down to the ledge. To keep his balance, he spread his arms wide, like that of a sailing kite.

This close, the sound of the falls was like a million separate small explosions in his ears. Fragments of history shattered into the air. He unknotted his tie as he looked out at the hotel he'd been living in for the past two years. Much had changed in those drawn-out days. And everything had stayed the same.

He unfolded the first Windsor knot, then the second, and slid the silk through his collar. He held the tie high in front of him. It lapped in the wind like a thirsty tongue. It was a traditional tie, diagonally striped. It was the tie of the Republic of Nkosi's parliament – a gift to the independent parliament's first members. The colours represented the riches of their soil. The wealth that had destroyed them. Sterling for coal, gold for the reason the White Man had stolen Nkosi in the first place, and silver for tantalum.

He noticed how the warm light from the Zimbabwean sky ignited the colours of his country. A short burst of laughter from the hotel pool slipped through the noise of the falls. It travelled across one of this world's greatest cavities just to hurt his heart. The laughter brought him to the climax of the melancholy that he had been feeling since he had awoken to the shrill ring of his hotel room's telephone. On the other end of the line came the sad, gruff voice of a comrade back in Nkosi. "Mfundisi, it is true ... the MM and the LLLS have joined forces. They are taking Baobab."

The laughter from the American children in the hotel's pool danced about his ears as his eyes followed the direction of the tie, which was making its dying descent into smoke and water. He felt a wave of nostalgia for his idyllic childhood. A youth that had been cut short by the tyranny of war. He remembered playing with his friends while keeping the kids safe from the hyenas. He remembered loving his mother, and his mother loving him back. He remembered how his brothers taught him how to track animals and how to hunt for ostrich eggs.

The laughter and his childhood were again drowned out by the pounding water. He sighed out the very last drop of breath within him as he watched his tie get pulled under the merciless rapids. Then he followed it, leaping away from his life and faith. Feeling relief during the scenic fall to his death.

. . . .

Back at the Victoria Falls Hotel, the officer spoke into the receiver. "Yes sir, he wrote a note and then excused himself. It says: "Do what you can for I am at a loss. It is too late for you, for me and for the Republic of Nkosi." Signed, "Mfundisi Majuto.[36]"

---

[36] Majuto means 'regret' in Swahili.

FEAR VERSUS HOPE

The beaches of Nkosi
September 18th, 2009

A shrill breeze came sweeping over the dunes. The wind picked up the sand and sent it stinging, like a thousand needles, into Babba's legs. Closing his eyes, he listened. A biting knowledge settled itself angrily inside of him. He felt a healing palm upon his shoulder. The Rra stood strong against the wind beside him.

"My child, you must not lose your hope."

Babba shook his head. "No, Rra ... I must not lose fear, because when there is no more fear, there is no need for hope. I have learned that they come together."

Chuckling affectionately, the Rra gave Babba's shoulder a squeeze. "You are becoming wiser than me in your old age, little boy!"

The Rra walked away from the philosophical child who was staring hard in the direction of the dunes. The wind was speaking to him. Under his breath he spoke back. "You can make it ... you can make it! Come ... I am waiting. The lions will come. They will tremble over the hills. They will thunder through the country, and they will save Nkosi. At night I can hear them roar."

EPILOGUE

This story of Nkosi's Little Warriors was pieced together from records retrieved in the aftermath of the slayings at Princess Marina Hospital. What has been retold in these pages was gathered from the therapy notes, from interviews with survivors at Princess Marina, surviving wives of the NAP, The Peace Officer whom met with Mfundisi the day of the genocide and the mandatory therapy journals of Paris, Dorian, Severin and Leoson. Without the efforts of Dr. Mandeep and his interest in Post-Traumatic Stress Disorder, and specifically REM therapy, there would be no recorded insight of these children's histories.

The insurgence of the Peace Keepers into Baobab came staggeringly late, too late to save the young men of Nkosi's capital city. Who were targets of the gender cleansing that took place on September 17th 2009. It took the UN seventeen days to pluck the courage to come to Baobab's aid. By the time they arrived, the militia had already retreated into hiding leaving the ladies of Baobab in mourning. The slaughter of Baobab has caused the ruination of Nkosi's solidarity and future.

The displacement camp was attacked first. The male recruits from CIDA, along with the younger male inhabitants, were massacred on the first day of the Freedom Fighters' arrival. For the length of their careers, these men advocated for the displaced, and in doing so, saved thousands of lives.

The hospital barricaded itself bravely but most of the male inhabitants were eventually slaughtered. The remains of hospital workers, Dr. Mandeep Jain, Shalini Jain and head nurse Sophie Le Roux, were discovered after the mass grave behind the hospital was unearthed upon the Peace Keepers' arrival. Their bodies have been sent back to their countries of origin, to be respectfully interred. Stefanus Abraham was taken by the united forces of the LLLS and the MM, as their hostage.

Now that the two forces – Militia for Minerals and the Liberating Land and Life Stealers – are fighting as a united front named The Militia of Nkosi, the challenges related to keeping Nkosian civilians safe are unfathomable. Healing will not take place in the manner it did in Rwanda. This nation is irreparably damaged. Perhaps late President Mfundisi was right in stating in his suicide note that it is too late for the Republic of Nkosi. With its young boys killed or killing, illiterate or diseased ... with its adults untrusting and exhausted ... with its old disillusioned and weakened, Nkosi has indeed failed.

Only one of the children from this story-told has been recovered – Leoson. He escaped Baobab and led a group of the youngsters north, across the border and found Deborah who fled with her family to a refugee camp. It is unknown whether Paris, Dorian, Severin and Nyla were recruited back into the militia during the attack on Baobab. One can only hope that any or all of them managed to run back through the Nothingness and find Babba and the Rra.

The empress of the Little Warriors, Helena, was indeed buried in Mokolodi, as Paris' records revealed. Her grave endures, adorned with an umbrella to protect her resting bones from the heat of Nkosi.

ABOUT THE AUTHOR

Lauren Camp grew up in Gaborone, Botswana. Having immigrated to Canada in the late 90's, she recognized and reveled in the lack of fear bred in her new country. Inspired by the human struggles on her mother continent, she writes about the dark and light shades of Africa.

She hopes to write a sequel to Nkosi's Little Warriors and is working on her next novel, Lowveld, about poaching in Southern Africa.

Made in the USA
San Bernardino, CA
06 March 2014